THE WAR
OF THE
WORLDS

PLUS BLOOD, GUTS AND ZOMBIES

Also by Eric S. Brown

Space Stations and Graveyards

Dying Days

Portals of Terror

Madmen's Dreams

Cobble

The Queen

The Wave

Waking Nightmares

Zombies II: Inhuman

Unabridged Unabashed and Undead:
The Best of Eric S. Brown

Season of Rot

Barren Earth (with Stephen North)

World War of the Dead

How the West Went to Hell

Bigfoot War

The Weaponer

THE WAR
OF THE
WORLDS
PLUS BLOOD, GUTS AND ZOMBIES

H. G. WELLS
AND
ERIC S. BROWN

G

GALLERY BOOKS

New York   London   Toronto   Sydney

Gallery Books
A Division of Simon & Schuster, Inc.
1230 Avenue of the Americas
New York, NY 10020

First Gallery Books trade paperback edition December 2010

GALLERY BOOKS and colophon are trademarks of Simon & Schuster, Inc.

For information about special discounts for bulk purchases, please contact Simon & Schuster Special Sales at 1-866-506-1949 or business@simonandschuster.com.

The Simon & Schuster Speakers Bureau can bring authors to your live event. For more information or to book an event contact the Simon & Schuster Speakers Bureau at 1-866-248-3049 or visit our website at www.simonspeakers.com.

Designed by Davina Mock-Maniscalco

Manufactured in the United States of America

10 9 8 7 6 5 4 3 2 1

Library of Congress Cataloging-in-Publication Data is available.

ISBN 978-1-4516-0975-2
ISBN 978-1-4516-1135-9 (ebook)

I would like to dedicate this book to my loving wife, Shanna, and my son, Merrick.
—Eric S. Brown

CONTENTS

Contents

But who shall dwell in these worlds if they be inhab
ited? . . . Are we or they Lords of the World? . . . And
how are all things made for man?

   —Kepler (quoted in *The Anatomy of Melancholy*)

BOOK ONE

———◆———

THE COMING
OF THE MARTIANS

1

THE EVE OF THE WAR

No one would have believed in the last years of the nineteenth century that this world was being watched keenly and closely by intelligences greater than man's and yet as mortal as his own; that as men busied themselves about their various concerns they were scrutinised and studied, perhaps almost as narrowly as a man with a microscope might scrutinise the transient creatures that swarm and multiply in a drop of water. With infinite complacency men went to and fro over this globe about their little affairs, serene in their assurance of their empire over matter. It is possible that the infusoria under the microscope do the same. No one gave a thought to the older worlds of space as sources of human danger, or thought of them only to dismiss the idea of life upon them as impossible or improbable. It is curious to recall some of the mental habits of those departed days. At most terrestrial men fancied there might be other men upon Mars, perhaps inferior to themselves and ready to welcome a missionary enterprise. Yet across the gulf of space, minds that are to our minds as ours are to those of the beasts that perish, intellects vast and cool and unsympathetic, regarded this earth with envious eyes, and slowly and surely drew their plans against us. And early in the twentieth century came the great disillusionment.

The planet Mars, I scarcely need remind the reader, revolves about the sun at a mean distance of 140,000,000 miles, and the light and heat it receives from the sun is barely half of that received by this world. It must be, if the nebular hypothesis has any truth, older than our world; and long before this earth ceased to be molten, life upon its surface must have begun its course. The fact that it is scarcely one seventh of the volume of the earth must have accelerated its cooling to the temperature at which life could begin. It has air and water and all that is necessary for the support of animated existence.

Yet so vain is man, and so blinded by his vanity, that no writer, up to the very end of the nineteenth century, expressed any idea that intelligent life might have developed there far, or indeed at all, beyond its earthly level. Nor was it generally understood that since Mars is older than our earth, with scarcely a quarter of the superficial area and remoter from the sun, it necessarily follows that it is not only more distant from time's beginning but nearer its end.

The secular cooling that must someday overtake our

planet has already gone far indeed with our neighbour. Its physical condition is still largely a mystery, but we know now that even in its equatorial region the midday temperature barely approaches that of our coldest winter. Its air is much more attenuated than ours, its oceans have shrunk until they cover but a third of its surface, and as its slow seasons change huge snowcaps gather and melt about either pole and periodically inundate its temperate zones. That last stage of exhaustion, which to us is still incredibly remote, has become a present-day problem for the inhabitants of Mars. The immediate pressure of necessity has brightened their intellects, enlarged their powers, and hardened their hearts. And looking across space with instruments, and intelligences such as we have scarcely dreamed of, they see, at its nearest distance only 35,000,000 of miles sunward of them, a morning star of hope, our own warmer planet, green with vegetation and grey with water, with a cloudy atmosphere eloquent of fertility, with glimpses through its drifting cloud wisps of broad stretches of populous country and narrow, navy-crowded seas.

And we men, the creatures who inhabit this earth, must be to them at least as alien and lowly as are the monkeys and lemurs to us. The intellectual side of man already admits that life is an incessant struggle for existence, and it would seem that this too is the belief of the minds upon Mars. Their world is far gone in its cooling and this world is still crowded with life, but crowded only with what they regard as inferior animals. To carry warfare sunward is, indeed, their only escape from the destruction that, generation after generation, creeps upon them.

I imagine that even they did not realize the full effect their war with us, the dwellers of this bright blue and green orb of light, would bring about or the utter terror it would unleash.

But before we judge of them too harshly we must remember what ruthless and utter destruction our own species has wrought, not only upon animals, such as the vanished bison and the dodo, but upon its inferior races. The Tasmanians, in spite of their human likeness, were entirely swept out of existence in a war of extermination waged by European immigrants, in the space of fifty years. Are we such apostles of mercy as to complain if the Martians warred in the same spirit?

The Martians seem to have calculated their descent with amazing subtlety—their mathematical learning is evidently far in excess of ours—and to have carried out their preparations with a well-nigh perfect unanimity. Had our instruments permitted it, we might have seen the gathering trouble far back in the nineteenth century. Men like Schiaparelli watched the red planet—it is odd, by-the-bye, that for countless centuries Mars has been the star of war—but failed to interpret the fluctuating appearances of the markings they mapped so well. All that time the Martians must have been getting ready.

During the opposition of 1894 a great light was seen on the illuminated part of the disk, first at the Lick Observatory, then by Perrotin of Nice, and then by other observers. English readers heard of it first in the issue of *Nature* dated August 2. I am inclined to think that this blaze may have been the casting of the huge gun, in the vast pit sunk into their planet, from which their shots were fired at us. Peculiar markings, as yet unexplained, were seen near the site of that outbreak during the next two oppositions.

The storm burst upon us six years ago now. As Mars approached opposition, Lavelle of Java set the wires of the astronomical exchange palpitating with the amazing intelligence of a huge outbreak of incandescent gas upon the planet. It had occurred towards midnight of the twelfth; and the spectroscope, to which he had at once resorted, indicated a mass of flaming gas, chiefly hydrogen, moving with an enormous velocity towards this earth. This jet of fire had become invisible about a quarter past twelve. He compared it to a colossal puff of flame suddenly and violently squirted out of the planet, "as flaming gases rushed out of a gun."

A singularly appropriate phrase it proved. Yet the next day there was nothing of this in the papers except a little note in the *Daily Telegraph,* and the world went in ignorance of one of the gravest dangers that ever threatened the human race. I might not have heard of the eruption at all had I not met Ogilvy, the well-known astronomer, at Ottershaw. He was immensely excited at the news, and in the excess of his feelings invited me up to take a turn with him that night in a scrutiny of the red planet.

In spite of all that has happened since, I still remember that vigil very distinctly: the black and silent observatory, the shadowed lantern throwing a feeble glow upon the floor in the corner, the steady ticking of the clockwork of the telescope, the little slit in the roof—an oblong profundity with the stardust streaked across it. Ogilvy moved about, invisible but audible. Looking through the telescope, one saw a circle of deep blue and the little round planet swimming in the field. It seemed such a little thing, so bright and small and still, faintly marked with transverse stripes, and slightly flattened from the perfect round. But so little it was, so silvery warm—a pin's-head of light! It was as if it quivered, but really this was the telescope vibrating with the activity of the clockwork that kept the planet in view.

As I watched, the planet seemed to grow larger and smaller and to advance and recede, but that was simply that my eye was tired. Forty millions of miles it was from us— more than forty millions of miles of void. Few people realise the immensity of vacancy in which the dust of the material universe swims.

Near it in the field, I remember, were three faint points of light, three telescopic stars infinitely remote, and all around it was the unfathomable darkness of empty space. You know how that blackness looks on a frosty starlight night. In a telescope it seems far profounder. And invisible to me because it was so remote and small, flying swiftly and steadily towards me across that incredible distance, drawing nearer every minute by so many thousands of miles, came the Thing they were sending us, the Thing that was to bring so much struggle and calamity and death to the earth. I never dreamed of it then as I watched; no one on earth dreamed of that unerring missile.

That night, too, there was another jetting out of gas from the distant planet. I saw it. A reddish flash at the edge, the slightest projection of the outline just as the chronometer struck midnight; and at that I told Ogilvy and he took my place. The night was warm and I was thirsty, and I went stretching my legs clumsily and feeling my way in the darkness, to the little table where the siphon stood, while Ogilvy exclaimed at the streamer of gas that came out towards us.

That night another invisible missile started on its way to the earth from Mars, just a second or so under twenty-four hours after the first one. I remember how I sat on the table there in the blackness, with patches of green and crimson swimming before my eyes. I wished I had a light to smoke by, little suspecting the meaning of the minute gleam I had seen and all that it would presently bring me. Ogilvy watched till one, and then gave it up; and we lit the lantern and walked over to his house. Down below in the darkness were Ottershaw and Chertsey and all their hundreds of people, sleeping in peace.

He was full of speculation that night about the condition of Mars, and scoffed at the vulgar idea of its having inhabitants who were signalling us. His idea was that meteorites might be falling in a heavy shower upon the planet, or that a huge volcanic explosion was in progress. He pointed out to me how unlikely it was that organic evolution had taken the same direction in the two adjacent planets.

"The chances against anything manlike on Mars are a million to one," he said.

Hundreds of observers saw the flame that night and the night after about midnight, and again the night after; and so for ten nights, a flame each night. Why the shots ceased after the tenth no one on earth has attempted to explain. It may be the gases of the firing caused the Martians inconvenience. Dense clouds of smoke or dust, visible through a powerful telescope on earth as little grey, fluctuating patches, spread through the clearness of the planet's atmosphere and obscured its more familiar features.

Even the daily papers woke up to the disturbances at last, and popular notes appeared here, there, and everywhere concerning the volcanoes upon Mars. The seriocomic periodical *Punch,* I remember, made a happy use of it in the political cartoon. And, all unsuspected, those missiles the Martians had fired at us drew earthward, rushing now at a pace of many miles a second through the empty gulf of space, hour by hour and day by day, nearer and nearer. It seems to me now almost incredibly wonderful that, with that swift fate hanging over us, men could go about their petty concerns as they did. I remember how jubilant Markham was at securing a new photograph of the planet for the illustrated paper he edited in those days. People in these latter times scarcely realise the abundance and enterprise of our nineteenth-century papers. For my own part, I was much occupied in learning to ride the bicycle, and busy upon a series of papers discussing the probable developments of moral ideas as civilisation progressed.

One night (the first missile then could scarcely have been 10,000,000 miles away) I went for a walk with my wife. It was starlight and I explained the Signs of the Zodiac to her, and pointed out Mars, a bright dot of light creeping zenithward, towards which so many telescopes were pointed. It was a warm night. Coming home, a party of excursionists from Chertsey or Isleworth passed us singing and playing music. There were lights in the upper windows of the houses as the people went to bed. From the railway station in the distance came the sound of shunting trains, ringing and rumbling, softened almost into melody by the distance. My wife pointed out to me the brightness of the red, green, and yellow signal lights hanging in a framework against the sky. It seemed so safe and tranquil.

2

———◦———

THE FALLING STAR

Then came the night of the first falling star. It was seen early in the morning, rushing over Winchester eastward, a line of flame high in the atmosphere. Hundreds must have seen it, and taken it for an ordinary falling star. Albin described it as leaving a greenish streak behind it that glowed for some seconds. Denning, our greatest authority on meteorites, stated that the height of its first appearance was about ninety or one hundred miles. It seemed to him that it fell to earth about one hundred miles east of him.

I was at home at that hour and writing in my study; and although my French windows face towards Ottershaw and the blind was up (for I loved in those days to look up at the night sky), I saw nothing of it. Yet this strangest of all things that ever came to earth from outer space must have fallen while I was sitting there, visible to me had I only looked up as it passed. Some of those who saw its flight say it travelled with a hissing sound. I myself heard nothing of that. Many people in Berkshire, Surrey, and Middlesex must have seen the fall of it, and, at most, have thought that another meteorite had descended. No one seems to have troubled to look for the fallen mass that night.

But very early in the morning poor Ogilvy, who had seen the shooting star and who was persuaded that a meteorite lay somewhere on the common between Horsell, Ottershaw, and Woking, rose early with the idea of finding it. Find it he did, soon after dawn, and not far from the sand pits. An enormous hole had been made by the impact of the projectile, and the sand and gravel had been flung violently in every direction over the heath, forming heaps visible a mile and a half away. The heather was on fire eastward, and a thin blue smoke rose against the dawn.

The Thing itself lay almost entirely buried in the sand, amidst the scattered splinters of a fir tree it had shivered to fragments in its descent. The uncovered part had the appearance of a huge cylinder, caked over and its outline softened by a thick scaly dun-coloured incrustation. It had a diameter of about thirty yards. He approached the mass, surprised at the size and more so at the shape, since most meteorites are rounded more or less completely. It was, however, still so hot from its flight through the air as to forbid his near approach. A stirring noise within its cylinder he ascribed to the unequal cooling of its surface; for at that time it had not occurred to him that it might be hollow.

He remained standing at the edge of the pit that the Thing had made for itself, staring at its strange appearance, astonished chiefly at its unusual shape and colour, and dimly perceiving even then some evidence of design in its arrival. The early morning was wonderfully still, and the sun, just clearing the pine trees towards Weybridge, was already warm. He did not remember hearing any birds that morning; there was certainly no breeze stirring, and the only sounds were the faint movements from within the cindery cylinder. He was all alone on the common.

Then suddenly he noticed with a start that some of the grey clinker, the ashy incrustation that covered the meteorite, was falling off the circular edge of the end. It was dropping off in flakes and raining down upon the sand. A large piece suddenly came off and fell with a sharp noise that brought his heart into his mouth.

For a minute he scarcely realised what this meant, and, although the heat was excessive, he clambered down into the pit close to the bulk to see the Thing more clearly. He fancied even then that the cooling of the body might account for this, but what disturbed that idea was the fact that the ash was falling only from the end of the cylinder.

And then he perceived that, very slowly, the circular top of the cylinder was rotating on its body. It was such a gradual movement that he discovered it only through noticing that a black mark that had been near him five minutes ago was now at the other side of the circumference. Even then he scarcely understood what this indicated, until he heard a muffled grating sound and saw the black mark jerk forward an inch or so. Then the thing came upon him in a flash. The cylinder was artificial—hollow—with an end that screwed out! Something within the cylinder was unscrewing the top!

"Good heavens!" said Ogilvy. "There's a man in it—men in it! Half roasted to death! Trying to escape!"

At once, with a quick mental leap, he linked the Thing with the flash upon Mars.

The thought of the confined creature was so dreadful to him that he forgot the heat and went forward to the cylinder to help turn it. But luckily the dull radiation arrested him before he could burn his hands on the still-glowing metal. Who could know the effect that such exposure would bring about in a human being? Would it kill as surely as the heat would have scarred him had he reached the craft? Would it change the very cells of his flesh? At that he stood irresolute for a moment, then turned, scrambled out of the pit, and set off running wildly into Woking. The time then must have been somewhere about six o'clock. He met a waggoner and tried to make him understand, but the tale he told and his appearance were so wild—his hat had fallen off in the pit—that the man simply drove on. He was equally unsuccessful with the potman who was just unlocking the doors of the public-house by Horsell Bridge. The fellow thought he was a lunatic at large and made an unsuccessful attempt to shut him into the taproom. That sobered him a little; and when he saw Henderson, the London journalist, in his garden, he called over the palings and made himself understood.

"Henderson," he called, "you saw that shooting star last night?"

"Well?" said Henderson.

"It's out on Horsell Common now."

"Good Lord!" said Henderson. "Fallen meteorite! That's good."

"But it's something more than a meteorite. It's a cylinder—an artificial cylinder, man! And there's something inside."

Henderson stood up with his spade in his hand.

"What's that?" he said. He was deaf in one ear.

Ogilvy told him all that he had seen. Henderson was a minute or so taking it in. Then he dropped his spade, snatched up his jacket, and came out into the road. The two men hurried back at once to the common, and found the cylinder still lying in the same position. But now the sounds inside had ceased, and a thin circle of bright metal showed between the top and the body of the cylinder. Air was either entering or escaping at the rim with a thin, sizzling sound.

They listened, rapped on the scaly burnt metal with a stick, and, meeting with no response, they both concluded the man or men inside must be insensible or dead.

Of course the two were quite unable to do anything. They shouted consolation and promises, and went off back to the town again to get help. One can imagine them, covered with sand, excited and disordered, running up the little street in the bright sunlight just as the shop folks were taking down their shutters and people were opening their bedroom windows. Henderson went into the railway station at once, in order to telegraph the news to London. The newspaper articles had prepared men's minds for the reception of the idea.

By eight o'clock a number of boys and unemployed men

had already started for the common to see the "dead men from Mars." That was the form the story took. I heard of it first from my newspaper boy about a quarter to nine when I went out to get my *Daily Chronicle*. I was naturally startled, and lost no time in going out and across the Ottershaw bridge to the sand pits.

3

ON HORSELL COMMON

I found a little crowd of perhaps twenty people surrounding the huge hole in which the cylinder lay. I have already described the appearance of that colossal bulk, embedded in the ground. The turf and gravel about it seemed charred as if by a sudden explosion. No doubt its impact had caused a flash of fire. Henderson and Ogilvy were not there. I think they perceived that nothing was to be done for the present, and had gone away to breakfast at Henderson's house.

There were four or five boys sitting on the edge of the pit, with their feet dangling, and amusing themselves—until I stopped them—by throwing stones at the giant mass. After I had spoken to them about it, they began playing at "touch" in and out of the group of bystanders.

Among these were a couple of cyclists, a jobbing gardener I employed sometimes, a girl carrying a baby, Gregg the butcher and his little boy, and two or three loafers and golf caddies who were accustomed to hanging about the railway station. There was very little talking. Few of the common people in England had anything but the vaguest astronomical ideas in those days. Most of them were staring quietly at the big tablelike end of the cylinder, which was still as Ogilvy and Henderson had left it. I fancy the popular expectation of a heap of charred corpses was disappointed at this inanimate bulk. Some went away while I was there, and other people came. I clambered into the pit and fancied I heard a faint movement under my feet. The top had certainly ceased to rotate.

It was only when I got thus close to it that the strangeness of this object was at all evident to me. At the first glance it was really no more exciting than an overturned carriage or a tree blown across the road. Not so much so, indeed. It looked like a rusty gas float. It required a certain amount of scientific education to perceive that the grey scale of the Thing was no common oxide, that the yellowish-white metal that gleamed in the crack between the lid and the cylinder had an unfamiliar hue. "Extra-terrestrial" had no meaning for most of the onlookers.

At that time it was quite clear in my own mind that the Thing had come from the planet Mars, but I judged it improbable that it contained any living creature. I thought the unscrewing might be automatic. In spite of Ogilvy, I still believed that there were men in Mars. My mind ran fancifully on the possibilities of its containing manuscript, on the difficulties in translation that might arise, whether we should find coins and models in it, and so forth. Yet it was a little too large for assurance on this idea. I felt an impatience to see it opened. About eleven, as nothing seemed happening, I walked back, full of such thought, to my home in Maybury. But I found it difficult to get to work upon my abstract investigations.

In the afternoon the appearance of the common had altered very much. The early editions of the evening papers had startled London with enormous headlines:

"A MESSAGE RECEIVED FROM MARS."

"REMARKABLE STORY FROM WOKING,"

and so forth. In addition, Ogilvy's wire to the Astronomical Exchange had roused every observatory in the three kingdoms.

There were half a dozen flies or more from the Woking station standing in the road by the sand pits, a basket-chaise from Chobham, and a rather lordly carriage. Besides that, there was quite a heap of bicycles. In addition, a large number of people must have walked, in spite of the heat of the day, from Woking and Chertsey, so that there was altogether quite a considerable crowd—one or two gaily dressed ladies among the others.

It was glaringly hot, not a cloud in the sky nor a breath of wind, and the only shadow was that of the few scattered pine trees. The burning heather had been extinguished, but the level ground towards Ottershaw was blackened as far as one could see, and still giving off vertical streamers of smoke. An enterprising sweet-stuff dealer in the Chobham Road had sent up his son with a barrow-load of green apples and ginger beer.

Going to the edge of the pit, I found it occupied by a group of about half a dozen men—Henderson, Ogilvy, and a tall, fair-haired man that I afterwards learned was Stent, the Astronomer Royal, with several workmen wielding spades and pickaxes. Stent was giving directions in a clear, high-pitched voice. He was standing on the cylinder, which was now evidently much cooler; his face was crimson and streaming with perspiration, and something seemed to have irritated him.

A large portion of the cylinder had been uncovered, though its lower end was still embedded. Ogilvy did not look well. It appeared to be more than the effort of his labor. His skin was pale and damp from a sweat that looked more born of fever than exhaustion. As soon as Ogilvy saw me among the staring crowd on the edge of the pit he called to me to come down, and asked me if I would mind going over to see Lord Hilton, the lord of the manor.

The growing crowd, he said, was becoming a serious impediment to their excavations, especially the boys. They wanted a light railing put up, and help to keep the people back. He told me that a faint stirring was occasionally still audible within the case, but that the workmen had failed to unscrew the top, as it afforded no grip to them. The case appeared to be enormously thick, and it was possible that the faint sounds we heard represented a noisy tumult in the interior.

I was very glad to do as he asked, and so become one of the privileged spectators within the contemplated enclosure. I failed to find Lord Hilton at his house, but I was told he was expected from London by the six o'clock train from Waterloo; and as it was then about a quarter past five, I went home, had some tea, and walked up to the station to waylay him.

4

THE CYLINDER OPENS

When I returned to the common the sun was setting. Scattered groups were hurrying from the direction of Woking, and one or two persons were returning. The crowd about the pit had increased, and stood out black against the lemon yellow of the sky—a couple of hundred people, perhaps. There were raised voices, and some sort of struggle appeared to be going on about the pit. Strange imaginings passed through my mind. As I drew nearer I heard Stent's voice:

"Keep back! Keep back!"

A boy came running towards me.

"It's a-movin'," he said to me as he passed; "a-screwin' and a-screwin' out. I don't like it. I'm a-goin' 'ome, I am."

I went on to the crowd. There were really, I should think, two or three hundred people elbowing and jostling one another, the one or two ladies there being by no means the least active.

"He's fallen in the pit!" cried some one.

"Keep back!" said several.

The crowd swayed a little, and I elbowed my way through. Every one seemed greatly excited. I heard a peculiar humming sound from the pit.

"I say!" said Ogilvy, looking on the verge of collapse; "help keep these idiots back. We don't know what's in the confounded thing, you know!"

I saw a young man, a shop assistant in Woking I believe he was, standing on the cylinder and trying to scramble out of the hole again. The crowd had pushed him in.

The end of the cylinder was being screwed out from within. Nearly two feet of shining screw projected. Somebody blundered against me, and I narrowly missed being pitched onto the top of the screw. I turned, and as I did so the screw must have come out, for the lid of the cylinder fell upon the gravel with a ringing concussion. I stuck my elbow into the person behind me, and turned my head towards the Thing again. For a moment that circular cavity seemed perfectly black. I had the sunset in my eyes.

I think everyone expected to see a man emerge—possibly something a little unlike us terrestrial men, but in all essentials a man. I know I did. But, looking, I presently saw something stirring within the shadow: greyish billowy movements, one above another, and then two luminous disks—like eyes. Then something resembling a little grey snake, about the thickness of a walking stick, coiled up out of the writhing middle, and wriggled in the air towards me—and then another.

A sudden chill came over me. There was a loud shriek from a woman behind. I half turned, keeping my eyes fixed upon the cylinder still, from which other tentacles were now projecting, and began pushing my way back from the edge of the pit. I saw astonishment giving place to horror on the faces of the people about me. I heard inarticulate exclamations on all sides. There was a general movement backwards. I saw the shopman struggling still on the edge of the pit. I found myself alone, and saw the people on the other side of the pit running off, Stent among them. I looked again at the cylinder, and ungovernable terror gripped me. I stood petrified and staring.

A big greyish rounded bulk, the size, perhaps, of a bear, was rising slowly and painfully out of the cylinder. As it bulged up and caught the light, it glistened like wet leather.

Two large dark-coloured eyes were regarding me steadfastly. The mass that framed them, the head of the thing, was rounded, and had, one might say, a face. There was a mouth under the eyes, the lipless brim of which quivered and panted, and dropped saliva. The whole creature heaved and pulsated convulsively. A lank tentacular appendage gripped the edge of the cylinder, another swayed in the air.

Those who have never seen a living Martian can scarcely imagine the strange horror of its appearance. The peculiar V-shaped mouth with its pointed upper lip, the absence of brow ridges, the absence of a chin beneath the wedgelike lower lip, the incessant quivering of this mouth, the Gorgon groups of tentacles, the tumultuous breathing of the lungs in a strange atmosphere, the evident heaviness and painfulness of movement due to the greater gravitational energy of the earth—above all, the extraordinary intensity of the immense eyes—were at once vital, intense, inhuman, crippled and monstrous. There was something fungoid in the oily brown skin, something in the clumsy deliberation of the tedious movements unspeakably nasty. Even at this first encounter, this first glimpse, I was overcome with disgust and dread.

Suddenly the monster vanished. It had toppled over the brim of the cylinder and fallen into the pit, with a thud like the fall of a great mass of leather. I heard it give a peculiar thick cry, and forthwith another of these creatures appeared darkly in the deep shadow of the aperture.

I turned and, running madly, made for the first group of trees, perhaps a hundred yards away; but I ran slantingly and stumbling, for I could not avert my face from these things.

There, among some young pine trees and furze bushes, I stopped, panting, and waited further developments. The common round the sand pits was dotted with people, standing like myself in a half-fascinated terror, staring at these creatures, or rather at the heaped gravel at the edge of the pit in which they lay. And then, with a renewed horror, I saw a round, black object bobbing up and down on the edge of the pit. It was the head of the shopman who had fallen in, but showing as a little black object against the hot western sun. Now he got his shoulder and knee up, and again he seemed to slip back until only his head was visible. Suddenly he vanished, and I could have fancied a faint shriek had reached me. I had a momentary impulse to go back and help him that my fears overruled.

Everything was then quite invisible, hidden by the deep pit and the heap of sand that the fall of the cylinder had made. Anyone coming along the road from Chobham or Woking would have been amazed at the sight—a dwindling multitude of perhaps a hundred people or more standing in a great irregular circle, in ditches, behind bushes, behind gates and hedges, saying little to one another and that in short, excited shouts, and staring, staring hard at a few heaps of sand. The barrow of ginger beer stood, a queer derelict, black against the burning sky, and in the sand pits was a row of deserted vehicles with their horses feeding out of nosebags or pawing the ground.

5

---❦---

THE HEAT-RAY

After the glimpse I had had of the Martians emerging from the cylinder in which they had come to the earth from their planet, a kind of fascination paralysed my actions. I remained standing knee-deep in the heather, staring at the mound that hid them. I was a battleground of fear and curiosity.

I did not dare to go back towards the pit, but I felt a passionate longing to peer into it. I began walking, therefore, in a big curve, seeking some point of vantage and continually looking at the sand heaps that hid these new-comers to our earth. Once a leash of thin black whips, like the arms of an octopus, flashed across the sunset and was immediately withdrawn, and afterwards a thin rod rose up, joint by joint, bearing at its apex a circular disk that spun with a wobbling motion. What could be going on there?

Most of the spectators had gathered in one or two groups—one a little crowd towards Woking, the other a knot of people in the direction of Chobham. Evidently they shared my mental conflict. There were few near me. One man I approached—he was, I perceived, a neighbour of mine, though I did not know his name—and accosted. But it was scarcely a time for articulate conversation.

"What ugly brutes!" he said. "What ugly brutes!" He repeated this over and over again.

"Did you see a man in the pit?" I said; but he made no answer to that. We became silent, and stood watching for a time side by side, deriving, I fancy, a certain comfort in one another's company. Then I shifted my position to a little knoll that gave me the advantage of a yard or more of elevation and when I looked for him presently he was walking towards Woking.

The sunset faded to twilight before anything further happened. The crowd far away on the left, towards Woking, seemed to grow, and I heard now a faint murmur from it. The little knot of people towards Chobham dispersed. There was scarcely an intimation of movement from the pit.

It was this, as much as anything, that gave people courage, and I suppose the new arrivals from Woking also helped to restore confidence. At any rate, as the dusk came on a slow, intermittent movement upon the sand pits began, a movement that seemed to gather force as the stillness of the evening about the cylinder remained unbroken. Vertical black figures in twos and threes would advance, stop, watch, and advance again, spreading out as they did so in a thin irregular crescent that promised to enclose the pit in its attenuated horns. I, too, on my side began to move towards the pit.

Then I saw some cabmen and others had walked boldly into the sand pits, and heard the clatter of hoofs and the gride of wheels. I saw a lad trundling off the barrow of apples. And then, within thirty yards of the pit, advancing from the direction of Horsell, I noted a little black knot of men, the foremost of whom was waving a white flag.

This was the Deputation. There had been a hasty consultation, and since the Martians were evidently, in spite of their repulsive forms, intelligent creatures, it had been resolved to show them, by approaching them with signals, that we too were intelligent.

Flutter, flutter, went the flag, first to the right, then to the left. It was too far for me to recognise anyone there, but afterwards I learned that Ogilvy, Stent, and Henderson were with others in this attempt at communication. This little group had in its advance dragged inward, so to speak, the circumference of the now almost complete circle of people, and a number of dim black figures followed it at discreet distances.

Suddenly there was a flash of light, and a quantity of luminous greenish smoke came out of the pit in three distinct puffs, which drove up, one after the other, straight into the still air.

This smoke (or flame, perhaps, would be the better word for it) was so bright that the deep blue sky overhead and the hazy stretches of brown common towards Chertsey, set with black pine trees, seemed to darken abruptly as these puffs arose, and to remain the darker after their dispersal. At the same time a faint hissing sound became audible.

Beyond the pit stood the little wedge of people with the white flag at its apex, arrested by these phenomena, a little knot of small vertical black shapes upon the black ground. As the green smoke arose, their faces flashed out pallid green, and faded again as it vanished. Then slowly the hissing passed into a humming, into a long, loud, droning noise. Slowly a humped shape rose out of the pit, and the ghost of a beam of light seemed to flicker out from it.

Forthwith flashes of actual flame, a bright glare leaping from one to another, sprang from the scattered group of men. It was as if some invisible jet impinged upon them and flashed into white flame. It was as if each man were suddenly and momentarily turned to fire.

Then, by the light of their own destruction, I saw them staggering and falling, and their supporters turning to run.

I stood staring, not as yet realising that this was death leaping from man to man in that little distant crowd. All I felt was that it was something very strange. An almost noiseless and blinding flash of light, and a man fell headlong and lay still; and as the unseen shaft of heat passed over them, pine trees burst into fire, and every dry furze bush became with one dull thud a mass of flames. And far away towards Knaphill I saw the flashes of trees and hedges and wooden buildings suddenly set alight.

It was sweeping round swiftly and steadily, this flaming death, this invisible, inevitable sword of heat. I perceived it coming towards me by the flashing bushes it touched, and was too astounded and stupefied to stir. I heard the crackle of fire in the sand pits and the sudden squeal of a horse that was as suddenly stilled. Then it was as if an invisible yet intensely heated finger were drawn through the heather between me and the Martians, and all along a curving line beyond the sand pits the dark ground smoked and crackled. Something fell with a crash far away to the left where the road from Woking station opens out on the common. Forthwith the hissing and humming ceased, and the black, dome-like object sank slowly out of sight into the pit.

All this had happened with such swiftness that I had stood motionless, dumbfounded and dazzled by the flashes of light. Had that death swept through a full circle, it must inevitably have slain me in my surprise. But it passed and spared me, and left the night about me suddenly dark and unfamiliar.

The undulating common seemed now dark almost to blackness, except where its roadways lay grey and pale under the deep blue sky of the early night. It was dark, and suddenly void of men. Overhead the stars were mustering, and in the west the sky was still a pale, bright, almost greenish blue. The tops of the pine trees and the roofs of Horsell came out sharp and black against the western afterglow. The Martians and their appliances were altogether invisible, save for that thin mast upon which their restless mirror wobbled. Patches of bush and isolated trees here and there smoked and glowed still, and the houses towards Woking station were sending up spires of flame into the stillness of the evening air.

Nothing was changed save for that and a terrible astonishment. The little group of black specks with the flag of white had been swept out of existence, and the stillness of the evening, so it seemed to me, had scarcely been broken.

It came to me that I was upon this dark common, helpless, unprotected, and alone. Suddenly, like a thing falling upon me from without, came—fear.

With an effort I turned and began a stumbling run through the heather.

The fear I felt was no rational fear, but a panic terror not only of the Martians, but of the dusk and stillness all about me. Such an extraordinary effect in unmanning me it had that I ran weeping silently as a child might do. Once I had turned, I did not dare to look back.

I remember I felt an extraordinary persuasion that I was being played with, that presently, when I was upon the very verge of safety, this mysterious death—as swift as the passage of light—would leap after me from the pit about the cylinder and strike me down.

6

❧◦❧

THE HEAT-RAY
IN THE CHOBHAM ROAD

It is still a matter of wonder how the Martians are able to slay men so swiftly and so silently. Many think that in some way they are able to generate an intense heat in a chamber of practically absolute non-conductivity. This intense heat they project in a parallel beam against any object they choose, by means of a polished parabolic mirror of unknown composition, much as the parabolic mirror of a lighthouse projects a beam of light. But no one has absolutely proved these details. However it is done, it is certain that a beam of heat is the essence of the matter. Heat, and invisible, instead of visible, light. Whatever is combustible flashes into flame at its touch, lead runs like water, it softens iron, cracks and melts glass, and when it falls upon water, incontinently that explodes into steam.

That night nearly forty people lay under the starlight about the pit, charred and distorted beyond recognition, and all night long the common from Horsell to Maybury was deserted and brightly ablaze. No one was there to see poor Ogilvy rise to his feet with the other slain men. In the deep shadows of the desolate dark, each and every one of the charred bodies sat up and got to their feet. How the Martians reacted to this unnatural occurrence, who could say? Perhaps on their world, they'd experienced something like this before but for whatever reason the Heat-Ray did not fire again on these animated corpses. Ogilvy and the others wandered off from the pit. They made their way through the deserted common, shambling along like mindless, soulless monsters. A pack of men, brave enough to venture back to the pit, came strolling up the way, carrying guns and other odd weapons intent on destroying the wretched creatures from another world only to see Ogilvy and the others. At first, cries of excitement and cheers arose among their ranks but this elation quickly turned to horror as the smell of burnt flesh reached them on the breeze and Ogilvy and his brethren drew closer, stepping into the light of their torches. The pack of men recoiled in fear. Many lost their nerve and simply fled back into town. Of those few who remained, watching the dead approach, only my longtime friend, Michael, was of strong enough resolve to take action. He raised his rifle and fired at the abomination of Ogilvy. His rifle cracked, spitting a round straight into the man's chest. Ogilvy spun from the impact but remained on his feet. Ogilvy unleashed an inhuman howl into the night and charged at Michael and the few remaining men of the party. The other dead followed in his wake, descending upon them. Michael and his men were attacked, pulled to the ground, and fed upon that night. Only one, a drunkard named Paul, managed to escape and when he spoke to me of the events, I did not believe him. I wrote his mad tale off to his beloved spirits and insanity of the day.

The news of the massacre probably reached Chobham, Woking, and Ottershaw about the same time though no one else to my knowledge heard Paul's seemingly deranged ravings. After he shared them with me and saw how I reacted, he turned to his drink more heavily than ever and I never saw him again. For my own part, I returned my attention to the alien visitors. In Woking the shops had closed when the tragedy happened, and a number of people, shop people and so forth, attracted by the stories they had heard, were walking over the Horsell Bridge and along the road between the hedges that runs out at last upon the common. You may imagine the young people brushed up after the labours of the day, and making this novelty, as they would make any novelty, the excuse for walking together and enjoying a trivial flirtation. You may figure to yourself the hum of voices along the road in the gloaming. . . .

As yet, of course, few people in Woking even knew that the cylinder had opened or that the dead had walked on the previous night, though poor Henderson had sent a messenger on a bicycle to the post office with a special wire to an evening paper.

As these folks came out by twos and threes upon the open, they found little knots of people talking excitedly and peering at the spinning mirror over the sand pits, and the new-comers were, no doubt, soon infected by the excitement of the occasion.

By half past eight, when the Deputation was destroyed, there may have been a crowd of three hundred people or more at this place, besides those who had left the road to approach the Martians nearer. It struck me as odd that no one mentioned the bodies of those who were slain the day before or questioned their absence. I could only assume everyone thought that the authorities or perhaps the loved ones of the dead had come and disposed of the bodies in a proper manner instead of simply leaving them to rot where they fell the day before. There were three policemen too, one of whom was mounted, doing their best, under instructions from Stent, to keep the people back and deter them from approaching the cylinder. There was some booing from those more thoughtless and excitable souls to whom a crowd is always an occasion for noise and horse-play.

Stent, anticipating some possibilities of a collision, had telegraphed from Horsell to the barracks as soon as the Martians emerged for the help of a company of soldiers to protect these strange creatures from violence, having heard rumors on an attempt to slay them the eve before and stories from the families of men who went missing this morning. After that he returned to lead that ill-fated advance. The description of their death, as it was seen by the crowd, tallies very closely with my own impressions: the three puffs of green smoke, the deep humming note, and the flashes of flame.

But that crowd of people had a far narrower escape than mine. Only the fact that a hummock of heathery sand intercepted the lower part of the Heat-Ray saved them. Had the elevation of the parabolic mirror been a few yards higher, none could have lived to tell the tale. They saw the flashes and the men falling and an invisible hand, as it were, lit the bushes as it hurried towards them through the twilight. Then, with a whistling note that rose above the droning of the pit, the beam swung close over their heads, lighting the tops of the beech trees that line the road, and splitting the bricks, smashing the windows, firing the window frames, and bringing down in crumbling ruin a portion of the gable of the house nearest the corner.

In the sudden thud, hiss, and glare of the igniting trees, the panic-stricken crowd seems to have swayed hesitatingly for some moments. Sparks and burning twigs began to fall into the road, and single leaves like puffs of flame. Hats and dresses caught fire. Then came a crying from the common. There were shrieks and shouts, and suddenly a mounted policeman came galloping through the confusion with his hands clasped over his head, screaming.

"They're coming!" a woman shrieked, and incontinently everyone was turning and pushing at those behind, in order to clear their way to Woking again. They must have bolted as blindly as a flock of sheep. Where the road grows narrow and black between the high banks the crowd jammed, and a desperate struggle occurred. All that crowd did not escape; three persons at least, two women and a little boy, were crushed and trampled there, and left to die amid the terror and the darkness. And they too rose like the men who were slain at the pit both this day and the night before. They reached out with battered, cold hands, clawing at others who raced by them. One of the women caught the ankle of a man fleeing for his life and tripped him, causing him to tumble to the ground. She rolled on top of him and buried her teeth into his neck. As blood spurted into her mouth with the air of every beat of his slowing and dying heart, a new fresh round of screams began from those at the rear of the mad rush away from the pit. I watched as the mounted policeman rode up and dismounted. He drew the club from his belt and advanced on the woman.

"Stop!" he cried, reaching out to pull her away from the now dead man underneath her.

She whirled on him in a fit of rage, fury, and hunger. Her earlier prey forgotten, she took a chunk from his arm as he pounded upon her head and shoulders with his weapon. His blows had little effect that I could see. A chorus of moans rose in the distance and drew my attention away from the grisly scene unfolding in front of me and those who still raced madly towards town. I stared at a group of charred and decaying men whom I had once known when they lived, as they came lumbering after the mob from the east. My throat caught as I saw poor Ogilvy leading them. My will broke and I too ran.

This time without looking back.

7

HOW I REACHED HOME

I raced through the streets as the sounds of screams and even the occasional crack of a rifle sounded behind me. The dead were alive once more and eating the living. It was unthinkable. It was horrific but it was true. Paul's tale haunted me as I saw the truth of it with my own eyes. I said a prayer for him as I ran.

For my own part, I remember nothing else of my flight except the stress of blundering against trees and stumbling through the heather as the dead roamed the streets. All about me gathered the invisible terrors of the Martians; that pitiless sword of heat seemed whirling to and fro, flourishing overhead before it descended and smote me out of life. I came into the road between the crossroads and Horsell, and ran along this to the crossroads.

At last I could go no farther; I was exhausted with the violence of my emotion and of my flight, and I staggered and fell by the wayside. That was near the bridge that crosses the canal by the gasworks. I fell and lay still.

I must have remained there some time.

I sat up, strangely perplexed. For a moment, perhaps, I could not clearly understand how I came there. My mind would not let me recall the woman's blood-smeared mouth as she clung to the struggling policeman so bravely trying to restrain her. My terror had fallen from me like a garment. My hat had gone, and my collar had burst away from its fastener. A few minutes before, there had only been three real things before me—the immensity of the night and space and nature, my own feebleness and anguish, and the near approach of death. Now it was as if something turned over, and the point of view altered abruptly. There was no sensible transition from one state of mind to the other. I was immediately the self of every day again—a decent, ordinary citizen. The silent common, the impulse of my flight, the starting flames, were as if they had been in a dream. I asked myself had these latter things indeed happened? I could not credit it.

I rose and walked unsteadily up the steep incline of the bridge. My mind was a blank wonder. The dead were gone as quickly as they had come. Calm had returned to the area. My muscles and nerves seemed drained of their strength. I dare say I staggered drunkenly. A head rose over the arch, and the figure of a workman carrying a basket appeared.

Beside him ran a little boy. He passed me, wishing me good night as if he too were in a fog of denial in regards to the events of the day. I was minded to speak to him, but did not. I answered his greeting with a meaningless mumble and went on over the bridge.

Over the Maybury arch a train, a billowing tumult of white, firelit smoke, and a long caterpillar of lighted windows, went flying south—clatter, clatter, clap, rap, and it had gone. A dim group of people talked in the gate of one of the houses in the pretty little row of gables that was called Oriental Terrace. It was all so real and so familiar. And that behind me! It was frantic, fantastic! Such things, I told myself, could not be. The dead did not walk and feast upon the living nor had creatures from another world truly come to our own.

Perhaps I am a man of exceptional moods. I do not know how far my experience is common. At times I suffer from the strangest sense of detachment from myself and the world about me; I seem to watch it all from the outside, from somewhere inconceivably remote, out of time, out of space, out of the stress and tragedy of it all. This feeling was very strong upon me that night. Here was another side to my dream.

But the trouble was the blank incongruity of this serenity and the swift death flying yonder, not two miles away. There was a noise of business from the gasworks, and the electric lamps were all alight. I stopped at the group of people.

"What news from the common?" said I.

There were two men and a woman at the gate.

"Eh?" said one of the men, turning.

"What news from the common?" I said.

"Ain't yer just *been* there?" asked the man.

"People seem fair silly about the common," said the woman over the gate. "What's it all about?"

"Haven't you heard of the men from Mars?" said I; "the creatures from Mars? What of the risen dead? Did they not come this way?"

"Quite enough," said the woman over the gate. "Thanks"; and all three of them laughed.

"Risen dead?" I heard them mutter. Clearly they looked upon me as I had Paul.

I felt foolish and angry. I tried and found I could not tell them what I had seen. They laughed again at my broken sentences.

"You'll hear more yet," I said, and went on to my home.

I startled my wife at the doorway, so haggard was I. I went into the dining room, sat down, drank some wine, and so soon as I could collect myself sufficiently I told her the things I had seen. The dinner, which was a cold one, had already been served, and remained neglected on the table while I told my story.

"There is one thing," I said, to allay the fears I had aroused; "they are the most sluggish things I ever saw crawl. They may keep the pit and kill people who come near them, but they cannot get out of it . . . . But the horror of them! Now the dead, they roam free. I do not know where they have vanished to or if perhaps the police and other good men have managed to contain them."

"Don't, dear!" said my wife, knitting her brows and putting her hand on mine.

"Poor Ogilvy!" I said. "I saw him, honey. All charred and burnt. His melted flesh hanging off him and yet he moved. His eyes were soulless and hungry like those of an animal!"

My wife at least did not find my experience incredible. When I saw how deadly white her face was, I ceased abruptly. There was no reason to worry her further. Surely, the authorities had dealt with the dead and the sluggish aliens were trapped within the confines of their pit, or at least I told myself so.

"They may come here," she said again and again.

I pressed her to take wine, and tried to reassure her.

"They can scarcely move," I said.

I began to comfort her and myself by repeating all that Ogilvy had told me of the impossibility of the Martians establishing themselves on the earth. In particular I laid stress on the gravitational difficulty. On the surface of the earth the force of gravity is three times what it is on the surface of Mars. A Martian, therefore, would weigh three times more than on Mars, albeit his muscular strength would be the same. His own body would be a cope of lead to him. That, indeed, was the general opinion. Both *The Times* and the *Daily Telegraph,* for instance, insisted on it the next morning, and both overlooked, just as I did, two obvious modifying influences and no mention of the dead was made within their pages.

The atmosphere of the earth, we now know, contains far more oxygen or far less argon (whichever way one likes to put it) than does Mars. The invigorating influences of this excess of oxygen upon the Martians indisputably did much to counterbalance the increased weight of their bodies. And, in the second place, we all overlooked the fact that such mechanical intelligence as the Martian possessed was quite able to dispense with muscular exertion at a pinch.

But I did not consider these points at the time, and so my reasoning was dead against the chances of the invaders. And as to the dead, my best guess was that poor Ogilvy had been changed from the radiation of the Martians' strange cylinder and this same energy had affected the rest of the dead as well, giving them life once more where no such thing should exist. I did not realize at the time the true danger of Ogilvy's infection or how rapidly it would spread. With wine and food, the confidence of my own table, and the necessity of reassuring my wife, I grew by insensible degrees courageous and secure.

"They have done a foolish thing," said I, fingering my wineglass. "They are dangerous because, no doubt, they are mad with terror. Perhaps they expected to find no living things—certainly no intelligent living things.

"A shell in the pit," said I, "if the worst comes to the worst will kill them all, the dead as well. If they can die once, they can do so again and be put into the earth for eternity." I just hoped that by obliterating them, they would not somehow resurrect themselves.

The intense excitement of the events had no doubt left my perceptive powers in a state of erethism. I remember that dinner table with extraordinary vividness even now. My dear wife's sweet anxious face peering at me from under the pink lamp shade, the white cloth with its silver and glass table furniture—for in those days even philosophical writers had many little luxuries—the crimson-purple wine in my glass, are photographically distinct. At the end of it I sat, tempering nuts with a cigarette, regretting Ogilvy's rashness and his demise, and denouncing the shortsighted timidity of the Martians.

So some respectable dodo in the Mauritius might have lorded it in his nest, and discussed the arrival of that shipful of pitiless sailors in want of animal food. "We will peck them to death tomorrow, my dear."

I did not know it, but that was the last civilised dinner I was to eat for very many strange and terrible days. And after I saw my wife off to bed, I proceeded to go around the house checking and rechecking the locks and making sure the windows were barred.

The images of the dead haunted me in my dreams and I heard their pitiful and inhuman howls in my mind throughout the night.

8

---◆◆◆◆◆---

FRIDAY NIGHT

The most extraordinary thing to my mind, of all the strange and wonderful things that happened upon that Friday, was the dovetailing of the commonplace habits of our social order with the first beginnings of the series of events that was to topple that social order headlong. If on Friday night you had taken a pair of compasses and drawn a circle with a radius of five miles round the Woking sand pits, I doubt if you would have had one human being outside it, unless it were some relation of Stent or of the three or four cyclists, whose emotions or habits were at all affected by the new-comers. Many people had heard of the cylinder, of course, and talked about it in their leisure, but it certainly did not make the sensation that an ultimatum to Germany would have done.

In London that night poor Henderson's telegram describing the gradual unscrewing of the shot was judged to be a canard, and his evening paper, after wiring for authentication from him and receiving no reply—the man was killed—decided not to print a special edition.

Still no one spoke of the happenings with the dead. It was as if such a topic was too unsavory and abominable to be discussed aloud or written about in print.

Even within the five-mile circle the great majority of people were inert. I have already described the behaviour of the men and women to whom I spoke. All over the district people were dining and supping; working men were gardening after the labours of the day, children were being put to bed, young people were wandering through the lanes love-making, students sat over their books.

Maybe there was a murmur in the village streets, a novel and dominant topic in the public-houses, and here and there a messenger, or even an eye-witness of the later occurrences with the Martians, caused a whirl of excitement, a shouting, and a running to and fro; but for the most part the daily routine of working, eating, drinking, sleeping, went on as it had done for countless years—as though no planet Mars existed in the sky. Even at Woking station and Horsell and Chobham that was the case.

In Woking junction, until a late hour, trains were stopping and going on, others were shunting on the sidings, passengers were alighting and waiting, and everything was proceeding in the most ordinary way. A boy from the town, trenching on Smith's monopoly, was selling papers with the afternoon's news. The ringing impact of trucks, the sharp whistle of the engines from the junction, mingled with their shouts of "Men from Mars!" Excited men came into the station about nine o'clock with incredible tidings, and caused no more disturbance than drunkards might have done. People rattling Londonwards peered into the darkness outside the carriage windows, and saw only a rare, flickering, vanishing spark dance up from the direction of Horsell, a red glow and a thin veil of smoke driving across the stars, and thought that nothing more serious than a heath fire was happening. It was only round the edge of the common that any disturbance was perceptible. There were half a dozen villas burning on the Woking border. There were lights in all the houses on the common side of the three villages, and the people there kept awake till dawn.

A curious crowd lingered restlessly, people coming and going but the crowd remaining, both on the Chobham and Horsell bridges. One or two adventurous souls, it was afterwards found, went into the darkness and crawled quite near the Martians; but they never returned, for now and again a light-ray, like the beam of a warship's searchlight swept the common, and the Heat-Ray was ready to follow. It is also possible they were eaten by the dead, who seemed to be keeping in the shadows and out of the spotlight. I wondered where the creatures could have disappeared to. Their number must have been nearing five dozen between the first forty who rose and those who died in the attack. A noise of hammering from the pit was heard by many people. It continued night and day. One lad who had managed to make it into the common and back claimed the aliens had retreated into their craft and the dead were pounding upon it relentlessly with their rotting fists, trying to get inside.

So you have the state of things on Friday night. In the centre, sticking into the skin of our old planet Earth like a poisoned dart, was this cylinder. But the poison was scarcely working yet. Around it was a patch of silent common, smouldering in places, and with a few dark, dimly seen objects lying in contorted attitudes here and there. Here and there was a burning bush or tree. Beyond was a fringe of excitement, and farther than that fringe the inflammation had not crept as yet. In the rest of the world the stream of life still flowed as it had flowed for immemorial years. The fever of war that would presently clog vein and artery, deaden nerve and destroy brain, had still to develop and none of us had even an inkling of the horror that the dead were to bring us as well. It was my belief that the dead were not of the Martians' doing but rather merely a side effect of their arrival and a single man's rashness, who would become the carrier of a plague unlike any the world had ever known in regards to its violence.

All night long the Martians' cylinder was being hammered upon by the dead, but also from inside the cylinder itself came the sounds of the work—stirring, sleepless, indefatigable—upon the machines they were making ready and ever and again a puff of greenish-white smoke whirled up to the starlit sky.

About eleven a company of soldiers came through Horsell, and deployed along the edge of the common to form a cordon. Later a second company marched through Chobham to deploy on the north side of the common. Several officers from the Inkerman barracks had spied upon the common earlier in the day, via handheld telescopes and such. One, Major Eden, who had ventured into the common on foot, was reported to be missing. The colonel of the regiment came to the Chobham bridge and was busy questioning the crowd at ten. The military authorities were certainly alive to the seriousness of the business.

Around eleven, a series of howls rose from the commons. The voices who issued the cries were at once hollow and filled with pain locked in a maddening paradox of human versus thing. Many believed it was the Martians at first until the first of the dead appeared. He was a common man wearing the tattered, burnt remains of a workman's clothes. Lumbering from the shadows, he advanced on the soldiers stationed at the edge of the common. Major Eden stared at him in disbelief as a young soldier shouted at the man to stop, warning him that he would be fired upon. The man paid the soldier no heed and continued on his path towards those gathered before him. A curly-haired soldier pushed the younger one aside and raised his rifle. A shot rang out. It struck the man, knocking his shoulder sideways as it impacted him, but the man did not scream or fall; he did not so much as flinch. Shaking his head, the soldier fired again. The man teetered, looking down at where the second round had entered his stomach, but still he did not fall. Before a third shot could be loosed, everyone noticed the man was no longer alone. From the shadows, the other dead emerged, numbering somewhere around fifty in all. Poor Ogilvy was still among their ranks. The breeze carried the stench of decay to the crowd and the line of soldiers.

Many of the crowd were now dispersing and losing their faith in the army's ability to stop the dead.

"Fire at will!" Major Eden yelled, running to the front line like some kind of epic hero one reads of in novels of warfare and swashbuckling adventure.

The cracks of the men's rifles were deafening as the whole company opened fire. The dead loosed a series of angry snarls, which could be heard above the cacophony of the battle. They charged into the soldiers' ranks. Many of the dead fell to the soldiers' fire but not all. Dozens poured into the firing line with clawing hands and gnashing teeth. The soldiers were terrified by what they faced but somehow managed to hold their ground, fighting the dead back in hand-to-hand combat the moment the monsters slammed into them. The gunfire and snarls became mixed with the cries of dying men. Rifles became clubs bashing into and slamming against rotten flesh. The dead were relentless and their fury only seemed to grow.

Finally the ranks broke.

Several of the dead made it through, running beyond the common, wild into the night. A lucky shot by the major himself to one of the things' skulls splattered grey matter onto the ground. The major noticed the creature stirred no more. Whereas wounds to anywhere else had little to no effect on the dead, his head shot dropped the creature cold and it did not move again. He ordered the soldiers all to aim for the heads of the dead men and women. The brave men, now knowing their enemy had a weakness, fought with renewed courage. The major himself charged into the melee, emptying his hand gun into the faces of the closest dead. He yelled a battle cry as he tossed aside his spent pistol and grabbed up the rifle of one of his fallen men. Screaming with a mixture of rage and determination, he swung it with all the strength he could muster, smashing in the skull of the closest dead man. As the corpse fell at his feet, he'd already moved on, engaging another of the things snarling and wailing before him. The major lost himself in this dance of death until at last there were no more of the things within his reach. As he paused, seeking another of the things to return to the grave, he realized the battle was over.

Corpses lay scattered everywhere, decayed ones and the freshly dead both. Major Eden was greatly concerned about the dead who had broken through and quickly dispatched squads of men to seek them out and eliminate them. Then the clean up began. As everyone set about trying to clear the field of the dead, another nightmare started. The freshly dead soldiers reanimated with hunger in their eyes and turned on those who had survived the other dead's assault. These newly risen monstrosities were put down with great haste and no withholding of ammunition. After this, Major Eden ordered all the bodies to be burnt to ashes and large pyres blazed under the stars as more and more bodies were tossed upon it.

About eleven, the next morning's papers were able to say, a squadron of hussars, two Maxims, and about four hundred men of the Cardigan regiment started from Aldershot to reinforce the demoralized and humbled troops who had faced the hungry dead. There was no covering it up now. The dead were real to all, though the papers mentioned time and time again that the commons were now clear of the deadly things and it was safer, if it could be called such, to come and witness the aliens from another world. The threat of being cooked alive by men from Mars held nowhere near the level of fear that being eaten alive by a former neighbor did.

A few seconds after midnight the crowd in the Chertsey road, Woking, saw a star fall from heaven into the pine woods to the northwest. It had a greenish colour, and caused a silent brightness like summer lightning. This was the second cylinder.

9

THE FIGHTING WITH THE ALIENS BEGINS

Saturday lives in my memory as a day of suspense. It was a day of lassitude too, hot and close, with, I am told, a rapidly fluctuating barometer. I had slept but little, still bothered by my encounters with the dead and the aliens alike, though my wife had succeeded in sleeping, and I rose early. I went into my garden before breakfast and stood listening, but towards the common there was nothing stirring but a lark.

The milkman came as usual. I heard the rattle of his chariot and I went round to the side gate to ask the latest news. He told me that during the night the Martians had been surrounded by troops and there was no word of what happened to the dead who'd broken through the army's ranks the night before. Many believed they were now hiding in the city and preying on those who happened to wander down the wrong street at the wrong time. Already, over a half dozen more men and three women had been reported missing. Then—a familiar, reassuring note—I heard a train running towards Woking.

"They aren't to be killed," said the milkman, "if that can possibly be avoided. They still want to talk to the Martians if they can. The dead though . . . I will be happy to see them put back in the grave."

I saw my neighbour gardening, chatted with him for a time, and then strolled in to breakfast. It was a most unexceptional morning. My neighbour was of the opinion that the troops would be able to capture or to destroy the Martians during the day. He feared, though, that the dead were the real threat. The Martians were still trapped in their pit, or so it seemed at the time, and the dead ran free.

"It's a pity they make themselves so unapproachable," he said. "It would be curious to know how they live on another planet; we might learn a thing or two."

I am amazed no one outright blamed the Martians for the dead. Perhaps it was a grand facade shared by all that even those creatures in the pit respected God and nature as we did and despite their hideous appearance, not even they would be capable of defying and defiling the very order of the world in such a manner.

He came up to the fence and extended a handful of strawberries, for his gardening was as generous as it was enthusiastic. At the same time he told me of the burning of the pine woods about the Byfleet Golf Links.

"They say," said he, "that there's another of those blessed things fallen there—number two. This time the dead have not risen around it . . . yet. That is a thing to be thankful for. But surely one's enough. This lot'll cost the insurance people a pretty penny before everything's settled." He laughed with an air of the greatest good humour as he said this. The woods, he said, were still burning, and pointed out a haze of smoke to me. "They will be hot under foot for days, on account of the thick soil of pine needles and turf," he said, and then grew serious over "poor Ogilvy." He had known Ogilvy as I had. It was sickening to think of our friend out there shambling around with blood-smeared lips and his soul lost.

After breakfast, instead of working, I decided to walk down towards the common. I couldn't bring myself to do this without being armed. I made my way back to the bedroom and opened the closet. There, tucked away in a dust-covered box, sat a Remington revolver which had belonged to a long dead relative of mine. It was an inheritance I had considered useless and my wife once every so often demanded I remove from the house, yet I had always kept it. Perhaps out of fear of a time such as this, I cannot say. I flipped its chamber open and loaded the six bullets in the waiting slots of its cylinder and closed it back up. Tucking the gun into the pocket of my coat, I set forth to face the day. Under the railway bridge I found a group of soldiers—sappers, I think, men in small round caps, dirty red jackets unbuttoned, and showing their blue shirts, dark trousers, and boots coming to the calf. They told me no one was allowed over the canal, and, looking along the road towards the bridge, I saw one of the Cardigan men standing sentinel there. I talked with these soldiers for a time; I told them of my sight of the Martians on the previous evening and of what had transpired with the dead. None of them had been present for that battle—they had only just arrived this morning—nor had they seen the Martians and had only the vaguest ideas of them, so that they plied me with questions. They said that they did not know who had authorised the movements of the troops; their idea was that a dispute had arisen at the Horse Guards. The ordinary sapper is a great deal better educated than the common soldier, and they discussed the peculiar conditions of the possible fight with some acuteness. I described the Heat-Ray to them, and they began to argue among themselves.

"Crawl up under cover and rush 'em, say I," said one.

"Get aht!," said another. "What's cover against this 'ere 'eat? Sticks to cook yer! What we got to do is to go as near as the ground'll let us, and then drive a trench."

"Blow yer trenches! You always want trenches; you ought to ha' been born a rabbit, Snippy. What if them dead things come back? You want to be stuck in a trench with them nippin' at ya?"

"Ain't they got any necks, then?" said a third, abruptly—a little, contemplative, dark man, smoking a pipe.

I repeated my description.

"Octopuses," said he, "that's what I calls 'em. Talk about fishers of men—fighters of fish it is this time!"

"It ain't no murder killing beasts like that," said the first speaker. "And it ain't no murder killin' the dead either. They just need to be reminded of what they are and I thinks a couple of rounds in them will do that!"

"Why not shell the darned things strite off and finish 'em?" said the little dark man. "You carn tell what they might do."

"Where's your shells?" said the first speaker. "There ain't no time. Do it in a rush, that's my tip, and do it at once."

So they discussed it. After a while I left them, and went on to the railway station to get as many morning papers as I could.

But I will not weary the reader with a description of that long morning and of the longer afternoon where in half of those I met were terrified the dead were coming after them and the other half spoke of nothing but the men from Mars and ranted on about them like men possessed. I did not succeed in getting a glimpse of the common, for even Horsell and Chobham church towers were in the hands of the military authorities. The soldiers I addressed didn't know anything; the officers were mysterious as well as busy. I found people in the town quite secure again in the presence of the military, and I heard for the first time from Marshall, the tobacconist, that his son was among the dead on the common. The soldiers had made the people on the outskirts of Horsell lock up and leave their houses.

I got back to lunch about two, very tired for, as I have said, the day was extremely hot and dull; and in order to refresh myself I took a cold bath in the afternoon. About half past four I went up to the railway station to get an evening paper, for the morning papers had contained only a very inaccurate description of the killing of Stent, Henderson, Ogilvy, and the others. But there was little I didn't know of this. However, it also contained a wild story of the dead's battle with the military and of the creatures' escape from the commons. The author of the article went on to ramble about how the dead carried a plague in their teeth and spread it to each person they attacked so that they too would rise and join the ranks of the unholy. This mad journalist feared the dead would sweep across our cities like a new Black Plague and leave very few alive in their wake.

The Martians did not show an inch of themselves. They seemed busy in their pit now that the dead no longer troubled them, and there was a sound of hammering and an almost continuous streamer of smoke. Apparently they were busy getting ready for a struggle. "Fresh attempts have been made to signal, but without success," was the stereotyped formula of the papers. A sapper told me it was done by a man in a ditch with a flag on a long pole. The Martians took as much notice of such advances as we should of the lowing of a cow.

I must confess the sight of all this armament, all this preparation, greatly excited me. My imagination became belligerent, and defeated the invaders in a dozen striking ways; something of my schoolboy dreams of battle and hero-ism came back. It hardly seemed a fair fight to me at that time. They seemed very helpless in that pit of theirs.

About three o'clock there began the thud of a gun at measured intervals from Chertsey or Addlestone. I learned that the smouldering pine wood into which the second cylinder had fallen was being shelled, in the hope of destroying that object before it opened. It was only about five, however, that a field gun reached Chobham for use against the first body of Martians.

About six in the evening, as I sat at tea with my wife in the summerhouse talking vigorously about the battle that was lowering upon us, I heard a muffled detonation from the common, and immediately after a gust of firing. Close on the heels of that came a violent rattling crash, quite close to us, that shook the ground; and, starting out upon the lawn, I saw the tops of the trees about the Oriental College burst into smoky red flame, and the tower of the little church beside it slide down into ruin. The pinnacle of the mosque had vanished, and the roof line of the college itself looked as if a hundred-ton gun had been at work upon it. One of our chimneys cracked as if a shot had hit it, flew, and a piece of it came clattering down the tiles and made a heap of broken red fragments upon the flower bed by my study window.

I and my wife stood amazed. Then I realised that the crest of Maybury Hill must be within range of the Martians' Heat-Ray now that the college was cleared out of the way.

At that I gripped my wife's arm, and without ceremony ran her out into the road. Then I fetched out the servant, telling her I would go upstairs myself for the box she was clamouring for.

"We can't possibly stay here," I said; and as I spoke the firing reopened for a moment upon the common. My hand felt around in my pocket for the reassuring feel of the hilt of the Remington tucked away there.

"But where are we to go?" said my wife in terror.

I thought, perplexed. Then I remembered her cousins at Leatherhead.

"Leatherhead!" I shouted above the sudden noise.

She looked away from me downhill. The people were coming out of their houses, astonished.

"How are we to get to Leatherhead?" she said.

Down the hill I saw a bevy of hussars ride under the railway bridge; three galloped through the open gates of the Oriental College; two others dismounted, and began running from house to house. The sun, shining through the smoke that drove up from the tops of the trees, seemed blood red, and threw an unfamiliar lurid light upon everything.

"Stop here," said I; "you are safe here"; and I started off at once for the Spotted Dog, for I knew the landlord had a horse and dog cart. I ran, for I perceived that in a moment everyone upon this side of the hill would be moving. I found him in his bar, quite unaware of what was going on behind his house. A man stood with his back to me, talking to him.

"I must have a pound," said the landlord, "and I've no one to drive it."

"I'll give you two," said I, over the stranger's shoulder.

"What for?"

"And I'll bring it back by midnight," I said.

"Lord!" said the landlord; "what's the hurry? I'm selling my bit of a pig. Two pounds, and you bring it back? What's going on now?"

I explained hastily that I had to leave my home, and so secured the dog cart. At the time it did not seem to me nearly so urgent that the landlord should leave his. I took care to have the cart there and then, drove it off down the road, and, leaving it in charge of my wife and servant, rushed into my house and packed a few valuables, such plate as we had, and so forth. The beech trees below the house were burning while I did this, and the palings up the road glowed red. While I was occupied in this way, one of the dismounted hussars came running up. He was going from house to house, warning people to leave. He was going on as I came out of my front door, lugging my treasures, done up in a tablecloth. I shouted after him:

"What news?"

He turned, stared, bawled something about "crawling out in a thing like a dish cover," and ran on to the gate of the house at the crest. A sudden whirl of black smoke driving across the road hid him for a moment. I ran to my neighbour's door and rapped to satisfy myself of what I already knew, that his wife had gone to London with him and had locked up their house. I went in again, according to my promise, to get my servant's box, lugged it out, clapped it beside her on the tail of the dog cart, and then caught the reins and jumped up into the driver's seat beside my wife. In another moment we were clear of the smoke and noise, and spanking down the opposite slope of Maybury Hill towards Old Woking.

In front was a quiet sunny landscape, a wheat field ahead on either side of the road, and the Maybury Inn with its swinging sign. I saw the doctor's cart ahead of me. At the bottom of the hill I turned my head to look at the hillside I was leaving. Thick streamers of black smoke shot with threads of red fire were driving up into the still air, and throwing dark shadows upon the green treetops eastward. The smoke already extended far away to the east and west—to the Byfleet pine woods eastward, and to Woking on the west. The road was dotted with people running towards us. And very faint now, but very distinct through the hot, quiet air, one heard the whirr of a machine-gun that was presently stilled, and an intermittent cracking of rifles. Apparently the Martians were setting fire to everything within range of their Heat-Ray.

I am not an expert driver, and I had immediately to turn my attention to the horse. When I looked back again the second hill had hidden the black smoke. I slashed the horse with the whip, and gave him a loose rein until Woking and Send lay between us and that quivering tumult. I overtook and passed the doctor between Woking and Send.

10

IN THE STORM

Leatherhead is about twelve miles from Maybury Hill. The scent of hay was in the air through the lush meadows beyond Pyrford, and the hedges on either side were sweet and gay with multitudes of dog-roses. The heavy firing that had broken out while we were driving down Maybury Hill ceased as abruptly as it began, leaving the evening very peaceful and still. We got to Leatherhead without misadventure about nine o'clock, and the horse had an hour's rest while I took supper with my cousins and commended my wife to their care.

My wife was curiously silent throughout the drive, and seemed oppressed with forebodings of evil. I talked to her reassuringly, pointing out that the Martians were tied to the

had been pierced as it were by a thread of green fire, suddenly lighting their confusion and falling into the field to my left. It was the third falling star!

Close on its apparition, and blindingly violet by contrast, danced out the first lightning of the gathering storm, and the thunder burst like a rocket overhead. The horse took the bit between his teeth and bolted.

A moderate incline runs towards the foot of Maybury Hill, and down this we clattered. Once the lightning had begun, it went on in as rapid a succession of flashes as I have ever seen. The thunderclaps, treading one on the heels of another and with a strange crackling accompaniment, sounded more like the working of a gigantic electric machine than the usual detonating reverberations. The flickering light was blinding and confusing, and a thin hail smote gustily at my face as I drove down the slope.

At first I regarded little but the road before me, but as a decaying man stepped out of the trees into my path, I was forced to pull back on the reins lest I collide with him. I stopped and stared, transfixed, as he loosed a wild howl and came running towards me. I whipped the Remington from my pocket to take aim but his hands were already upon me. He pulled me out into the roadway and we wrestled in the dirt. His yellow teeth snapped at me as I pressed an arm under his chin to keep his mouth at bay. I felt his hands clawing upon the shoulders of my coat as I forced the pistol up and pressed it to his forehead. I squeezed the trigger and the gun bucked in my hand, discharging its brand of death into his skull. His blood sprayed onto me. I leaped to my feet, brushing it off with panicked hands. I ran back to my transportation and prepared to flee, fearing where there was one of the dead there would be others, but then abruptly my attention was arrested by something that was moving rapidly down the opposite slope of Maybury Hill. At first I took it for the wet roof of a house, but one flash following another showed it to be in swift rolling movement. It was an elusive vision—a moment of bewildering darkness, and then, in a flash like daylight, the red masses of the Orphanage near the crest of the hill, the green tops of the pine trees, and this problematical object came out clear and sharp and bright.

And this Thing I saw! How can I describe it? A monstrous tripod, higher than many houses, striding over the young pine trees, and smashing them aside in its career; a walking engine of glittering metal, striding now across the heather; articulate ropes of steel dangling from it, and the clattering tumult of its passage mingling with the riot of the thunder. A flash, and it came out vividly, heeling over one way with two feet in the air, to vanish and reappear almost instantly as it seemed, with the next flash, a hundred yards nearer. Can you imagine a milking stool tilted and bowled violently along the ground? That was the impression those instant flashes gave. But instead of a milking stool imagine it a great body of machinery on a tripod stand.

Then suddenly the trees in the pine wood ahead of me were parted, as brittle reeds are parted by a man thrusting through them; they were snapped off and driven headlong, and a second huge tripod appeared, rushing, as it seemed, headlong towards me. And I was galloping hard to meet it! At the sight of the second monster my nerve went altogether. Not stopping to look again, I wrenched the horse's head hard round to the right and in another moment the dog cart had heeled over upon the horse; the shafts smashed noisily, and I was flung sideways and fell heavily into a shallow pool of water.

I crawled out almost immediately, and crouched, my feet still in the water, under a clump of furze. The horse lay motionless (his neck was broken, poor brute!) and by the lightning flashes I saw the black bulk of the overturned dog cart and the silhouette of the wheel still spinning slowly. In another moment the colossal mechanism went striding by me, and passed uphill towards Pyrford.

Seen nearer, the Thing was incredibly strange, for it was no mere insensate machine driving on its way. Machine it was, with a ringing metallic pace, and long, flexible, glittering tentacles (one of which gripped a young pine tree) swinging and rattling about its strange body. It picked its road as it went striding along, and the brazen hood that surmounted it moved to and fro with the inevitable suggestion of a head looking about. Behind the main body was a huge mass of white metal like a gigantic fisherman's basket, and puffs of green smoke squirted out from the joints of the limbs as the monster swept by me. And in an instant it was gone.

So much I saw then, all vaguely for the flickering of the lightning, in blinding highlights and dense black shadows.

As it passed it set up an exultant deafening howl that drowned the thunder—"Aloo! Aloo!"—and in another minute it was with its companion, half a mile away, stooping over something in the field. I have no doubt this Thing in the field was the third of the ten cylinders they had fired at us from Mars.

For some minutes I lay there in the rain and darkness watching, by the intermittent light, these monstrous beings of metal moving about in the distance over the hedge tops. A thin hail was now beginning, and as it came and went their figures grew misty and then flashed into clearness again. Now and then came a gap in the lightning, and the night swallowed them up.

I was soaked with hail above and puddle water below. It was some time before my blank astonishment would let me struggle up the bank to a drier position, or think at all of my imminent peril. Then things took yet another turn for the worse. They came from everywhere in the woods around me. The dead ran, howling and wailing as the passing of the Martians' machines spooked them as well. In truth, though, I believe this is merely the dead's nature. They are driven by instinct alone and the greatest of their drives is hunger. I watched as dozens, beyond the point of numbering, emerged in the cooked uniforms of military men. I ducked and prayed they would not see me. I had no means with which to defend myself against their numbers. My mind raced. I knew I had to find shelter or help.

Not far from me was a little one-roomed squatter's hut of wood, surrounded by a trampled patch of potato garden. I struggled to my feet at last, and, crouching and making use of every chance of cover, I made a run for this. When I reached the hut, my stealth gave way to panic. I hammered at the door, but I could not make the people hear (if there were any people inside), and after a time I desisted, and, availing myself of a ditch for the greater part of the way, succeeded in crawling, unobserved by these monstrous machines and the roaming dead, into the pine woods towards Maybury.

Under cover of this I pushed on, wet and shivering now, towards my own house. I walked among the trees trying to find the footpath. It was very dark indeed in the wood, for the lightning was now becoming infrequent, and the hail, which was pouring down in a torrent, fell in columns through the gaps in the heavy foliage.

If I had fully realised the meaning of all the things I had seen I should have immediately worked my way round through Byfleet to Street Cobham, and so gone back to rejoin my wife at Leatherhead. I told myself she was safe there. The dead were here in these woods with me. They had a place to defend and I know our people there kept a few weapons tucked away if for nothing more than hunting. Any rifle or firearm was better than none in these dark times. I longed to join her but that night the strangeness of things about me, and my physical wretchedness, prevented me, for I was bruised, weary, wet to the skin, deafened and blinded by the storm.

I had a vague idea of going on to my own house, and that was as much motive as I had. I knew, though, it may offer no protection from the mighty machines; it would, at least, if boarded and secured properly, hold off the dead lest they attack in numbers such as those I had just witnessed among the trees. I staggered through the woods, fell into a ditch and bruised my knees against a plank, and finally splashed out into the lane that ran down from the College Arms. I say splashed, for the storm water was sweeping the sand down the hill in a muddy torrent. There in the darkness a man blundered into me and sent me reeling back.

He gave a cry of terror, sprang sideways, and rushed on before I could gather my wits sufficiently to speak to him and show him I was human and breathing. He must have thought I was one of the unholy, rotting monsters that filled these woods. I made no attempt to stop him for if he was armed as I was I might have found a bullet in my skull. So heavy was the stress of the storm just at this place that I had the hardest task to win my way up the hill. I went close up to the fence on the left and worked my way along its palings.

Near the top I stumbled upon something soft, and, by a flash of lightning, saw between my feet a heap of black broadcloth and a pair of boots. Before I could distinguish clearly how the man lay, the flicker of light had passed. I stood over him waiting for the next flash. When it came, I saw that he was a sturdy man, cheaply but not shabbily dressed; his head was bent under his body, and he lay crumpled up close to the fence, as though he had been flung violently against it.

Overcoming the repugnance natural to one who had been forced to slay the dead before, I stooped and turned him over to feel for his heart. This was rather as a mistake. I do not know what I was thinking. Even days before such a thing would not have been a danger but now it nearly cost me my life. He was quite dead but nonetheless, his eyes sprang open and were filled with an unspeakable rage. Apparently his neck had been broken for his head dangled limply to one side. The lightning flashed for a third time, and he leaped upon me. I sprang to my feet, shoving him off and back to the mud. It was the landlord of the Spotted Dog, whose conveyance I had taken.

I bashed his face with the butt of my pistol as I fell upon him, striking him again and again until I heard the crunching sound of bone and he lay still once more. I wiped the pistol's butt on my pants and shoved it back inside my coat as I pushed on up the hill. I made my way by the police station and the College Arms towards my own house. It was clear a battle had been fought around it. Many a body with gaping wounds bleeding from their heads lay about and the ground was covered in gnawed-upon body parts and empty shell casings. Nothing was burning on the hillside, though from the common there still came a red glare and a rolling tumult of ruddy smoke beating up against the drenching hail. So far as I could see by the flashes, the houses about me were mostly uninjured. By the College Arms a dark heap lay in the road. I made sure to steer clear of it.

Down the road towards Maybury Bridge there were voices and the sound of feet, but I had not the courage to shout or to go to them. I was filled with fear that they might not be alive and I could simply not stand to stare into another rotting, snarling face. It would break me even if I survived the encounter. I let myself in with my latchkey, closed, locked and bolted the door, staggered to the foot of the staircase, and sat down. My imagination was full of those striding metallic monsters, and of the dead body smashed against the fence.

I crouched at the foot of the staircase with my back to the wall, shivering violently. Then I heard the screams from outside, down the road. The voices I had heard belonged to the living and now the dead had found them.

I shuddered and prayed for their souls.

11

⤖⬥⬤⬥⬗

AT THE WINDOW

I have already said that my storms of emotion have a trick of exhausting themselves. After a time I discovered that I was cold and wet, and with little pools of water and blood not my own about me on the stair carpet. I got up almost mechanically, went into the dining room and drank some whiskey, and then I was moved to change my clothes and make sure the house was as secure as it could be. I bolted the door and closed the shutters over all the barred windows on the ground level. I did this as quietly as possible, hoping not to draw the attention of unwelcome and potential guests.

After I had done that I went upstairs to my study, but why I did so I do not know. The window of my study looks over the trees and the railway towards Horsell Common. In the hurry of our departure this window had been left open, I closed it just in case the dead could climb but remained staring through its wet glass. The passage was dark, and, by contrast with the picture the window frame enclosed, the side of the room seemed impenetrably dark. I turned and stopped short in the doorway as the sounds of the chaos outside called me back to the window.

The thunderstorm had passed. The towers of the Oriental College and the pine trees about it had gone, and very far away, lit by a vivid red glare, the common about the sand pits was visible. Across the light huge black shapes, grotesque and strange, moved busily to and fro. At their feet the dead ran about in scores. Some were crushed under the feet of the Martian machines but their brothers and sisters took no warning from this and continued in their mindless, inhuman hunt for the living. Mayhap the dead thought the machines would flush the living out into their waiting arms?

It seemed indeed as if the whole country in that direction was on fire—a broad hillside set with minute tongues of flame, swaying and writhing with the gusts of the dying storm, and throwing a red reflection upon the cloud scud above. Every now and then a haze of smoke from some nearer conflagration drove across the window and hid the Martian shapes. I could not see what they were doing, nor the clear form of them, nor recognise the black objects they were busied upon. Neither could I see the nearer fire, though the reflections of it danced on the wall and ceiling of the study. A sharp, resinous tang of burning wood and flesh was in the air.

I opened the window and leaned out, too curious to stop myself. As I did so, the view opened out until, on the one hand, it reached to the houses about Woking station, and on the other to the charred and blackened pine woods of Byfleet. There was a light down below the hill, on the railway, near the arch, and several of the houses along the Maybury road and the streets near the station were glowing ruins. The light upon the railway puzzled me at first; there were a black heap and a vivid glare, and to the right of that a row of yellow oblongs. Then I perceived this was a wrecked train, the fore part smashed and on fire, the hinder carriages still upon the rails. I could make out the shapes of the dead around it, feasting on the bodies of those who'd been too wounded in the wreck to run from the creatures.

Between these three main centres of light—the houses, the train, and the burning county towards Chobham—stretched irregular patches of dark country, broken here and there by intervals of dimly glowing and smoking ground where the Martians had turned their strange beams of death on the living and dead alike. It was the strangest spectacle, that black expanse set with fire. It reminded me, more than anything else, of the Potteries at night. At first I could distinguish no living people at all, though I peered intently for them. Later I saw against the light of Woking station a number of black figures hurrying one after the other across the line. Their movements made them appear alive at least, but I had no hard evidence to support this other than my own desperate longing to hope that I was not the only one left here who was still breathing.

And this was the little world in which I had been living

securely for years, this fiery chaos! What had happened in the last seven hours I still did not know; nor did I know, though I was beginning to guess, the relation between these mechanical colossi and the sluggish lumps I had seen disgorged from the cylinder. With a queer feeling of impersonal interest I turned my desk chair to the window, sat down, and stared at the blackened country, and particularly at the three gigantic black things that were going to and fro in the glare about the sand pits.

They seemed amazingly busy. I began to ask myself what they could be. Were they intelligent mechanisms? Such a thing I felt was impossible. Or did a Martian sit within each, ruling, directing, using, much as a man's brain sits and rules in his body? I began to compare the things to human machines, to ask myself for the first time in my life how an ironclad or a steam engine would seem to an intelligent lower animal. I also wondered about the dead. The men from Mars seldom bothered to destroy the creatures with their rays. They seemed only to strike at them when the walking corpses interfered directly with their intentions, otherwise they left the rotting things be. Could it be that the Martians did not see them as a real threat? Could their only target be mankind itself? In a way, it made as much sense as anything as of late had. The dead were unreasoning animals and could be easily eradicated once the threat of mankind had been extinguished.

The storm had left the sky clear, and over the smoke of the burning land the little fading pinpoint of Mars was dropping into the west, when a soldier came into my garden. I heard a slight scraping at the fence, and rousing myself from the lethargy that had fallen upon me, I looked down and saw him dimly, clambering over the palings. At the sight of another human being my torpor passed, and I leaned out of the window eagerly.

"Hist!" said I, in a whisper. "The dead are about, man! You need to find cover before they spot you!"

He stopped astride of the fence in doubt. Then he came over and across the lawn to the corner of the house. He bent down and stepped softly, trying to stay as invisible as he could to the street beyond.

"Who's there?" he said, also whispering, standing under the window and peering up.

"Where are you going?" I asked.

"God knows."

"Are you trying to hide? If so, it will not work out there."

"What else am I to do?"

"Come into the house," I said.

I went down, unfastened the door, and let him in, and locked the door again. I could not see his face. He was hatless, and his coat was unbuttoned.

"My word!" he said, as I drew him in.

"What has happened?" I asked.

"What hasn't?" In the obscurity I could see he made a gesture of despair. "They wiped us out—simply wiped us out," he repeated again and again.

"Who?" I rasped. "The dead or the Martians?"

"Both."

He followed me, almost mechanically, into the dining room.

"Take some whiskey," I said, pouring out a stiff dose.

He drank it. Then abruptly he sat down before the table, put his head on his arms, and began to sob and weep like a little boy, in a perfect passion of emotion, while I, with a curious forgetfulness of my own recent despair, stood beside him, wondering. What horrors had this military man seen to break him so?

It was a long time before he could steady his nerves to answer my questions, and then he answered perplexingly and brokenly. He was a driver in the artillery, and had only come into action about seven. At that time firing was going on across the common, and it was said the first party of Martians were crawling slowly towards their second cylinder under cover of a metal shield.

Later this shield staggered up on tripod legs and became the first of the fighting-machines I had seen. The gun he drove had been unlimbered near Horsell, in order to command the sand pits, and its arrival it was that had precipitated the action. As the limber gunners went to the rear, his horse trod in a rabbit hole and came down, throwing him into a depression of the ground. At the same moment the gun exploded behind him, the ammunition blew up, there was fire all about him, and he found himself lying under a heap of charred dead men and dead horses.

"I lay still," he said, "scared out of my wits, with the fore quarter of a horse atop of me. We'd been wiped out. And the smell! Like burnt meat! I was hurt across the back by the fall of the horse, and there I had to lie until I felt better. Just like a parade it had been a minute before—then stumble, bang, swish!

"Wiped out!" he said.

He had hid under the dead horse for a long time, peeping out furtively across the common. The Cardigan men had tried a rush, in skirmishing order, at the pit, simply to be swept out of existence. Then the monster had risen to its feet and had begun to walk leisurely to and fro across the common among the few fugitives, with its headlike hood turning about exactly like the head of a cowled human being. A kind of arm carried a complicated metallic case, about which green flashes scintillated, and out of the funnel of this there smoked the Heat-Ray.

In a few minutes there was, so far as the soldier could see, not a living thing left upon the common, and every bush and tree upon it that was not already a blackened skeleton was burning. The hussars had been on the road beyond the curvature of the ground, and he saw nothing of them. He heard the Martians rattle for a time and then become still. The giant saved Woking station and its cluster of houses until the last; then in a moment the Heat-Ray was brought to bear, and the town became a heap of fiery ruins. Then the Thing shut off the Heat-Ray, and turning its back upon the artillery-man, began to waddle away towards the smouldering pine woods that sheltered the second cylinder. As it did so a second glittering Titan built itself up out of the pit.

The second monster followed the first, and at that the artilleryman began to crawl very cautiously across the hot heather ash towards Horsell. He managed to get alive into the ditch by the side of the road, and so escaped to Woking. There his story became ejaculatory. The place was impassable. It seems there were a few people alive there, frantic for the most part and many burned and scalded or set upon by the dead and bearing the wounds of bites, some missing large chunks of their arms and legs which were bandaged over with whatever scraps they could cobble together to cover those wounds. He was turned aside by the fire, and hid among some almost scorching heaps of broken wall as one of the Martian giants returned. He saw this one pursue a man—though he could not tell if the man was living or dead—catch him up in one of its steely tentacles, and knock his head against the trunk of a pine tree. At last, after nightfall, the artilleryman made a rush for it and got over the railway embankment.

Since then he had been skulking along towards Maybury, in the hope of getting out of danger Londonward. The few living people he saw signs of were hiding in trenches and cellars, and many of the survivors had made off towards Woking village and Send. He had been consumed with thirst until he found one of the water mains near the railway arch smashed, and the water bubbling out like a spring upon the road. He pushed himself on as hard and as fast as he could until his flight had led him to me.

That was the story I got from him, bit by bit. He grew calmer telling me and trying to make me see the things he had seen. He had eaten no food since midday, he told me early in his narrative, and I found some mutton and bread in the pantry and brought it into the room. We lit no lamp for fear of attracting the Martians, or more likely the dead, and ever and again our hands would touch upon bread or meat. As he talked, things about us came darkly out of the darkness, and the trampled bushes and broken rose trees outside the window grew distinct. It would seem that a number of men or animals had rushed across the lawn and our hearts had frozen in our chests until we were sure that it was not the dead, having caught our scent, come to feed on our skin and blood. I began to see his face, blackened, haggard, and spotted with stale blood, as no doubt mine was also.

When we had finished eating we went softly upstairs to my study, and I looked again out of the open window. In one night the valley had become a valley of ashes. The fires had dwindled now. Where flames had been there were now streamers of smoke; but the countless ruins of shattered and gutted houses and blasted and blackened trees that the night had hidden stood out now gaunt and terrible in the pitiless light of dawn. Yet here and there some object had had the luck to escape—a white railway signal here, the end of a greenhouse there, white and fresh amid the wreckage. Never before in the history of warfare had destruction been so indiscriminate and so universal. And shining with the growing light of the east, three of the metallic giants stood about the pit, their cowls rotating as though they were surveying the desolation they had made.

It seemed to me that the pit had been enlarged, and ever and again puffs of vivid green vapour streamed up and out of it towards the brightening dawn—streamed up, whirled, broke, and vanished.

Beyond were the pillars of fire about Chobham. They became pillars of bloodshot smoke at the first touch of day.

12

WHAT I SAW OF THE DESTRUCTION OF WEYBRIDGE AND SHEPPERTON

As the dawn grew brighter we withdrew from the window from which we had watched the Martians and the dead, and went very quietly downstairs.

The artilleryman agreed with me that the house was no place to stay in. Not only was it useless against the men from Mars and their Heat-Ray, it was in the center of a place ruled by the dead. At any moment, we could be discovered and attacked. He proposed, he said, to make his way Londonward, and thence rejoin his battery—No. 12, of the Horse Artillery, if they were still there and alive. My plan was to return at once to Leatherhead; and so greatly had the strength of the Martians and the speed of the dead plague impressed me that I had determined to take my wife to New-haven, and go with her out of the country forthwith. For I already perceived clearly that the country about London must inevitably be the scene of a disastrous struggle before such creatures as these could be destroyed.

Between us and Leatherhead, however, lay the third cyl-inder, with its guarding giants and untold waiting numbers of the dead. Had I been alone, I think I should have taken my chance and struck across country. But the artilleryman dissuaded me: "It's no kindness to the right sort of wife," he said, "to make her a widow"; and in the end I agreed to go with him, under cover of the woods, northward as far as Street Cobham before I parted with him. Thence I would make a big detour by Epsom to reach Leatherhead.

I should have started at once, but my companion had been in active service and he knew better than that. He made me ransack the house for a flask, which he filled with whiskey; and we lined every available pocket with packets of biscuits and slices of meat. I went upstairs to the bedroom closet and placed all the bullets I had for the Remington into my pocket with the gun and made sure it was fully loaded again. Then we crept out of the house, and ran as quickly and quietly as we could down the ill-made road by which I had come overnight. The houses seemed deserted. In the road lay a group of three charred bodies close together, struck dead, truly dead, by the Heat-Ray. Their tissue had been heated so much their brains must have cooked inside their skulls like eggs frying in a pan. Here and there were things that people had dropped—a clock, a slipper, a silver spoon, and the like poor valuables. At the corner turning up towards the post office a little cart, filled with boxes and furniture, and horseless, heeled over on a broken wheel. A cash box had been hastily smashed open and thrown under the debris. As we passed the cart, a dead man sprang at us from behind it. He leaped onto me, knocking my Remington aside as I tried to pull it from my coat. The artilleryman's speedy reaction was all that saved me. He grabbed up a piece of debris from the road and swung it like a club into the creature's face. I leaped to retrieve my weapon as the dead man toppled and my companion bashed his head to a pulp. We moved on at an even faster pace, leaving the thing to rot where it lay.

Except the lodge at the Orphanage, which was still on fire, none of the houses had suffered very greatly here. The Heat-Ray had shaved the chimney tops and passed. Yet, save ourselves, there did not seem to be a living soul on Maybury Hill, only the occasional dead man or woman who by the grace of God we were able to elude. The majority of the inhabitants had escaped or been found by the dead, I suppose, by way of the Old Woking road—the road I had taken when I drove to Leatherhead—or they had hidden inside a house behind barred doors and shuttered windows covered in boards.

We went down the lane, by the body of the man in black, sodden now from the overnight hail, whose skull leaked blood into the puddle of rain around him, and broke into the woods at the foot of the hill. We pushed through these towards the railway without meeting a soul, living or dead. The woods across the line were but the scarred and blackened ruins of woods; for the most part the trees had fallen, but a certain proportion still stood, dismal grey stems, with dark brown foliage instead of green. Here and there lay bodies of the true dead burnt to a crisp or devoured to the point that they had not reanimated from the infection.

On our side the fire had done no more than scorch the nearer trees; it had failed to secure its footing. In one place the woodmen had been at work on Saturday; trees, felled and freshly trimmed, lay in a clearing, with heaps of sawdust by the sawing-machine and its engine. Hard by was a temporary hut, deserted. There was not a breath of wind this morning, and everything was strangely still. Even the birds were hushed, and as we hurried along I and the artilleryman talked in whispers and looked now and again over our shoulders. It was as if death embraced the land in her cold arms. Once or twice we stopped to listen to the nothingness around us.

After a time we drew near the road, and as we did so we heard the clatter of hoofs and saw through the tree stems three cavalry soldiers riding slowly towards Woking. Their guns were held ready and they nearly mistook us for the creatures we ourselves were so desperately trying to avoid. We hailed them, letting them know we were alive, and they halted while we hurried towards them. It was a lieutenant and a couple of privates of the 8th Hussars, with a stand like a theodolite, which the artilleryman told me was a heliograph.

"You are the first living men I've seen coming this way this morning," said the lieutenant.

His voice and face were eager. The men behind him stared curiously. The artilleryman jumped down the bank into the road and saluted.

"Gun destroyed last night, sir. Have been hiding, attempting to avoid the dead. Trying to rejoin battery, sir. You'll come in sight of the Martians, I expect, about half a mile along this road."

"What the dickens are they like?" asked the lieutenant.

"Giants in armour, sir. Hundred feet high. Three legs and a body like 'luminium, with a mighty great head in a hood, sir."

"Get out!" said the lieutenant. "What confounded nonsense!"

"You'll see, sir. They carry a kind of box, sir, that shoots fire and strikes you dead."

"What d'ye mean—a gun?"

"No, sir." And the artilleryman began a vivid account of the Heat-Ray. Halfway through, the lieutenant interrupted him and looked up at me. I was still standing on the bank by the side of the road.

"It's perfectly true," I said.

"Well," said the lieutenant, "I suppose it's my business to see it too. Look here"—to the artilleryman—"we're detailed here clearing people out of their houses, so many people just holed up with the dead mucking about. It's our job to find them and get them to safety. You'd better go along and report yourself to Brigadier-General Marvin, and tell him all you know. He's at Weybridge. Know the way?"

"I do," I said; and he turned his horse southward again.

"Half a mile, you say?" said he.

"At most," I answered, and pointed over the treetops southward. He thanked me, warned us to take care, and rode on, and we saw them no more.

Farther along we came upon a group of three women and two children in the road, busy clearing out a labourer's cottage. A shotgun was strapped to the tallest woman's back and one of the others held onto an old-fashioned-looking pistol despite her work. They had got hold of a little hand truck, and were piling it up with unclean-looking bundles and shabby furniture. They were all too assiduously engaged to talk to us as we passed. It made me think how foolish humans are. In times like these, it was insane to cling to such petty and material belongings but these women seemed determined to salvage something of their former lives.

By Byfleet station we emerged from the pine trees, and found the country calm and peaceful under the morning sunlight. We were far beyond the range of the Heat-Ray there, and had it not been for the silent desertion of some of the houses, the stirring movement of packing or boarding up in others, and the knot of soldiers standing on the bridge over the railway and staring down the line towards Woking, the day would have seemed very like any other Sunday. The soldiers were on edge and a couple of them smoked, discarding one fag to light up another in its place. They were all heavily armed and looked to have seen combat with the dead already this day.

Several farm waggons and carts were moving creakily along the road to Addlestone, and suddenly through the gate of a field we saw, across a stretch of flat meadow, six twelve-pounders standing neatly at equal distances pointing towards Woking. The gunners stood by the guns with a handful of soldiers, tasked to protect them from the dead, waiting, and the ammunition waggons were at a business-like distance. The men stood almost as if under inspection.

"That's good!" said I. "They will get one fair shot, at any rate."

The artilleryman hesitated at the gate.

"I shall go on," he said.

Farther on towards Weybridge, just over the bridge, there were a number of men in white fatigue jackets throwing up a long rampart, and more guns behind.

"It's bows and arrows against the lightning, anyhow," said the artilleryman. "They 'aven't seen that fire-beam yet."

The officers who were not actively engaged stood and stared over the treetops southwestward, and the men digging would stop every now and again to stare in the same direction.

Byfleet was in a tumult; people packing, and a score of hussars, some of them dismounted, some on horseback, were hunting them about. Three or four black government waggons, with crosses in white circles, and an old omnibus, among other vehicles, were being loaded in the village street. Around this morbid scene, there were scores of people, most of them sufficiently sabbatical to have assumed their best clothes. The soldiers were having the greatest difficulty in making them realise the gravity of their position and get them to leave their possessions behind. We saw one shrivelled old fellow with a huge box and a score or more of flower pots containing orchids, angrily expostulating with the corporal who would leave them behind. I stopped and gripped his arm.

"Do you know what's over there?" I said, pointing at the pine tops that hid the Martians.

"Eh?" said he, turning. "I was explainin' these is vally-ble."

"Death!" I shouted. "Death is coming! Death!" and leaving him to digest that if he could, I hurried on after the artillery-man. At the corner I looked back. The soldier had left him, and he was still standing by his box, with the pots of orchids on the lid of it, and staring vaguely over the trees.

No one in Weybridge could tell us where the headquarters were established; the whole place was in such confusion as I had never seen in any town before. Carts, carriages everywhere, the most astonishing miscellany of conveyances and horseflesh. The respectable inhabitants of the place, men in golf and boating costumes, wives prettily dressed, were packing, river-side loafers energetically helping, children excited, and, for the most part, highly delighted at this astonishing variation of their Sunday experiences. In the midst of it all the worthy vicar was very pluckily holding an early celebration, and his bell was jangling out above the excitement as if he'd gone mad from the events of the last day.

I and the artilleryman, seated on the step of the drinking fountain, made a very passable meal upon what we had brought with us. Patrols of soldiers—here no longer hussars, but grenadiers in white—were warning people to move now or to take refuge in their cellars if they could not, as soon as the firing began. We saw as we crossed the railway bridge that a growing crowd of people had assembled in and about the railway station, and the swarming platform was piled with boxes and packages. The ordinary traffic had been stopped, I believe, in order to allow of the passage of troops and guns to Chertsey, and I have heard since that a savage struggle occurred for places in the special trains that were put on at a later hour to help clear this area of people before the dead plague worsened or the Martians annihilated the town.

We remained at Weybridge until midday, and at that hour we found ourselves at the place near Shepperton Lock where the Wey and Thames join. Part of the time we spent helping two old women to pack a little cart as an armed man stood watch over them. The Wey has a treble mouth, and at this point boats are to be hired, and there was a ferry across the river. On the Shepperton side was an inn with a lawn, and beyond that the tower of Shepperton Church—it has been replaced by a spire—rose above the trees.

Here we found an excited and noisy crowd of fugitives. As yet the flight had not grown to a panic; some people simply refused to believe that the dead walked and most thought the Martians were no real threat, but there were already far more people than all the boats going to and fro could enable to cross. Everyone was terrified the dead would come and break through the soldiers' defensive lines whether they showed it or not. There was an underlying current of fear amidst the excitement. People came panting along under heavy burdens; one husband and wife were even carrying a small outhouse door between them, with some of their household goods piled thereon. One man told us he meant to try to get away from Shepperton station.

There was a lot of shouting, and one man was even jesting. He joked about the end of the world in an odd kind of black humor. The idea people seemed to have here was that the Martians were simply formidable human beings, who might attack and sack the town, to be certainly destroyed in the end. Every now and then people would glance nervously across the Wey, at the meadows towards Chertsey, but everything over there was still.

Across the Thames, except just where the boats landed, everything was quiet, in vivid contrast with the Surrey side. The people who landed there from the boats went tramping off down the lane. The big ferryboat had just made a journey. Three or four soldiers stood on the lawn of the inn, staring and jesting at the fugitives to ease their own fear, without offering to help. The inn was closed, as it was now within prohibited hours.

"What's that?" cried a boatman, and "Shut up, you fool!" said a man near me to a yelping dog. Then the sound came again, this time from the direction of Chertsey, a muffled thud—the sound of a gun.

The fighting was beginning. Almost immediately unseen batteries across the river to our right, unseen because of the trees, took up the chorus, firing heavily one after the other. A woman screamed. Everyone stood arrested by the sudden stir of battle, near us and yet invisible to us. Nothing was to be seen save flat meadows, cows feeding unconcernedly for the most part, and silvery pollard willows motionless in the warm sunlight.

"The sojers'll stop 'em," said a woman beside me, doubt-fully. A haziness rose over the treetops.

Then suddenly we saw a rush of smoke far away up the river, a puff of smoke that jerked up into the air and hung; and forthwith the ground heaved under foot and a heavy explosion shook the air, smashing two or three windows in the houses near, and leaving us astonished.

"Here they are!" shouted a man in a blue jersey. "Yonder! D'yer see them? Yonder!"

Quickly, one after the other, one, two, three, four of the armoured Martians appeared, far away over the little trees, across the flat meadows that stretched towards Chertsey, and striding hurriedly towards the river. Little cowled fig-ures they seemed at first, going with a rolling motion and as fast as flying birds.

Then, advancing obliquely towards us, came a fifth. Their armoured bodies glittered in the sun as they swept swiftly forward upon the guns, growing rapidly larger as they drew nearer. One on the extreme left, the remotest that is, flourished a huge case high in the air, and the ghostly, terrible Heat-Ray I had already seen on Friday night smote towards Chertsey, and struck the town.

At the sight of these strange, swift, and terrible crea-tures the crowd near the water's edge seemed to me to be for a moment horror-struck. There was no screaming or shout-ing, but a silence. Then a hoarse murmur and a movement of feet—a splashing from the water. A man, too frightened to drop the portmanteau he carried on his shoulder, swung round and sent me staggering with a blow from the corner of his burden. A woman thrust at me with her hand and rushed past me. I turned with the rush of the people, but I was not too terrified for thought. The terrible Heat-Ray was in my mind. To get under water! That was it!

"Get under water!" I shouted, unheeded.

I faced about again, and rushed towards the approaching Martian, rushed right down the gravelly beach and headlong into the water. Others did the same. A boatload of people putting back came leaping out as I rushed past. The stones under my feet were muddy and slippery, and the river was so low that I ran perhaps twenty feet scarcely waist-deep. Then, as the Martian towered overhead scarcely a couple of hundred yards away, I flung myself forward under the surface. The splashes of the people in the boats leaping into the river sounded like thunderclaps in my ears. People were landing hastily on both sides of the river.

But the Martian machine took no more notice for the moment of the people running this way and that than a man would of the confusion of ants in a nest against which his foot has kicked. When, half suffocated, I raised my head above water, the Martian's hood pointed at the batteries that were still firing across the river, and as it advanced it swung loose what must have been the generator of the Heat-Ray.

In another moment it was on the bank, and in a stride wading halfway across. The knees of its foremost legs bent at the farther bank, and in another moment it had raised itself to its full height again, close to the village of Shepperton. Forthwith the six guns which, unknown to anyone on the right bank, had been hidden behind the outskirts of that village, fired simultaneously. The sudden near concussion, the last close upon the first, made my heart jump. The monster was already raising the case generating the Heat-Ray as the first shell burst six yards above the hood.

I gave a cry of astonishment. I saw and thought nothing of the other four Martian monsters; my attention was riveted upon the nearer incident. Simultaneously two other shells burst in the air near the body as the hood twisted round in time to receive, but not in time to dodge, the fourth shell.

The shell burst clean in the face of the Thing. The hood bulged, flashed, was whirled off in a dozen tattered fragments of red flesh and glittering metal.

"Hit!" shouted I, with something between a scream and a cheer.

I heard answering shouts from the people in the water about me. I could have leaped out of the water with that momentary exultation.

The decapitated colossus reeled like a drunken giant; but it did not fall over. It recovered its balance by a miracle, and, no longer heeding its steps and with the camera that fired the Heat-Ray now rigidly upheld, it reeled swiftly upon Shepperton. The living intelligence, the Martian within the hood, was slain and splashed to the four winds of heaven, and the Thing was now but a mere intricate device of metal whirling to destruction. It drove along in a straight line, incapable of guidance. It struck the tower of Shepperton Church, smashing it down as the impact of a battering ram might have done, swerved aside, blundered on and collapsed with tremendous force into the river out of my sight.

A violent explosion shook the air, and a spout of water, steam, mud, and shattered metal shot far up into the sky.

As the camera of the Heat-Ray hit the water, the latter had immediately flashed into steam. In another moment a huge wave, like a muddy tidal bore but almost scaldingly hot, came sweeping round the bend upstream. I saw people struggling shorewards, and heard their screaming and shouting faintly above the seething and roar of the Martian's collapse.

For a moment I heeded nothing of the heat, forgot the patent need of self-preservation. I splashed through the tumultuous water, pushing aside a man in black to do so, until I could see round the bend. Half a dozen deserted boats pitched aimlessly upon the confusion of the waves. The fallen Martian came into sight downstream, lying across the river, and for the most part submerged.

Thick clouds of steam were pouring off the wreckage, and through the tumultuously whirling wisps I could see, intermittently and vaguely, the gigantic limbs churning the water and flinging a splash and spray of mud and froth into the air. The tentacles swayed and struck like living arms, and, save for the helpless purposelessness of these movements, it was as if some wounded thing were struggling for its life amid the waves. Enormous quantities of a ruddy-brown fluid were spurting up in noisy jets out of the machine.

My attention was diverted from this death flurry by a furious yelling, like that of the thing called a siren in our manufacturing towns. A man, knee-deep near the towing path, shouted inaudibly to me and pointed. Looking back, I saw the other Martians advancing with gigantic strides down the riverbank from the direction of Chertsey. The Shepperton guns spoke this time unavailingly.

At that I ducked at once under water, and, holding my breath until movement was an agony, blundered painfully ahead under the surface as long as I could. The water was in a tumult about me, and rapidly growing hotter.

When for a moment I raised my head to take breath and throw the hair and water from my eyes, the steam was rising in a whirling white fog that at first hid the Martians altogether. The noise was deafening. Then I saw them dimly, colossal figures of grey, magnified by the mist. They had passed by me, and two were stooping over the frothing, tumultuous ruins of their comrade.

The third and fourth stood beside him in the water, one perhaps two hundred yards from me, the other towards Laleham. The generators of the Heat-Rays waved high, and the hissing beams smote down this way and that.

The air was full of sound, a deafening and confusing conflict of noises—the clangorous din of the Martians, the crash of falling houses, the thud of trees, fences, sheds flashing into flame, and the crackling and roaring of fire. Dense black smoke was leaping up to mingle with the steam from the river, and as the Heat-Ray went to and fro over Weybridge its impact was marked by flashes of incandescent white, that gave place at once to a smoky dance of lurid flames. The nearer houses still stood intact, awaiting their fate, shadowy, faint and pallid in the steam, with the fire behind them going to and fro.

For a moment perhaps I stood there, breast-high in the almost boiling water, dumbfounded at my position, hopeless of escape. Through the reek I could see the people who had been with me in the river scrambling out of the water through the reeds, like little frogs hurrying through grass from the advance of a man, or running to and fro in utter dismay on the towing path.

Then suddenly the white flashes of the Heat-Ray came leaping towards me. The houses caved in as they dissolved at its touch, and darted out flames; the trees changed to fire with a roar. The Ray flickered up and down the towing path, licking off the people who ran this way and that, and came down to the water's edge not fifty yards from where I stood. It swept across the river to Shepperton, and the water in its track rose in a boiling weal crested with steam. I turned shoreward.

In another moment the huge wave, well-nigh at the boiling-point had rushed upon me. I screamed aloud, and scalded, half blinded, agonised, I staggered through the leaping, hissing water towards the shore. Had my foot stumbled, it would have been the end. I fell helplessly, in full sight of the Martians, upon the broad, bare gravelly spit that runs down to mark the angle of the Wey and Thames. I expected nothing but death.

I have a dim memory of the foot of a Martian coming down within a score of yards of my head, driving straight into the loose gravel, whirling it this way and that and lifting again; of a long suspense, and then of the four carrying the debris of their comrade between them, now clear and then presently faint through a veil of smoke, receding interminably, as it seemed to me, across a vast space of river and meadow. And then, very slowly, I realised that by a miracle I had escaped.

13

HOW I FELL
IN WITH THE CURATE

After getting this sudden lesson in the power of terrestrial weapons, the Martians retreated to their original position upon Horsell Common; and in their haste, and encumbered with the debris of their smashed companion, they no doubt overlooked many such a stray and negligible victim as myself. Had they left their comrade and pushed on forthwith, there was nothing at that time between them and London but batteries of twelve-pounder guns, and they would certainly have reached the capital in advance of the tidings of their approach; as sudden, dreadful, and destructive their advent would have been as the earthquake that destroyed Lisbon a century ago.

But they were in no hurry. Cylinder followed cylinder on its interplanetary flight; every twenty-four hours brought them reinforcement. And meanwhile the military and naval authorities, now fully alive to the tremendous power of their antagonists, worked with furious energy. Almost all of their efforts and manpower where now directed at the Martians. The dead were still very much a threat and a terrible one, but the Martians' sheer capacity for destruction was appalling to the point that they, for the moment, outweighed the threat of the dead. Every minute a fresh gun came into position reinforced by a squad of armed infantry to guard against the rotting men and women of the dead plague should they make a move as well before twilight, every row of suburban villas on the hilly slopes about Kingston and Richmond, masked an expectant black muzzle. Other soldiers made their rounds disposing of the corpses in the streets before they had a chance to clamor to their feet. Gunshots rang out under the harsh rays of the sun. Here and there, a corpse rose before the soldiers reached it. The corpse would cry out and charge the closest of the living, coming at them with tooth and nails in a mad frenzy of hunger. All of these were dealt with a panicked flurry of rifle cracks from all directions instead of a calm point blank shot to the head. Often the corpse would be so riddled from the barrage its shredded body would collapse into a pool of blood, unable to move, as the men closed in on it to make sure it stayed down. And through the charred and desolated area—perhaps twenty square miles altogether—that encircled the Martian encampment on Horsell Common, through charred and ruined villages among the green trees, through the blackened and smoking arcades that had been but a day ago pine spinneys, crawled the devoted scouts with the heliographs that were presently to warn the gunners of the Martian approach. But the Martians now understood our command of artillery and the danger of human proximity, and not a man ventured within a mile of either cylinder, save at the price of his life.

It would seem that these giants spent the earlier part of the afternoon in going to and fro, transferring everything from the second and third cylinders—the second in Addlestone Golf Links and the third at Pyrford—to their original pit on Horsell Common. Over that, above the blackened heather and ruined buildings that stretched far and wide, stood one as sentinel, while the rest abandoned their vast fighting-machines and descended into the pit. They were hard at work there far into the night, and the towering pillar of dense green smoke that rose therefrom could be seen from the hills about Merrow, and even, it is said, from Banstead and Epsom Downs.

And while the Martians behind me were thus preparing for their next sally, and in front of me Humanity gathered for the battle, I made my way with infinite pains and labour from the fire and smoke of burning Weybridge towards London.

I could only look in horror at the bodies of the dead and the pyres of bodies that burned in the streets as soldiers and volunteers hauled men and women unlucky enough to be struck down or trampled into their flames. The air stunk of cooked meat and it made me sick to my stomach. I fell to my knees and fought not to retch onto the dirt. The day had taken its toll. I was exhausted and weary. As the sickness passed, I rose and continued on my way.

I saw an abandoned boat, very small and remote, drifting downstream; and throwing off the most of my sodden clothes, I went after it, gained it, and so escaped out of that destruction. There were no oars in the boat, but I contrived to paddle, as well as my parboiled hands would allow, down the river towards Halliford and Walton, going very tediously and continually looking behind me, as you may well understand. I followed the river, because I considered that the water gave me my best chance of escape should these giants return.

The hot water from the Martian's overthrow drifted downstream with me, so that for the best part of a mile I could see little of either bank. Once, however, I made out a string of black figures hurrying across the meadows from the direction of Weybridge. Their strides told me at once they were not alive. I prayed for the souls of anyone who they might find in their search for the living. Weybridge, it seemed, was deserted, and several of the houses facing the river were on fire. It was strange to see the place quite tranquil, quite desolate under the hot blue sky, with the smoke and little threads of flame going straight up into the heat of the afternoon. Never before had I seen houses burning without the accompaniment of an obstructive crowd. A little farther on the dry reeds up the bank were smoking and glowing, and a line of fire inland was marching steadily across a late field of hay.

For a long time I drifted, so painful and weary was I after the violence I had been through, and so intense the heat upon the water. Then my fears got the better of me again. A horrible thought crossed my mind. The dead didn't need to breathe. Those who died in the water may very well still be there beneath the current, either being swept along by it or fighting their way to shore across the muddy bottom of the river, slowly inching along with the unstoppable determination of creatures who no longer felt pain or exhaustion. I resumed my paddling. I had no intention of discovering if there were dead in the river. I convinced myself that merely staying on the move would keep me safe from groping hands reaching up from below the bottom of the boat.

The sun scorched my bare back. At last, as the bridge at Walton was coming into sight round the bend, my fever and faintness overcame my fears, and I landed on the Middlesex bank and lay down, deadly sick, amid the long grass. I longed for my pistol but I had lost it in the turmoil of my flight. I suppose the time was then about four or five o'clock. I got up presently, walked perhaps half a mile without meeting a soul, and then lay down again in the shadow of a hedge. I did not want to stop. I knew there were likely dead men in the area but I was so overwrought, my fatigue left me no choice. I seem to remember talking, wanderingly, to myself during that last spurt. I was also very thirsty, and bitterly regretful I had drunk no more water. It is a curious thing that I felt angry with my wife; I cannot account for it, but my impotent desire to reach Leatherhead worried me excessively.

I do not clearly remember the arrival of the curate, so that probably I dozed. I became aware of him as a seated figure in soot-smudged shirt sleeves, and with his upturned, clean-shaven face staring at a faint flickering that danced over the sky. The sky was what is called a mackerel sky— rows and rows of faint down-plumes of cloud, just tinted with the midsummer sunset.

I sat up, and at the rustle of my motion he looked at me quickly.

"Have you any water?" I asked abruptly.

He shook his head.

"You have been asking for water for the last hour," he said. "If I were one of the dead, you'd have been my dinner by now."

For a moment we were silent, taking stock of each other. I dare say he found me a strange enough figure, naked, save for my water-soaked trousers and socks, scalded, and my face and shoulders blackened by the smoke. His face was a fair weakness, his chin retreated, and his hair lay in crisp, almost flaxen curls on his low forehead; his eyes were rather large, pale blue, and blankly staring. He spoke abruptly, looking vacantly away from me.

"What does it mean?" he said. "What do these things mean?"

I stared at him and made no answer.

He extended a thin white hand and spoke in almost a complaining tone.

"Why are these things permitted? What sins have we done? The morning service was over, I was walking through the roads to clear my brain for the afternoon, and then—fire, earthquake, death! As if it were Sodom and Gomorrah! All our work undone, all the work—What are these Martians?

Do they hold so much that not only can they bring death but raise us from it as well so that our own departed turn on us like animals?"

"What are we?" I answered, clearing my throat.

He gripped his knees and turned to look at me again. For half a minute, perhaps, he stared silently.

"I was walking through the roads to clear my brain," he said. "And suddenly—fire, earthquake, death!"

He relapsed into silence, with his chin now sunken almost to his knees.

Presently he began waving his hand.

"All the work—all the Sunday schools—What have we done?—what has Weybridge done? Everything gone—everything destroyed. The church! We rebuilt it only three years ago. Gone! Swept out of existence! Why?"

Another pause, and he broke out again like one demented.

"The smoke of her burning goeth up for ever and ever!" he shouted. "The dead have risen from their tombs and we are all damned! Behold, the end of days are come!"

His eyes flamed, and he pointed a lean finger in the direction of Weybridge.

By this time I was beginning to take his measure. The tremendous tragedy in which he had been involved—it was evident he was a fugitive from Weybridge—had driven him to the very verge of his reason.

"Are we far from Sunbury?" I said, in a matter-of-fact tone.

"What are we to do?" he asked. "Are these creatures everywhere? Has the earth been given over to them?"

"Are we far from Sunbury?"

"Only this morning I officiated at early celebration—"

"Things have changed," I said, quietly. "You must keep your head. There is still hope."

"Hope!"

"Yes. Plentiful hope—for all this destruction!"

I began to explain my view of our position. He listened at first, but as I went on the interest dawning in his eyes gave place to their former stare, and his regard wandered from me.

"This must be the beginning of the end," he said, interrupting me. "The end! The great and terrible day of the Lord! When men shall call upon the mountains and the rocks to fall upon them and hide them—hide them from the face of Him that sitteth upon the throne! I tell you again, the end has come. If the dead do not claim us all then these metal giants shall wipe us from the Earth and make it their own!"

I began to understand the position. I ceased my laboured reasoning, struggled to my feet, and, standing over him, laid my hand on his shoulder. I knew we were in danger where we sat. At any moment roving packs of the decaying creatures might wander upon us and I had no desire to die from such foolish inaction.

"Be a man!" said I. "You are scared out of your wits! What good is religion if it collapses under calamity? Think of what earthquakes and floods, wars and volcanoes, have done before to men! Did you think God had exempted Weybridge? He is not an insurance agent. We must move. Here in the open like this . . . . We must move!"

For a time he sat in blank silence.

"But how can we escape?" he asked, suddenly. "They are invulnerable, they are pitiless."

"Neither the one nor, perhaps, the other," I answered. "And the mightier they are the more sane and wary should we be. One of them was killed yonder not three hours ago."

"Killed!" he said, staring about him. "How can God's ministers be killed?"

"I saw it happen." I proceeded to tell him. "We have chanced to come in for the thick of it," said I, "and that is all."

"What is that flicker in the sky?" he asked abruptly.

I told him it was the heliograph signalling—that it was the sign of human help and effort in the sky.

"We are in the midst of it," I said, "quiet as it is. That flicker in the sky tells of the gathering storm. Yonder, I take it are the Martians, and Londonward, where those hills rise about Richmond and Kingston and the trees give cover, earthworks are being thrown up and guns are being placed. Presently the Martians will be coming this way again."

And even as I spoke he sprang to his feet and stopped me by a gesture

"Listen!" he said.

From beyond the low hills across the water came the dull resonance of distant guns and a remote weird crying, mixing with the howls of the hungry dead. Then everything was still. A cockchafer came droning over the hedge and past us. High in the west the crescent moon hung faint and pale above the smoke of Weybridge and Shepperton and the hot, still splendour of the sunset.

"We had better follow this path," I said, "northward."

We set out as quick as we could on foot. No sooner than

we were on the move, the dead found us. We had waited too long. There were three of them. A man whose neck was torn open and the front of his business suit covered in dried blood; a woman whose skin was cooked and peeling off her body in long strips; and a soldier, who brought up the rear. The soldier looked to have been trampled on by one of the Martian machines. That the creature was standing, let alone moving, was miraculous. One of the soldier's legs was broken, as were both his arms, and he dragged it along behind him as he shambled towards us. The white of bone protruded from underneath his fractured and crushed ribs. The business man and the woman were fast. They were on us almost by the time we saw them coming. The woman tackled my companion. She and the curate went toppling to the ground. I dodged the business man as he made his move at me, sidestepping his lunge. I never imagined myself a hero or truly to be a man of action yet I grabbed a piece of rubble from the ground, spinning to face him as he came at me again. I struck out, smashing his face inward. Teeth and spittle flew from his mouth as he reeled, and I advanced on him for another blow. I swung the heavy piece of wood, smashing it into the side of the man's head. Finally, he went down. I dropped with my knees on his body and swung the wood several more times, blood splashing over me, until he lay still. Leaping to my feet, I saw the dead soldier inches from me. The smell of his internal fluids leaking from his battered form made me gag. I retreated a step then eyed him. Taking careful aim, I lashed out and broke his remaining leg at the knee with my swing.

The curate was still wrestling with the woman. He,

however, had the upper hand. Like me, he had improvised a weapon from the debris around us and stabbed the woman again and again with a sharp piece of stone the size of a dagger.

"The head!" I yelled. "You can only kill them if you destroy their brain!"

With a mighty plunge, the rock in his hand shoved through her left eye as the curate laid all his weight behind the blow. The woman creature cried out then lay still. I raced to his side, leaving the soldier vainly trying to crawl after me as he pulled himself along the roadway with his hands.

The curate looked more deranged now than ever but I took his hand and pulled him along as we ran into the night. I could only pray his mind would return to him as we struggled to leave those scenes of horror behind us.

14

IN LONDON

My younger brother was in London when the Martians fell at Woking. He was a medical student working for an imminent examination, and he heard nothing of the arrival until Saturday morning, but if he had, it was unlikely he would've taken the time to dwell on it. Many of the bodies used by the students in their studies had come to life once more. Two of his fellows had died before the bodies were dealt with. The mess had been kept quiet from the public and the doctors were frantically trying to discern the cause of such a bizarre and deadly occurrence. The morning papers on Saturday contained, in addition to lengthy special articles on the planet Mars, on life in the planets, and so forth, a brief and vaguely worded telegram, all the more striking for its brevity.

The Martians, alarmed by the approach of a crowd, had killed a number of people with a quick-firing gun, but worse, these people and many others had risen from the grave to turn on the living, so the story ran. The writers made no connection between the Martians and the living dead, treating each as their own separate wonder and horror. The telegram concluded with the words: *"Formidable as they seem to be, the Martians have not moved from the pit into which they have fallen, and, indeed, seem incapable of doing so. Probably this is due to the relative strength of the earth's gravitational energy."* On that last text their leader-writer expanded very comfortingly.

Of course all the students in the crammer's biology class, to which my brother went that day, were intensely interested given their own dealings with the risen dead in the school, but there were no signs of any unusual excitement in the streets. More than a few people had gone missing in the last few days but there was no air of panic. No one yet realized the dead were already among them and growing in number. The afternoon papers puffed scraps of news under big headlines. They had nothing to tell beyond the movements of troops about the common, and the burning of the pine woods between Woking and Weybridge, until eight. It was as if the government itself wished to deny the existence of the dead plague or at least shield the public from it. Perhaps they feared a state panic so vast they would not be able to deal with it. Then the *St. James's Gazette,* in an extra-special edition, announced the bare fact of the interruption of telegraphic communication. This was thought to be due to the falling of burning pine trees across the line. Nothing more of the fighting was known that night, the night of my drive to Leatherhead and back.

My brother felt no anxiety about us, as he knew from the description in the papers that the cylinder was a good two miles from my house. He made up his mind to run down that night to me, in order, as he says, to see the Things before they were killed. He despatched a telegram, which never reached me, about four o'clock, and spent the evening at a music hall.

In London, also, on Saturday night there was a thunderstorm, and my brother reached Waterloo in a cab. On the platform from which the midnight train usually starts he learned, after some waiting, that an accident prevented trains from reaching Woking that night. The nature of the accident he could not ascertain; indeed, the railway authorities did not clearly know at that time. There was very little excitement in the station, as the officials, failing to realise that anything further than a breakdown between Byfleet and Woking junction had occurred, were running the theatre trains which usually passed through Woking round by Virginia Water or Guildford. They were busy making the necessary arrangements to alter the route of the Southampton and Portsmouth Sunday League excursions. A nocturnal newspaper reporter, mistaking my brother for the traffic manager, to whom he bears a slight resemblance, waylaid and tried to interview him. Few people, excepting the railway officials, connected the breakdown with the Martians.

I have read, in another account of these events, that on

Sunday morning "all London was electrified by the news from Woking." As a matter of fact, there was nothing to justify that very extravagant phrase. Plenty of Londoners did not hear of the Martians until the panic of Monday morning. Those who did took some time to realise all that the hastily worded telegrams in the Sunday papers conveyed. The majority of people in London do not read Sunday papers.

The habit of personal security, moreover, is so deeply fixed in the Londoner's mind, and startling intelligence so much a matter of course in the papers, that they could read without any personal tremors: *"About seven o'clock last night the Martians came out of the cylinder, and, moving about under an armour of metallic shields, have completely wrecked Woking station with the adjacent houses, and massacred an entire battalion of the Cardigan Regiment. No details are known. Maxims have been absolutely useless against their armour; the field guns have been disabled by them. Flying hussars have been galloping into Chertsey. The Martians appear to be moving slowly towards Chertsey or Windsor. Great anxiety prevails in West Surrey, and earthworks are being thrown up to check the advance Londonward."* That was how the Sunday *Sun* put it, and a clever and remarkably prompt "handbook" article in the *Referee* compared the affair to a menagerie suddenly let loose in a village.

No one in London knew positively of the nature of the armoured Martians, and there was still a fixed idea that these monsters must be sluggish: "crawling," "creeping painfully"—such expressions occurred in almost all the earlier reports. And in terms of the dead plague, ignorance prevailed. None of the telegrams could have been written by an eyewitness of their advance. The Sunday papers printed separate editions as further news came to hand, some even in default of it. But there was practically nothing more to tell people until late in the afternoon, when the authorities gave the press agencies the news in their possession. It was stated that the people of Walton and Weybridge, and all the district were pouring along the roads Londonward, and that was all.

My brother went to church at the Foundling Hospital in the morning, still in ignorance of what had happened on the previous night. There he heard allusions made to the invasion, and a special prayer for peace. Coming out, he bought a *Referee*. He became alarmed at the news in this, and went again to Waterloo station to find out if communication were restored. The omnibuses, carriages, cyclists, and innumerable people walking in their best clothes seemed scarcely affected by the strange intelligence that the news venders were disseminating. People were interested, or, if alarmed, alarmed only on account of the local residents. At the station he heard for the first time that the Windsor and Chertsey lines were now interrupted. The porters told him that several remarkable telegrams had been received in the morning from Byfleet and Chertsey stations, but that these had abruptly ceased. My brother could get very little precise detail out of them.

"There's fighting going on about Weybridge" was the extent of their information.

The train service was now very much disorganised. Quite a number of people who had been expecting friends from places on the South-Western network were standing about the station. One grey-headed old gentleman came and abused the South-Western Company bitterly to my brother. "It wants showing up," he said.

One or two trains came in from Richmond, Putney, and Kingston, containing people who had gone out for a day's boating and found the locks closed and a feeling of panic in the air. A man in a blue and white blazer addressed my brother, full of strange tidings.

"There's hosts of people driving into Kingston in traps and carts and things, with boxes of valuables and all that," he said. "They come from Molesey and Weybridge and Walton, and they say there's been guns heard at Chertsey, heavy firing, and that mounted soldiers have told them to get off at once because the Martians are coming. We heard guns firing at Hampton Court station, but we thought it was thunder. What the dickens does it all mean? The Martians can't get out of their pit, can they?"

My brother could not tell him.

Afterwards he found that the vague feeling of alarm had spread to the clients of the underground railway, and that the Sunday excursionists began to return from all over the South-Western "lung"—Barnes, Wimbledon, Richmond Park, Kew, and so forth—at unnaturally early hours; but not a soul had anything more than vague hearsay to tell of. Everyone connected with the terminus seemed ill-tempered.

About five o'clock the gathering crowd in the station was immensely excited by the opening of the line of communication, which is almost invariably closed, between the South-Eastern and the South-Western stations, and the passage of carriage trucks bearing huge guns and carriages crammed with soldiers. These were the guns that were brought up from Woolwich and Chatham to cover Kingston. There was an exchange of pleasantries: "You'll get eaten!" "We're the beast-tamers!" and so forth. A little while after that a squad of police came into the station and began to clear the public off the platforms, and my brother went out into the street again.

The church bells were ringing for evensong, and a squad of Salvation Army lassies came singing down Waterloo Road. On the bridge a number of loafers were watching a curious brown scum that came drifting down the stream in patches. The sun was just setting, and the Clock Tower and the Houses of Parliament rose against one of the most peaceful skies it is possible to imagine, a sky of gold, barred with long transverse stripes of reddish-purple cloud. There was talk of a floating body that once disturbed when trying to retrieve it attacked those around it. Mere bullets seemed to do it no harm until a trained marksman became involved in the conflict and put it down with a single shot to its head. One of the men there, a reservist he said he was, told my brother he had seen the heliograph flickering in the west.

In Wellington Street my brother met a couple of sturdy roughs who had just been rushed out of Fleet Street with still-wet newspapers and staring placards. "Dreadful catastrophe!" they bawled one to the other down Wellington Street. "Fighting at Weybridge! Full description! Repulse of the Martians! London in Danger!" He had to give threepence for a copy of that paper.

Then it was, and then only, that he realised something of the full power and terror of these monsters. He learned that they were not merely a handful of small sluggish creatures, but that they were minds swaying vast mechanical bodies; and that they could move swiftly and smite with such power that even the mightiest guns could not stand against them.

They were described as "vast spiderlike machines, nearly a hundred feet high, capable of the speed of an express train, and able to shoot out a beam of intense heat." Masked batteries, chiefly of field guns, had been planted in the country about Horsell Common, and especially between the Woking district and London. Five of the machines had been seen moving towards the Thames, and one, by a happy chance, had been destroyed. In the other cases the shells had missed, and the batteries had been at once annihilated by the Heat-Rays. Heavy losses of soldiers were mentioned and for the first time he read of events similar to those that had occurred at his school with the dead. The article spoke of a "plague" unlike anyone could dream of in their worst nightmares. The dead were returning to life and not as people, but rather monsters of snarling faces and gnashing teeth. All of the towns and cities closest to the arrival of the first Martian cylinders were now overrun by packs of corpses, reanimated by some unknown force. To many, this horror was far greater than that of the Martians but the papers still gave the beings from Mars their main focus. It was believed the Martians were the real threat given their speed and vastly superior weaponry. Being a medical student, however, it sent a cold shiver along his spine as he read of these happenings. I believe some part of him knew in that moment the dead plague would spread far faster and further than the authorities let on in the papers. They assured folks through the words of the article's author that the dead were merely a side issue and one that could easily be dealt with once the massive alien machines were stopped. The tone of the despatch was optimistic towards its end.

The Martians had been repulsed; they were not invulnerable. They had retreated to their triangle of cylinders again, in the circle about Woking. Signallers with heliographs were pushing forward upon them from all sides. Guns were in rapid transit from Windsor, Portsmouth, Aldershot, Woolwich—even from the north; among others, long wire-guns of ninety-five tons from Woolwich. Altogether one hundred and sixteen were in position or being hastily placed, chiefly covering London. Never before in England had there been such a vast or rapid concentration of military material. Added to even this were untold numbers of soldiers to stem the spread of the dead as the gunners made their stand against the Martian machines.

Any further cylinders that fell, it was hoped, could be destroyed at once by high explosives, which were being rapidly manufactured and distributed. No doubt, ran the report, the situation was of the strangest and gravest description, but the public was exhorted to avoid and discourage panic.

People were warned to stay inside and limit their contact with others. They were told to avoid strangers who acted in any abnormal manner as these individuals could be carriers of the dead plague. Few took these warnings to heart, however, as most still transfixed on the fear of the coming of the Martian machines and the tales of their deadly Heat-Rays from which there would be no escape if they reached the city. No doubt the Martians were strange and terrible in the extreme, but at the outside there could not be more than twenty of them against our millions. The dead too were limited in number, or so many believed, and the poor creatures couldn't reason, so to many this alone assured mankind's victory against them.

The authorities had reason to suppose, from the size of the Martian cylinders, that at the outside there could not be more than five in each cylinder—fifteen altogether. And one at least was disposed of—perhaps more. The public would be fairly warned of the approach of danger, and elaborate measures were being taken for the protection of the people in the threatened southwestern suburbs. Armed soldiers and police patrolled the streets with orders to kill and burn any of the dead who turned up on sight. And so, with reiterated assurances of the safety of London and the ability of the authorities to cope with the difficulty, this quasi-proclamation closed.

This was printed in enormous type on paper so fresh that it was still wet, and there had been no time to add a word of comment. It was curious, my brother said, to see how ruthlessly the usual contents of the paper had been hacked and taken out to give this place.

All down Wellington Street people could be seen fluttering out the pink sheets and reading, and the Strand was suddenly noisy with the voices of an army of hawkers following these pioneers. Men came scrambling off buses to secure copies. Certainly this news excited people intensely, whatever their previous apathy. The shutters of a map shop in the Strand were being taken down, my brother said, and a man in his Sunday raiment, lemon-yellow gloves even, was visible inside the window hastily fastening maps of Surrey to the glass.

Going on along the Strand to Trafalgar Square, the paper in his hand, my brother saw some of the fugitives from West Surrey. There was a man with his wife and two boys and some articles of furniture in a cart such as green-grocers use. He was driving from the direction of Westminster Bridge; and close behind him came a hay waggon with five or six respectable-looking people in it, and some boxes and bundles. The faces of these people were haggard, and their entire appearance contrasted conspicuously with the Sabbath-best appearance of the people on the omnibuses. Most of these refugees were armed in some way from guns that looked military in issue, though my brother had no idea how they could have come to possess such, to holding shovels like spears in their arms. People in fashionable clothing peeped at them out of cabs. They stopped at the Square as if undecided which way to take, and finally turned eastward along the Strand. Some way behind these came a man in workday clothes, riding one of those old-fashioned tricycles with a small front wheel. There was a shotgun strapped to his back and he was dirty and white in the face.

My brother turned down towards Victoria, and met a number of such people. He had a vague idea that he might see something of me. He noticed an unusual number of police regulating the traffic. Some of the refugees were exchanging news with the people on the omnibuses. One was professing to have seen the Martians. "Boilers on stilts, I tell you, striding along like men." Most of them were excited and animated by their strange experience. But by and large the authorities present mostly seemed to be checking this influx of people for bite marks and wounds. It made sense to my brother. They did not want to let anyone who may perhaps being carrying the plague in their blood into London.

Beyond Victoria the public-houses were doing a lively trade with these arrivals. At all the street corners groups of people were reading papers, talking excitedly, or staring at these unusual Sunday visitors. They seemed to increase as night drew on as did the number of soldiers in the city, until at last the roads, my brother said, were like Epsom High Street on a Derby Day. My brother addressed several of these fugitives and got unsatisfactory answers from most.

None of them could tell him any news of Woking except one man, who assured him that Woking had been entirely destroyed on the previous night. The man said it was a place which belonged solely to the dead now.

"I come from Byfleet," he said; "man on a bicycle came through the place in the early morning, and ran from door to door warning us to come away. Then came soldiers. We went out to look, and there were clouds of smoke to the south— nothing but smoke, and not a soul coming that way. Then we heard the guns at Chertsey, and folks coming from Wey- bridge. So I've locked up my house and come on. I am very glad I departed as quickly as I did. As I was leaving, I saw dead men and women in the streets, running wild with feral, hollow eyes. Their skin was grey and many showed signs of decay. The soldiers were trying to make a stand against them even as guns were being hauled up to stave off the Martian advance, if it was possible. Gunshots echoed behind me amid screams and howls as I biked away from that place."

At the time there was a strong feeling in the streets that the authorities were to blame for their incapacity to dispose of the invaders without all this inconvenience. Many claimed they had acted too slowly not only in regards to the Martians but to the dead as well. They cursed the fools who first made contact with the aliens for not chucking their pit full of explosives and detonating them the second it was known the men from Mars were not men at all. Mankind was now fighting a war on two fronts thanks to the delayed reactions of those in Woking and the surrounding areas.

About eight o'clock a noise of heavy firing was distinctly audible all over the south of London. My brother could not hear it for the traffic in the main thoroughfares, but by striking through the quiet back streets to the river he was able to distinguish it quite plainly.

He walked from Westminster to his apartments near Regent's Park, about two. He was now very anxious on my account, and disturbed at the evident magnitude of the trouble. His mind was inclined to run, even as mine had run on Saturday, on military details. He thought of all those silent, expectant guns, of the suddenly nomadic countryside; he tried to imagine "boilers on stilts" a hundred feet high. He thought of the unfortunate soldiers who stood guard against the dead and prayed they would not have to kill someone they knew. The American Civil War was by many called the war of brothers but this was far worse. Any who died rose. A soldier may find himself standing against his neighbor, father, or even his own wife and children. He found himself extremely grateful not to be out on those front lines with a rifle in his hands for he knew he would not have had the heart to stop me had I been one of the dead.

There were one or two cartloads of refugees passing along Oxford Street, and several in the Marylebone Road, but so slowly was the news spreading that Regent Street and Portland Place were full of their usual Sunday-night promenaders, albeit they talked in groups and most carried hidden arms beneath their fancy dress, and along the edge of Regent's Park there were as many silent couples "walking out" together under the scattered gas lamps as ever there had been. The night was warm and still, and a little oppressive; the sound of guns continued intermittently, and after midnight there seemed to be sheet lightning in the south.

He read and re-read the paper, fearing the worst had happened to me. He was restless, and after supper prowled out again aimlessly. He returned and tried in vain to divert his attention to his examination notes. He made sure the place he was staying was secure, taking careful effort to place his heavy desk against the door and close the shutters of his window. These he strengthened as well by tying them shut with bits of cloth twisted up into a makeshift rope. Only then did he try to rest. He went to bed a little after midnight, and was awakened from lurid dreams in the small hours of Monday by the sound of door knockers, feet running in the street, distant drumming, and a clamour of bells. Red reflections danced on the ceiling. For a moment he lay astonished, wondering whether day had come or the world gone mad. Then he jumped out of bed and ran to the window.

His room was an attic and as he thrust his head out,

up and down the street there were a dozen echoes to the noise of his window sash, and heads in every kind of night disarray appeared. Enquiries were being shouted. "They are coming!" bawled a policeman, hammering at the door; "the Martians are coming! The dead are here!" and hurried to the next door.

The sound of drumming and trumpeting came from the Albany Street Barracks, and every church within earshot was hard at work killing sleep with a vehement disorderly tocsin. There was a noise of doors opening, and window after window in the houses opposite flashed from darkness into yellow illumination.

Up the street came galloping a closed carriage, bursting abruptly into noise at the corner, rising to a clattering climax under the window, and dying away slowly in the distance. Close on the rear of this came a couple of cabs, the forerunners of a long procession of flying vehicles, going for the most part to Chalk Farm station, where the North-Western special trains were loading up, instead of coming down the gradient into Euston. In their wake, chasing after them, came a dozen or so men and women dressed in tattered, bloodstained clothes. One of them looked up at my brother and showed its teeth before passing on into the night.

For a long time my brother stared out of the window in blank astonishment and fear, watching the policemen hammering at door after door, and delivering their incomprehensible message. The pack of creatures came pouring towards them. The police, now armed, turned to meet the things with a blaze of bullets. Then the door behind him opened, and the man who lodged across the landing came in, dressed only in shirt, trousers, and slippers, his braces loose about his waist, his hair disordered from his pillow.

"What the devil is it?" he asked. "A fire? What a devil of a row!"

They both craned their heads out of the window, straining to hear what the policemen were shouting. The dead lay still in puddles of blood where they'd been dispatched and the police had returned to their original job that had brought them to this street. People were coming out of the side streets, and standing in groups at the corners talking. All of them took great care to avoid the corpses.

"What the devil is it all about?" said my brother's fellow lodger.

My brother answered him vaguely and began to dress, running with each garment to the window in order to miss nothing of the growing excitement and horror outside. Presently men selling unnaturally early newspapers came bawling into the street. My brother almost laughed at the insanity of it, selling papers in the middle of such danger and chaos.

"London in danger of suffocation! The Kingston and Richmond defences forced! Fearful massacres in the Thames Valley! The dead plague spreading! Dead men in London!"

And all about him—in the rooms below, in the houses on each side and across the road, and behind in the Park Terraces and in the hundred other streets of that part of Marylebone, and the Westbourne Park district and St. Pancras, and westward and northward in Kilburn and St. John's Wood and Hampstead, and eastward in Shoreditch and Highbury and Haggerston and Hoxton, and, indeed, through all the vastness of London from Ealing to East Ham—people were rubbing their eyes, and opening windows to stare out and ask aimless questions, dressing hastily as the first breath of the coming storm of Fear blew through the streets. It was the dawn of the great panic. London, which had gone to bed on Sunday night oblivious and inert, was awakened, in the small hours of Monday morning, to a vivid sense of danger. The dead were in their streets and the Martians at their doorstep.

Unable from his window to learn what was happening, my brother went down and out into the street, just as the sky between the parapets of the houses grew pink with the early dawn. He wished he held some kind—any kind—of weapon, but he did not. The flying people on foot and in vehicles grew more numerous every moment. "Black Smoke!" he heard people crying, and again "Black Smoke!" The contagion of such a unanimous fear was inevitable. As my brother hesitated on the door-step, he saw another news vender approaching, and got a paper forthwith. The man was running away with the rest, and selling his papers for a shilling each as he ran—a grotesque mingling of profit and panic. Here and there among the crowd was a dead man or woman giving chase, the police unable to blast them to shreds for fear of hitting the civilians they intermingled with. My brother hastily removed himself from the throng to a safer spot on the steps of his building where he could see any threat as it approached and could duck inside straight away if so needed.

And from this paper my brother read that catastrophic despatch of the Commander-in-Chief:

"The Martians are able to discharge enormous clouds of a black and poisonous vapour by means of rockets. They have smothered our batteries, destroyed Richmond, Kingston, and Wimbledon, and are advancing slowly towards London, destroying everything on the way. It is impossible to stop them. There is no safety from the Black Smoke but in instant flight. Worse still, as the Black Smoke kills instantly, no troops are able to advance and deal with the dead before they arise. The number of the dead is now beyond measure and sweeping outward from these sights like wildfire."

That was all, but it was enough. The whole population of the great six-million city was stirring, slipping, running; presently it would be pouring *en masse* northward.

"Black Smoke!" the voices cried. "Fire!" as others shouted of the dead in the streets. "Run! Run the dead have come! The end of days are at hand!"

The bells of the neighbouring church made a jangling tumult, a cart carelessly driven smashed, amid shrieks and curses, against the water trough up the street as a dead man leaped onto it, attacking the driver. Sickly yellow lights went to and fro in the houses, and some of the passing cabs flaunted unextinguished lamps. And overhead the dawn was growing brighter, clear and steady and calm.

He heard footsteps running to and fro in the rooms, and up and down stairs behind him. His landlady came to the door, loosely wrapped in dressing gown and shawl; her husband followed ejaculating.

As my brother began to realise the import of all these things, he turned hastily to his own room, put all his available money—some ten pounds altogether—into his pockets, and went out again into the streets. He was determined to find a way out of the city and, Lord willing, find a weapon with which to defend himself should he come face to face with one of the dead creatures.

15

WHAT HAD HAPPENED
IN SURREY

It was while the curate had sat and talked so wildly to me under the hedge in the flat meadows near Halliford, and while my brother was watching the fugitives stream over Westminster Bridge, that the Martians had resumed the offensive. So far as one can ascertain from the conflicting accounts that have been put forth, the majority of them remained busied with preparations in the Horsell pit until nine that night, hurrying on some operation that disengaged huge volumes of green smoke. The Things from Mars had erected strange fences composed of lightning around each of their pits to hold out the dead as they worked. When the dead tried to cross through to reach the working Martians, they were fried to a crisp and fell, this time truly dead, to the ground.

But three certainly came out about eight o'clock and, advancing slowly and cautiously, made their way through Byfleet and Pyrford towards Ripley and Weybridge, and so came in sight of the expectant batteries against the setting sun. The military had fought their way back into some of these places through the ranks of the dead in order to reestablish a better line to attempt to halt the Martian advance. These Martians did not advance in a body, but in a line, each perhaps a mile and a half from his nearest fellow. They communicated with one another by means of sirenlike howls, running up and down the scale from one note to another.

It was this howling and firing of the guns at Ripley and St. George's Hill that we had heard at Upper Halliford. The Ripley gunners, unseasoned artillery volunteers who ought never to have been placed in such a position, fired one wild, premature, ineffectual volley, and bolted on horse and foot through the deserted village, while the Martian, without using his Heat-Ray, walked serenely over their guns, stepped gingerly among them, passed in front of them, and so came unexpectedly upon the guns in Painshill Park, which he destroyed.

The St. George's Hill men, however, were better led or of a better mettle. Hidden by a pine wood as they were, they seem to have been quite unsuspected by the Martian nearest to them. They laid their guns as deliberately as if they had been on parade, and fired at about a thousand yards' range.

The shells flashed all round him, and he was seen to advance a few paces, stagger, and go down. Everybody yelled together, and the guns were reloaded in frantic haste. The overthrown Martian set up a prolonged ululation, and immediately a second glittering giant, answering him, appeared over the trees to the south. It would seem that a leg of the tripod had been smashed by one of the shells. The whole of the second volley flew wide of the Martian on the ground, and, simultaneously, both his companions brought their Heat-Rays to bear on the battery. The ammunition blew up, the pine trees all about the guns flashed into fire, and only one or two of the men who were already running over the crest of the hill escaped.

After this it would seem that the three took counsel together and halted, and the scouts who were watching them report that they remained absolutely stationary for the next half hour. The Martian who had been overthrown crawled tediously out of his hood, a small brown figure, oddly suggestive from that distance of a speck of blight, and apparently engaged in the repair of his support. During this time, the gunners and other men who had died in the battle arose and made a move against the brown creature. The other tripods danced, squashing many of the dead to the point of immobility and one brought its Heat-Ray to bear on the remaining creatures, keeping it pouring on them until there was nothing left of the dead but ash. About nine he had finished, for his cowl was then seen above the trees again.

It was a few minutes past nine that night when these three sentinels were joined by four other Martians, each carrying a thick black tube. A similar tube was handed to each of the three, and the seven proceeded to distribute themselves at equal distances along a curved line between St. George's Hill, Weybridge, and the village of Send, southwest of Ripley. By then more dead had wandered into the area but with all of them safe once again inside their tripods, the Martians paid no heed to the few random dead who wandered to and fro beneath their feet.

A dozen rockets sprang out of the hills before them as soon as they began to move, and warned the waiting batteries about Ditton and Esher. At the same time four of their fighting machines, similarly armed with tubes, crossed the river, and two of them, black against the western sky, came into sight of myself and the curate as we hurried wearily and painfully along the road that runs northward out of Halliford. They moved, as it seemed to us, upon a cloud, for a milky mist covered the fields and rose to a third of their height.

At this sight the curate cried faintly in his throat, and began running; but I knew it was no good running from a Martian, and I turned aside and crawled through dewy nettles and brambles into the broad ditch by the side of the road. He looked back, saw what I was doing, and turned to join me. It was my unfortunate luck that a dead man already called the ditch home. His legs were smashed to bits but his cold hands took hold of me before I saw him. He pulled me towards his waiting teeth. I smashed a fist into his jaw, twisting free of his grasp. How I managed to do so without his nails digging into my flesh, I do not know. As he opened his mouth to howl in anger, the curate had pushed passed me and was upon him. He grabbed the dead man's head in his hands and twisted his neck sharply. I heard more than saw the creature's neck snap. The curate quickly kicked the body aside and motioned for me to get down as the Martian machines drew closer. I nodded my thanks to him as we heard the machines slowing.

The two halted, the nearer to us standing and facing Sunbury, the remoter being a grey indistinctness towards the evening star, away towards Staines.

The occasional howling of the Martians had ceased; they took up their positions in the huge crescent about their cylinders in absolute silence. It was a crescent with twelve miles between its horns. Never since the devising of gunpowder was the beginning of a battle so still. To us and to an observer about Ripley it would have had precisely the same effect—the Martians seemed in solitary possession of the darkling night, lit only as it was by the slender moon, the stars, the afterglow of the daylight, and the ruddy glare from St. George's Hill and the woods of Painshill.

But facing that crescent everywhere—at Staines, Hounslow, Ditton, Esher, Ockham, behind hills and woods south of the river, and across the flat grass meadows to the north of it, wherever a cluster of trees or village houses gave sufficient cover—the guns were waiting. The signal rockets burst and rained their sparks through the night and vanished, and the spirit of all those watching batteries rose to a tense expectation. The Martians had but to advance into the line of fire, and instantly those motionless black forms of men, those guns glittering so darkly in the early night, would explode into a thunderous fury of battle.

No doubt the thought that was uppermost in a thousand

of those vigilant minds, even as it was uppermost in mine, was the riddle—how much they understood of us. Did they grasp that we in our millions were organized, disciplined, working together? Or did they interpret our spurts of fire, the sudden stinging of our shells, our steady investment of their encampment, as we should the furious unanimity of onslaught in a disturbed hive of bees? Did they dream they might exterminate us? (At that time no one knew what food they needed.) A hundred such questions struggled together in my mind as I watched that vast sentinel shape. And in the back of my mind was the sense of all the huge unknown and hidden forces Londonward. Had they prepared pitfalls? Were the powder mills at Hounslow ready as a snare? Would the Londoners have the heart and courage to make a greater Moscow of their mighty province of houses?

Then, after an interminable time, as it seemed to us, crouching and peering through the hedge, came a sound like the distant concussion of a gun. Another nearer, and then another. And then the Martian beside us raised his tube on high and discharged it, gunwise, with a heavy report that made the ground heave. The one towards Staines answered him. There was no flash, no smoke, simply that loaded detonation.

I was so excited by these heavy minute-guns following one another that I so far forgot my personal safety and my scalded hands as to clamber up into the hedge and stare towards Sunbury. As I did so a second report followed, and a big projectile hurtled overhead towards Hounslow. I expected at least to see smoke or fire, or some such evidence of its work. But all I saw was the deep blue sky above, with one solitary star, and the white mist spreading wide and low beneath. And there had been no crash, no answering explosion. The silence was restored; the minute lengthened to three.

"What has happened?" said the curate, standing up beside me.

"Heaven knows!" said I.

A bat flickered by and vanished. A distant tumult of shouting began and ceased. I looked again at the Martian, and saw he was now moving eastward along the riverbank, with a swift, rolling motion.

Every moment I expected the fire of some hidden battery to spring upon him; but the evening calm was unbroken. The figure of the Martian grew smaller as he receded, and presently the mist and the gathering night had swallowed him up. By a common impulse we clambered higher. Towards Sunbury was a dark appearance, as though a conical hill had suddenly come into being there, hiding our view of the farther country; and then, remoter across the river, over Walton, we saw another such summit. These hill-like forms grew lower and broader even as we stared.

Moved by a sudden thought, I looked northward, and there I perceived a third of these cloudy black kopjes had risen.

Everything had suddenly become very still. Far away to the southeast, marking the quiet, we heard the Martians hooting to one another, and then the air quivered again with the distant thud of their guns. But the earthly artillery made no reply.

Now at the time we could not understand these things,

but later I was to learn the meaning of these ominous kopjes that gathered in the twilight. Each of the Martians, standing in the great crescent I have described, had discharged, by means of the gunlike tube he carried, a huge canister over whatever hill, copse, cluster of houses, or other possible cover for guns, chanced to be in front of him. Some fired only one of these, some two—as in the case of the one we had seen; the one at Ripley is said to have discharged no fewer than five at that time. These canisters smashed on striking the ground—they did not explode—and incontinently disengaged an enormous volume of heavy, inky vapour, coiling and pouring upward in a huge and ebony cumulus cloud, a gaseous hill that sank and spread itself slowly over the surrounding country. And the touch of that vapour, the inhaling of its pungent wisps, was death to all that breathes.

It was heavy, this vapour, heavier than the densest smoke, so that, after the first tumultuous uprush and outflow of its impact, it sank down through the air and poured over the ground in a manner rather liquid than gaseous, abandoning the hills, and streaming into the valleys and ditches and watercourses even as I have heard the carbonic-acid gas that pours from volcanic clefts is wont to do. And where it came upon water some chemical action occurred, and the surface would be instantly covered with a powdery scum that sank slowly and made way for more. The scum was absolutely insoluble, and it is a strange thing, seeing the instant effect of the gas, that one could drink without hurt the water from which it had been strained. The vapour did not diffuse as a true gas would do. It hung together in banks, flowing sluggishly down the slope of the land and driving reluctantly before the wind, and very slowly it combined with the mist and moisture of the air, and sank to the earth in the form of dust. Save that an unknown element giving a group of four lines in the blue of the spectrum is concerned, we are still entirely ignorant of the nature of this substance.

Once the tumultuous upheaval of its dispersion was over, the black smoke clung so closely to the ground, even before its precipitation, that fifty feet up in the air, on the roofs and upper stories of high houses and on great trees, there was a chance of escaping its poison altogether, as was proved even that night at Street Cobham and Ditton.

The man who escaped at the former place tells a wonderful story of the strangeness of its coiling flow, and how he looked down from the church spire and saw the houses of the village rising like ghosts out of its inky nothingness. Untold numbers of dead men rose to their feet under the cover of this black smoke. He heard their hungry howls like a constant symphony of pain. For a day and a half he remained there, weary, starving and sun-scorched, the earth under the blue sky and against the prospect of the distant hills a velvet-black expanse, with red roofs, green trees, and, later, black-veiled shrubs and gates, barns, outhouses, and walls, rising here and there into the sunlight. The dead, at first, kept him trapped in the high place which saved his life but soon they wandered off in search of prey. Finally, when enough of them had departed, he had managed to escape to tell his tale of the Black Smoke.

But that was at Street Cobham, where the black vapour

was allowed to remain until it sank of its own accord into the ground. As a rule the Martians, when it had served its purpose, cleared the air of it again by wading into it and directing a jet of steam upon it.

This they did with the vapour banks near us, as we saw in the starlight from the window of a deserted house at Upper Halliford, whither we had returned. Our journey there was both fast and treacherous. We could only marvel at the packs upon packs of the dead, who bled out from under the cover of the Black Smoke. It, at times, appeared as if our entire military had fallen to the deadly gas. We crept through the trees with the greatest of caution and utmost stealth as an encounter with the dead would surely cost us our lives. We had no weapons beyond our hands and wits. Even if we had, it would have made no difference. The number of the dead was so vast that if we stopped to engage one of them, the others would have heard or seen us and came in numbers so great guns would not have mattered.

As soon as we entered the deserted house and made sure it was clear of rotting guests, we secured it as best as possible then found ourselves drawn to the window with longing to see what was happening with the creatures from another world and what their actions would now be. From there we could see the searchlights on Richmond Hill and Kingston Hill going to and fro, and heard the crack of rifles in an unending barrage. The gunnery stations on these hills must have been too high for the gas to reach as it crept its way across the land. Now the souls stationed at them with the heavy guns were to face the legions of the dead as well as the Martian invaders. Somehow, those brave men were able to hold against the dead.

About eleven, the windows rattled, and we heard the sound of the huge siege guns that had been put in position there. These continued intermittently for the space of a quarter of an hour, sending chance shots at the invisible Martians at Hampton and Ditton, and then the pale beams of the electric light vanished, and were replaced by a bright red glow.

Then the fourth cylinder fell—a brilliant green meteor— as I learned afterwards, in Bushey Park. Before the guns on the Richmond and Kingston line of hills began, there was a fitful cannonade far away in the southwest, due, I believe, to guns being fired haphazard before the black vapour could overwhelm the gunners as Martians launched a second round of tubes to make sure the bulk of the area had not been reinforced by fresh men.

So, setting about it as methodically as men might smoke out a wasps' nest, the Martians spread this strange stifling vapour over the Londonward country. The horns of the crescent slowly moved apart, until at last they formed a line from Hanwell to Coombe and Malden. All night through their destructive tubes advanced. Never once, after the Martian at St. George's Hill was brought down, did they give the artillery the ghost of a chance against them. Wherever there was a possibility of guns being laid for them unseen, a fresh canister of the black vapour was discharged, and where the guns were openly displayed the Heat-Ray was brought to bear. Thus they traveled on, leaving swarms of the dead in their wake.

By midnight the blazing trees along the slopes of Richmond Park and the glare of Kingston Hill threw their light upon a network of black smoke, blotting out the whole valley of the Thames and extending as far as the eye could reach. And through this two Martians slowly waded, and turned their hissing steam jets this way and that.

They were sparing of the Heat-Ray that night, either because they had but a limited supply of material for its production or because they did not wish to destroy the country but only to crush and overawe the opposition they had aroused. In the latter aim they certainly succeeded. Sunday night was the end of the organised opposition to their movements. After that no body of men would stand against them, so hopeless was the enterprise. The dead also played their part in this. They were so numerous that if guns were brought forward again into these areas, their gunners and defenders would be overwhelmed by the dead long before the Martians need bring their weapons to bear. Any resistance here left to be mounted would be done so solely by the navy. It was not to happen. Even the crews of the torpedo-boats and destroyers that had brought their quick-firers up the Thames refused to stop, mutinied, and went down again. Who can say if they were afraid of the Martians' Heat-Rays or the dead reaching them? I can't imagine what those sailors might have seen under the water along its muddy bottom. Were the dead down there as numerous as those on the land? I am sure, though, that they thanked God many a time that the dead could not truly swim. The only offensive operation men ventured upon after that night was the preparation of mines and pitfalls, and even in that their energies were frantic and spasmodic. Many a man was lost to the dead and these traps were laid poorly in great haste.

One has to imagine, as well as one may, the fate of those batteries towards Esher, waiting so tensely in the twilight. Survivors there were none. One may picture the orderly expectation, the officers alert and watchful, the gunners ready, the ammunition piled to hand, the limber gunners with their horses and waggons, the groups of civilian spectators standing as near as they were permitted, the evening stillness, the ambulances and hospital tents with the burned, wounded, and those ravaged by the dead from Weybridge; then the dull resonance of the shots the Martians fired, and the clumsy projectile whirling over the trees and houses and smashing amid the neighbouring fields.

One may picture, too, the sudden shifting of the attention, the swiftly spreading coils and bellyings of that blackness advancing headlong, towering heavenward, turning the twilight to a palpable darkness, a strange and horrible antagonist of vapour striding upon its victims, men and horses near it seen dimly, running, shrieking, falling headlong, shouts of dismay, the guns suddenly abandoned, men choking and writhing on the ground, and the swift broadening-out of the opaque cone of smoke. And then night and extinction—nothing but a silent mass of impenetrable vapour hiding those killed by it and their return to an unnatural state of existence.

Before dawn the black vapour was pouring through the streets of Richmond, and the disintegrating organism of government was, with a last expiring effort, rousing the population of London to the necessity of flight.

I heard stories of one general named Alves who made a great stand against the dead flocking towards civilization in advance of the Martians themselves. Like the Spartans of ages before, this general and several hundred men made a stand against the dead. As the creatures came charging out of the lands smote by the black vapours of the Martians, they stood their ground to the last man, forming a firing line.

The distance of the dead as the things made their advance gave a great advantage to the men with rifles. The riflemen had time to pick their targets and carefully aim their shots, at first dropping rows of the enemy with each volley of death. As the dead grew closer, the rate of their fire increased into a frantic defensive crescendo. The tide of the dead was unstoppable, however. As soon as one creature fell, two more from the area of devastation took its place. A witness, most likely a deserter, watched from afar as the creatures struck the firing line like a juggernaut. Alves and his men engaged them with bayonets and rifles used as clubs, slaying even more but in the end the gesture was futile. The dead poured over Alves and his brave platoon, claiming many of them as their own and devouring the others down to their bones. Yet, Alves and his men may have bought us all time as warnings of the dead swept ahead of the battle.

16

THE EXODUS FROM

LONDON

So you understand the roaring wave of fear that swept through the greatest city in the world just as Monday was dawning—the stream of flight rising swiftly to a torrent, lashing in a foaming tumult round the railway stations, banked up into a horrible struggle about the shipping in the Thames, and hurrying by every available channel northward and eastward. Armed soldiers and regular men alike fending off the dead wherever and whenever they appeared. By ten o'clock the police organisation, and by midday even the railway organisations, were losing coherency, losing shape and efficiency, guttering, softening, running at last in that swift liquefaction of the social body. It was a hopeless seeming struggle. Men and women died each passing minute at the teeth of the dead as the police and soldiers couldn't be everywhere at once. Most of what remained of the actual police were skittish and panicked themselves.

All the railway lines north of the Thames and the South-Eastern people at Cannon Street had been warned by midnight on Sunday, and trains were being filled, the trains no longer sane by the standards of the old world which existed mere days before. Makeshift armor covered their windows and rifle stands rode atop every third car occupied by the best marksmen the government of the area could spare from the defensive lines. People were fighting savagely for standing-room in the carriages even at two o'clock. By three, people were being trampled and crushed even in Bishopsgate Street, a couple of hundred yards or more from Liverpool Street station; revolvers were fired, people stabbed, and the policemen who had been sent to direct the traffic, exhausted and infuriated, were breaking the heads of the people they were called out to protect. The only difference from this madness the officers experienced was that each person they murdered in self-defense or fear now had to be murdered twice if they wanted to survive.

And as the day advanced and the engine drivers and stokers refused to return to London, the pressure of the flight drove the people in an ever-thickening multitude away from the stations and along the northward-running roads. By midday a Martian had been seen at Barnes, and a cloud of slowly sinking black vapour drove along the Thames and across the flats of Lambeth, cutting off all escape over the bridges in its sluggish advance. Another bank drove over Ealing, and surrounded a little island of survivors on Castle Hill, alive, but unable to escape.

After a fruitless struggle to get aboard a North-Western train at Chalk Farm—the engines of the trains that had loaded in the goods yard there *ploughed* through shrieking people, and a dozen stalwart men fought to keep the crowd from crushing the driver against his furnace—my brother emerged upon the Chalk Farm road, dodged across through a hurrying swarm of vehicles, and had the luck to be foremost in the sack of a cycle shop. The front tire of the machine he got was punctured in dragging it through the window, but he got up and off, notwithstanding, with no further injury than a cut wrist. The steep foot of Haverstock Hill was impassable owing to several overturned horses, and my brother struck into Belsize Road.

So he got out of the fury of the panic, and, skirting the Edgware Road, reached Edgware about seven, fasting and wearied, but well ahead of the crowd. Along the road people were standing in the roadway, curious, wondering. It looked as if he'd outrun the dead. He was passed by a number of cyclists, some horsemen, and two motor cars. A mile from Edgware the rim of the wheel broke, and the machine became unridable. He left it by the roadside and trudged through the village. There were shops half opened in the main street of the place, and people crowded on the pavement and in the doorways and windows, staring astonished at this extraordinary procession of fugitives that was beginning. He succeeded in getting some food at an inn.

For a time he remained in Edgware not knowing what next to do. The flying people increased in number. Many of them, like my brother, seemed inclined to loiter in the place. There was no fresh news of the invaders from Mars and for the time being it seemed the dead were content to stay in the streets he'd left behind. None the less, the people here were on guard against them. Law was a joke. Only in establishments like where my brother had gained food, where things were kept in check by the owner's shotgun, was there any semblance of order.

At that time the road was crowded, but as yet far from congested. Most of the fugitives at that hour were mounted on cycles, but there were soon motor cars, hansom cabs, and carriages hurrying along, and the dust hung in heavy clouds along the road to St. Albans.

It was perhaps a vague idea of making his way to Chelmsford, where some friends of his lived, that at last induced my brother to strike into a quiet lane running eastward. Presently he came upon a stile, and, crossing it, followed a footpath northeastward. He passed near several farmhouses and some little places whose names he did not learn. He saw few fugitives until, in a grass lane towards High Barnet, he happened upon two ladies who became his fellow travellers. He came upon them just in time to save them.

He heard their screams, and, hurrying round the corner, saw a couple of men struggling to drag them out of the little pony-chaise in which they had been driving, while a third with difficulty held the frightened pony's head. One of the ladies, a short woman dressed in white, was simply screaming; the other, a dark, slender figure, slashed at the man who gripped her arm with a whip she held in her disengaged hand.

My brother immediately grasped the situation, shouted, and hurried towards the struggle. One of the men desisted and turned towards him, and my brother, realising from his antagonist's face that a fight was unavoidable, and being an expert boxer, went into him forthwith and sent him down against the wheel of the chaise.

It was no time for pugilistic chivalry and my brother laid him quiet with a kick, and gripped the collar of the man who pulled at the slender lady's arm. He heard the clatter of hoofs, the whip stung across his face, a third antagonist struck him between the eyes, and the man he held wrenched himself free and made off down the lane in the direction from which he had come.

Partly stunned, he found himself facing the man who had held the horse's head, and became aware of the chaise receding from him down the lane, swaying from side to side, and with the women in it looking back. The man before him, a burly rough, tried to close, and he stopped him with a blow in the face. Then, realising that he was deserted, he dodged round and made off down the lane after the chaise, with the sturdy man close behind him, and the fugitive, who had turned now, following remotely.

Suddenly he stumbled and fell; his immediate pursuer went headlong, and he rose to his feet to find himself with a couple of antagonists again. He would have had little chance against them had not the slender lady very pluckily pulled up and returned to his help. It seems she had had a revolver all this time, but it had been under the seat when she and her companion were attacked. She fired at six yards' distance, narrowly missing my brother. The less courageous of the robbers made off, and his companion followed him, cursing his cowardice. They both stopped in sight down the lane, where the third man lay insensible.

"Take this!" said the slender lady, and she gave my brother her revolver.

"Go back to the chaise," said my brother, wiping the blood from his split lip.

She turned without a word—they were both panting—and they went back to where the lady in white struggled to hold back the frightened pony.

The robbers had evidently had enough of it. When my brother looked again they were retreating.

"I'll sit here," said my brother, "if I may"; and he got upon the empty front seat. The lady looked over her shoulder.

"Give me the reins," she said, and laid the whip along the pony's side. In another moment a bend in the road hid the three men from my brother's eyes.

So, quite unexpectedly, my brother found himself, panting, with a cut mouth, a bruised jaw, and bloodstained knuckles, driving along an unknown lane with these two women.

He learned they were the wife and the younger sister of a surgeon living at Stanmore, who had come in the small hours from a dangerous case at Pinner, and heard at some railway station on his way of the Martian advance. He had hurried home, roused the women—their servant had left them two days before—packed some provisions, put his revolver under the seat—luckily for my brother—and told them to drive on to Edgware, with the idea of getting a train there. He stopped behind to tell the neighbours. He would overtake them, he said, at about half past four in the morning, and now it was nearly nine and they had seen nothing of him. It was likely the dead had claimed him as one of their own. The women my brother traveled with were distraught about this chance and wanted to wait for him. They could not stop in Edgware because of the growing traffic through the place, and so they had come into this side lane. In the end, despite their desires, they were left with no option but to keep moving.

That was the story they told my brother in fragments when presently they stopped again, nearer to New Barnet. He promised to stay with them, at least until they could determine what to do, or until the missing man arrived, and professed to be an expert shot with the revolver—a weapon strange to him—in order to give them confidence. He knew the weapon would be utterly useless against the Martians and their mighty tripods and equally useless against the dead should the rotting things show themselves in any kind of decent number. Yet, the feel of the weapon in his grasp gave him new hope. His chances were far better now than they were on his own. His bruised jaw hurt ferociously and he rubbed at it while he rode with the women. He could not bring himself to ask the ladies if they held any extra ammunition for the revolver beyond what rested in its chamber. He was sure he would not like the answer.

They made a sort of encampment by the wayside, and the pony became happy in the hedge. My brother kept a watchful eye for the dead but so far none were to be seen.

He told them of his own escape out of London, and all that he knew of these Martians and their ways.

He also told them his theories on the dead plague. He believed now the plague was not a plague or infection at all. After long thought, he had deduced that he'd been wrong before and the plague was indeed linked with the coming of the Martians though he was still sure it was not something the sluggish creatures had planned. The women listened to his rant but soon grew weary of his attempts to apply science to something as nature-defying as the risen dead. The sun crept higher in the sky, and after a time their talk died out and gave place to an uneasy state of anticipation. Several wayfarers came along the lane, and of these my brother gathered such news as he could. Every broken answer he had deepened his impression of the great disaster that had come on humanity, deepened his persuasion of the immediate necessity for prosecuting this flight. It was only a matter of time until the dead caught up with them all. There seemed to be nowhere to run from the foul things. They always followed and found you in the end. He urged the matter upon them.

"We have money," said the slender woman, and hesitated.

Her eyes met my brother's, and her hesitation ended.

"So have I," said my brother.

She explained that they had as much as thirty pounds in gold, besides a five-pound note, and suggested that with that they might get upon a train at St. Albans or New Barnet. My brother thought that was hopeless, seeing the fury of the Londoners to crowd upon the trains, and broached his own idea of striking across Essex towards Harwich and thence escaping from the country altogether.

Mrs. Elphinstone—that was the name of the woman in white—would listen to no reasoning, and kept calling upon "George"; but her sister-in-law was astonishingly quiet and deliberate, and at last agreed to my brother's suggestion. So, designing to cross the Great North Road, they went on towards Barnet, my brother leading the pony to save it as much as possible. Not long thereafter they spotted the first dead man my brother had seen in some time. He lay on the side of the road, legs crushed by a wagon, his back twisted at an unnatural angle. He wailed and extended his arms towards them but the ditch he rested in was too steep for him to pull himself out of with his mangled hands. It looked as if he'd been run over and trampled then simply tossed out of the path of the refugees fleeing northward into the ditch. My brother considered expending a bullet to stop the man's maddening inhuman cries but instead urged his party on at a greater speed.

As the sun crept up the sky the day became excessively hot, and under foot a thick, whitish sand grew burning and blinding, so that they travelled only very slowly. They encountered more of the dead who had perished from hunger, exertion, and the like. Luckily, there were others traveling the road with them who were better equipped to deal with the monsters and they made short work of it when they appeared. The hedges were grey with dust. And as they advanced towards Barnet a tumultuous murmuring grew stronger.

They began to meet more people. For the most part these

were staring before them, murmuring indistinct questions, jaded, haggard, unclean. One man in evening dress passed them on foot, his eyes on the ground. They heard his voice, and, looking back at him, saw one hand clutched in his hair and the other beating invisible things. My brother was quick to notice that the man bore several bite marks along his right arm underneath the tattered cloth of his sleeve. Blood dripped and was flung from these wounds as he walked and threw his fit. When his paroxysm of rage was over, he went on his way without once looking back. The ladies were upset by the man's apparent madness and my brother warned them not to stop and offer help.

As my brother's party went on towards the crossroads to the south of Barnet they saw a woman approaching the road across some fields on their left, carrying a child and with two other children; and then passed a man in dirty black, with a thick stick in one hand and a small portmanteau in the other. Then round the corner of the lane, from between the villas that guarded it at its confluence with the high road, came a little cart drawn by a sweating black pony and driven by a sallow youth in a bowler hat, grey with dust. There were three girls, East End factory girls, and a couple of little children crowded in the cart. One of the girls was bound, head to toe, and her flesh was a sick greyish color.

"Is she dead?" Mrs. Elphinstone had whispered to my brother, who nodded and motioned her to silence. As a medical student, he knew that sometimes the grief of losing a loved one was too much to handle. Clearly for these folk, that was the case. After the girl had died and reanimated, they'd tied her up. Perhaps they were in denial, claiming she was "ill" and kept her with them rather than let the army deal with her by breaking her skull open and tossing her into a pyre. My brother's heart went out to the children who were riding with her for she must have stunk greatly from the heat of the midday sun.

"This'll tike us rahnd Edgware?" asked the driver of the cart with the dead girl in the back, wild-eyed, white-faced; and when my brother told him it would if he turned to the left, he whipped up at once without the formality of thanks.

My brother noticed a pale grey smoke or haze rising among the houses in front of them, and veiling the white facade of a terrace beyond the road that appeared between the backs of the villas. Mrs. Elphinstone suddenly cried out at a number of tongues of smoky red flame leaping up above the houses in front of them against the hot, blue sky. The tumultuous noise resolved itself now into the disorderly mingling of many voices, the grind of many wheels, the creaking of waggons, and the staccato of hoofs. The lane came round sharply not fifty yards from the crossroads.

"Good heavens!" cried Mrs. Elphinstone. "What is this you are driving us into?"

My brother stopped.

For the main road was a boiling stream of people, a torrent of human beings rushing northward, one pressing on another. Among them were a few of the dead, raging through the crowd, attacking anyone and everyone they could reach. The air was full of screams. A great bank of dust, white and luminous in the blaze of the sun, made everything within twenty feet of the ground grey and indistinct and was perpetually renewed by the hurrying feet of a dense crowd of horses and of men and women on foot, and by the wheels of vehicles of every description.

"Way!" my brother heard voices crying. "Make way!"

It was like riding into the smoke of a fire to approach the meeting point of the lane and road; the crowd roared like a fire and cried out as the dead moved through them. The dust was hot and pungent. And, indeed, a little way up the road a villa was burning and sending rolling masses of black smoke across the road to add to the confusion.

Two men came past them. They carried military issued rifles though they were not soldiers. My brother guessed they'd looted them from the dead. Then a dirty woman, carrying a heavy bundle and weeping. A lost retriever dog, with hanging tongue, circled dubiously round them, scared and wretched, and fled at my brother's threat.

So much as they could see of the road Londonward between the houses to the right was a tumultuous stream of dirty, hurrying people, racing for their lives, pent in between the villas on either side; the black heads, the crowded forms, grew into distinctness as they rushed towards the corner, hurried past, and merged their individuality again in a receding multitude that was swallowed up at last in a cloud of dust.

"Go on! Go on!" cried the voices. "Way! Way!"

One man's hands pressed on the back of another. My brother stood at the pony's head. Irresistibly attracted, he advanced slowly, pace by pace, down the lane. He held his revolver as best as he could as he led the pony through the chaos, keeping it ready should the dead make their way through the crowd to him.

Edgware had been a scene of confusion, Chalk Farm a riotous tumult, but this was a whole population in movement. It is hard to imagine that host. It had no character of its own. The figures poured out past the corner, and receded with their backs to the group in the lane. Along the margin came those who were on foot threatened by the wheels, stumbling in the ditches, blundering into one another.

The carts and carriages crowded close upon one another, making little way for those swifter and more impatient vehicles that darted forward every now and then when an opportunity showed itself of doing so, sending the people scattering against the fences and gates of the villas.

"Push on!" was the cry. "Push on! They are coming!" My brother was unsure if the people who were crying the warnings meant the Martians or the dead already with them.

In one cart stood a blind man in the uniform of the Salvation Army, gesticulating with his crooked fingers and bawling, "Eternity! Eternity!" His face was filthy and blood leaked from a wound on the side of his forehead. His voice was hoarse and very loud so that my brother could hear him long after he was lost to sight in the dust. Some of the people who crowded in the carts whipped stupidly at their horses and quarrelled with other drivers; some sat motionless, staring at nothing with miserable eyes; some gnawed their hands with thirst, or lay prostrate in the bottoms of their conveyances. The horses' bits were covered with foam, their eyes bloodshot. Gunshots were erupting throughout the press now. People were turning on people as some fools took shots at the rotting monsters without regard to those in the crowd around them.

There were cabs, carriages, shop cars, waggons, beyond counting; a mail cart, a road-cleaner's cart marked "Vestry of St. Pancras," a huge timber waggon crowded with roughs. A brewer's dray rumbled by with its two near wheels splashed with fresh blood.

"Clear the way!" cried the voices. "Clear the way!"

"Eter-nity! Eter-nity!" came echoing down the road.

There were sad, haggard women tramping by, well dressed, with children that cried and stumbled, their dainty clothes smothered in dust, their weary faces smeared with tears. With many of these came men, sometimes helpful, sometimes lowering and savage. Fighting side by side with them pushed some weary street outcast in faded black rags, wide-eyed, loud-voiced, and foul-mouthed. There were sturdy workmen thrusting their way along, wretched, unkempt men, clothed like clerks or shopmen, struggling spasmodically; a wounded soldier my brother noticed, men dressed in the clothes of railway porters, one wretched creature in a nightshirt with a coat thrown over it.

But varied as its composition was, certain things all that host had in common. There were fear and pain on their faces, and fear behind them. The dead were coming. A tumult up the road, a quarrel for a place in a waggon, sent the whole host of them quickening their pace; even a man so scared and broken that his knees bent under him was galvanised for a moment into renewed activity. The heat and dust had already been at work upon this multitude. Their skins were dry, their lips black and cracked. They were all thirsty, weary, and footsore. And amid the various cries one heard disputes, reproaches, groans of weariness and fatigue; the voices of most of them were hoarse and weak. Through it all ran a refrain:

"Way! Way! The Martians are coming! Save yourselves from the dead!"

Few stopped and came aside from that flood. Mostly these looked to be trained soldiers with rifles. They began to take careful aim at the dead and the worst of the idiots who were still blasting away carelessly amidst the others. The soldiers' rifles rang out with well-placed shots, likely saving the lives of many in the crowd. The lane opened slantingly into the main road with a narrow opening, and had a delusive appearance of coming from the direction of London. Yet a kind of eddy of people drove into its mouth; weaklings elbowed out of the stream, who for the most part rested but a moment before plunging into it again. A little way down the lane, with two friends bending over him, lay a man with a bare leg, wrapped about with bloody rags. He was a lucky man to have friends. My brother hoped his friends wouldn't be unlucky to have him. If he died, they may find themselves in rather unexpected trouble.

A little old man, with a grey military moustache and a filthy black frock coat, limped out and sat down beside the trap, removed his boot—his sock was blood-stained—shook out a pebble, and hobbled on again; and then a little girl of eight or nine, all alone, threw herself under the hedge close by my brother, weeping.

"I can't go on! I can't go on!"

My brother woke from his torpor of astonishment and

lifted her up, speaking gently to her, and carried her to Miss Elphinstone. So soon as my brother touched her she became quite still, as if frightened.

"Ellen!" shrieked a woman in the crowd, with tears in her voice—"Ellen!" And the child suddenly darted away from my brother, crying "Mother!"

"They are coming," said a man on horseback, riding past along the lane. This time there was no doubt he was referring to the dead. At the rear of the mass of people in flight, pushing and shoving against one another, there came a pack of the things howling with mad eyes.

"Out of the way, there!" bawled a coachman, towering high; and my brother saw a closed carriage turning into the lane.

The people crushed back on one another to avoid the horse. My brother pushed the pony and chaise back into the hedge, and the man drove by and stopped at the turn of the way. It was a carriage, with a pole for a pair of horses, but only one was in the traces. My brother saw dimly through the dust that two men lifted out something on a white stretcher and put it gently on the grass beneath the privet hedge.

One of the men came running to my brother.

"Where is there any water?" he said. "He is dying fast, and very thirsty. It is Lord Garrick."

"Lord Garrick!" said my brother; "the Chief Justice?"

"The water?" he said.

"There may be a tap," said my brother, "in some of the houses. We have no water. I dare not leave my people." My brother's gaze lingered on the man in the stretcher. He had

The War of the Worlds, Plus Blood, Guts and Zombies

not the heart to tell them the man was already dead. In moments, likely, the man would awaken and make short work of these determined caretakers who so vainly sought to save him. My brother's heart felt cold as he watched them go, shaking his head. "Be careful!" he called after them. "Watch him closely." My brother told me that was all he could bring himself to say at the time.

The man pushed against the crowd towards the gate of the corner house.

"Go on!" said the people, thrusting at him. "They are coming! Go on!"

Then my brother's attention was distracted by a bearded, eagle-faced man lugging a small handbag, which split even as my brother's eyes rested on it and disgorged a mass of sovereigns that seemed to break up into separate coins as it struck the ground. They rolled hither and thither among the struggling feet of men and horses. The man stopped and looked stupidly at the heap, and the shaft of a cab struck his shoulder and sent him reeling. He gave a shriek and dodged back, and a cartwheel shaved him narrowly.

"Way!" cried the men all about him. "Make way!"

So soon as the cab had passed, he flung himself, with both hands open, upon the heap of coins, and began thrusting handfuls in his pocket. A horse rose close upon him, and in another moment, half rising, he had been borne down under the horse's hoofs.

"Stop!" screamed my brother, and pushing a woman out of his way, tried to clutch the bit of the horse.

Before he could get to it, he heard a scream under the wheels, and saw through the dust the rim passing over the poor wretch's back. The driver of the cart slashed his whip at my brother, who ran round behind the cart. The multitudinous shouting confused his ears. The man was writhing in the dust among his scattered money, unable to rise, for the wheel had broken his back, and his lower limbs lay limp and dead. My brother stood up and yelled at the next driver, and a man on a black horse came to his assistance.

"Get him out of the road," said he; and, clutching the man's collar with his free hand, my brother lugged him sideways. But he still clutched after his money, and regarded my brother fiercely, hammering at his arm with a handful of gold. "Go on! Go on!" shouted angry voices behind.

"Way! Way!"

"Get him into a house!" my brother ordered. "At least there he might have a chance of the dead passing him by!"

The man nodded.

There was a smash as the pole of a carriage crashed into the cart that the man on horseback stopped. My brother looked up, and the man with the gold twisted his head round and bit the wrist that held his collar. There was a concussion, and the black horse came staggering sideways, and the carthorse pushed beside it. A hoof missed my brother's foot by a hair's breadth. He released his grip on the fallen man and jumped back. He saw anger change to terror on the face of the poor wretch on the ground, and in a moment he was hidden and my brother was borne backward and carried past the entrance of the lane, and had to fight hard in the torrent to recover it.

He saw Miss Elphinstone covering her eyes, and a little child, with all a child's want of sympathetic imagination, staring with dilated eyes at a dusty something that lay black and still, ground and crushed under the rolling wheels. The only blessing was that a hoof had shattered its skull so that it would not rise. "Let us go back!" he shouted, and began turning the pony round. "We cannot cross this—hell," he said and they went back a hundred yards the way they had come, until the fighting crowd was hidden. As they passed the bend in the lane my brother saw the face of the dying man in the ditch under the privet, deadly white and drawn, and shining with perspiration. This time my brother's heart could take the pain no longer. He walked over to the man and stood above him, pistol in hand. The man looked up at my brother with pleading eyes. My brother cocked the pistol and placed it to the man's temple, pulling the trigger before he lost his nerve. The man slumped to the dirt and my brother, with tears in his eyes, returned to where he was needed. The two women sat silent, crouching in their seat and shivering.

Then beyond the bend my brother stopped again. Miss Elphinstone was white and pale, and her sister-in-law sat weeping, too wretched even to call upon "George." My brother was horrified and perplexed. So soon as they had retreated he realised how urgent and unavoidable it was to attempt this crossing. He turned to Miss Elphinstone, suddenly resolute.

"We must go that way," he said, and led the pony round again.

For the second time that day this girl proved her quality. To force their way into the torrent of people, my brother plunged into the traffic and held back a cab horse, while she drove the pony across its head. A waggon locked wheels for a moment and ripped a long splinter from the chaise. In another moment they were caught and swept forward by the stream. My brother, with the cabman's whip marks red across his face and hands, scrambled into the chaise and took the reins from her.

"Point the revolver at the man behind," he said, giving it to her, "if he presses us too hard. No!—point it at his horse."

Then he began to look out for a chance of edging to the right across the road. But once in the stream he seemed to lose volition, to become a part of that dusty rout. They swept through Chipping Barnet with the torrent; they were nearly a mile beyond the centre of the town before they had fought across to the opposite side of the way. Only God's grace kept them from the dead who still pushed their way forward, deeper into those fleeing. It was din and confusion indescribable; but in and beyond the town the road forks repeatedly, and this to some extent relieved the stress.

They struck eastward through Hadley, and there on either side of the road, and at another place farther on they came upon a great multitude of people drinking at the stream, some fighting to come at the water. The dead were not among them . . . yet. And farther on, from a lull near East Barnet, they saw two trains running slowly one after the other without signal or order—trains swarming with people, with men even among the coals behind the engines—going northward along the Great Northern Railway. The soldiers in the rifle emplacements at the cars took pop shots at any one who strayed too close. My brother supposes they must have filled outside London, for at that time the furious terror of the people had rendered the central termini impossible.

Near this place, they found a deserted home and there they halted for the rest of the afternoon, for the violence of the day had already utterly exhausted all three of them. They began to suffer the beginnings of hunger; the night was cold, and none of them dared to sleep despite their securing of the doors and windows. And in the evening many people came hurrying along the road nearby their stopping place in the deserted home, fleeing from unknown dangers before them, and going in the direction from which my brother had come. Hour after hour, they heard gunshots, screams, and the mad raging of the dead outside. Once the screams were so close my brother positioned himself at the house's front door in fear the dead were coming for them at last. His knuckles remained white from his death grip upon the weapon until another scream sounded far away and the noise makers on the other side of the door ran off into the night at its call.

17

THE "THUNDER CHILD"

Had the Martians aimed only at destruction, they might on Monday have annihilated the entire population of London, as it spread itself slowly through the home counties. The dead were doing well enough of a job on their own and it would have only taken the slightest effort on the Martians' part to ensure the eradication of humanity in the area. The murdering of those on not only the road through Barnet, but also through Edgware and Waltham Abbey, and along the roads eastward to South-end and Shoeburyness, and south of the Thames to Deal and Broadstairs, would have made easy targets. They all would have been ready for the taking that June morning. If the scene had been witnessed from a balloon in the blazing blue above London every northward and eastward road running out of the tangled maze of streets would have seemed stippled black with the streaming fugitives, each dot a human agony of terror and physical distress. I have set forth at length in the last chapter my brother's account of the road through Chipping Barnet, in order that my readers may realise how that swarming of black dots appeared to one of those concerned. Never before in the history of the world had such a mass of human beings moved and suffered together. The legendary hosts of Goths and Huns, the hugest armies Asia has ever seen, would have been but a drop in that current. And this was no disciplined march; it was a stampede—a stampede gigantic and terrible—without order and without a goal, six million people unarmed and unprovisioned, driving headlong. It was the beginning of the rout of civilisation, of the massacre of mankind. The Martians alone would have been enough to achieve this and wipe out our race but the dead were overkill, taking away any hope that may have existed.

Directly below him the balloonist would have seen the network of streets far and wide, houses, churches, squares, crescents, gardens—already derelict—spread out like a huge map, and in the southward *blotted*. Over Ealing, Richmond, Wimbledon, it would have seemed as if some monstrous pen had flung ink upon the chart. Steadily, incessantly, each black splash grew and spread, shooting out ramifications this way and that, now banking itself against rising ground, now pouring swiftly over a crest into a new-found valley, exactly as a gout of ink would spread itself upon blotting paper.

And beyond, over the blue hills that rise southward of

the river, the glittering Martians went to and fro, calmly and methodically spreading their poison cloud over this patch of country and then over that, laying it again with their steam jets when it had served its purpose, and taking possession of the conquered country. And any poor souls who still remained in those parts met a painful death and rose to join the ranks of the already seemingly endless hordes of the dead. They do not seem to have aimed at extermination so much as at complete demoralisation and the destruction of any opposition. They exploded any stores of powder they came upon, cut every telegraph, and wrecked the railways here and there. They were hamstringing mankind. They seemed in no hurry to extend the field of their operations, and did not come beyond the central part of London all that day. It is possible that a very considerable number of people in London stuck to their houses through Monday morning, having been trapped in them by the dead before the Martians' arrival to the city proper. Certain it is that many died at home suffocated by the Black Smoke as their boarded up and barricaded doors could not save them from the very air itself.

Until about midday the Pool of London was an astonishing scene. Steamboats and shipping of all sorts lay there, tempted by the enormous sums of money offered by fugitives, and it is said that many who swam out to these vessels were thrust off with boathooks and drowned. It also said that many who entered the waters, swimming for these beacons of hope, never reached them at all. Below the surface, there was surely a number of dead who had their fun with those brave or foolish enough to swim through the muddy and blood-tainted waters. About one o'clock in the afternoon the thinning remnant of a cloud of the black vapour appeared between the arches of Blackfriars Bridge. At that the Pool became a scene of mad confusion, fighting, and collision, and for some time a multitude of boats and barges jammed in the northern arch of the Tower Bridge, and the sailors and lightermen had to fight savagely against the people who swarmed upon them from the riverfront. People were actually clambering down the piers of the bridge from above. The dead mixed into these struggles as well, sopping wet corpses climbing from the water onto the docks and to the shore only to be put down by the crews of the ships or armed civilians from the crowd who scored lucky shots.

When, an hour later, a Martian appeared beyond the Clock Tower and waded down the river, nothing but wreckage floated above Limehouse.

Of the falling of the fifth cylinder I have presently to tell. The sixth star fell at Wimbledon. My brother, keeping watch beside the women in the chaise in a meadow, saw the green flash of it far beyond the hills. On Tuesday the little party, still set upon getting across the sea, made its way through the swarming country towards Colchester. The news that the Martians were now in possession of the whole of London was confirmed. They had been seen at Highgate, and even, it was said, at Neasden. But they did not come into my brother's view until the morrow.

That day the scattered multitudes began to realise the urgent need of provisions. As they grew hungry the rights of property ceased to be regarded. Farmers were out to defend their cattle-sheds, granaries, and ripening root crops with arms in their hands. Many of these hired thugs and deserters from the army with the promise of food and shelter in exchange for helping them defend what was theirs. A number of people now, like my brother, had their faces eastward, and there were some desperate souls even going back towards London to get food. These were chiefly people from the northern suburbs, whose knowledge of the Black Smoke came by hearsay or those so starved and desperate that death was a better alternative than the existence they were living. He heard that about half the members of the government had gathered at Birmingham, and that enormous quantities of high explosives were being prepared to be used in automatic mines across the Midland counties.

He was also told that the Midland Railway Company had replaced the desertions of the first day's panic, had resumed traffic, and was running northward trains from St. Albans to relieve the congestion of the home counties. These trains were now fully armored and carried each their own contingent of soldiers who were out for vengeance against the dead. There was also a placard in Chipping Ongar announcing that large stores of flour were available in the northern towns and that within twenty-four hours bread would be distributed among the starving people in the neighbourhood. But this intelligence did not deter him from the plan of escape he had formed, and the three pressed eastward all day, and heard no more of the bread distribution than this promise. Nor, as a matter of fact, did anyone else hear more of it. That night fell the seventh star, falling upon Primrose Hill. It fell while Miss Elphinstone was watching, for she took that duty alternately with my brother. She saw it.

On Wednesday the three fugitives—they had passed the night in a field of unripe wheat, all staying awake and praying the dead would not discover them inside the field—reached Chelmsford, and there a body of the inhabitants, calling itself the Committee of Public Supply, seized the pony as provisions, and would give nothing in exchange for it but the promise of a share in it the next day. Here there were rumours of Martians at Epping, and news of the destruction of Waltham Abbey Powder Mills in a vain attempt to blow up one of the invaders. There were also tales of armies of the dead storming lesser known towns in force and devouring entire populations within hours if not minutes.

People were watching for Martians here from the church towers and snipers took shots at any of the dead that could be spotted as they approached. My brother, very luckily for him as it chanced, preferred to push on at once to the coast rather than wait for food, although all three of them were very hungry. By midday they passed through Tillingham, which, strangely enough, seemed to be quite silent and deserted, save for a few furtive plunderers hunting for food. Near Tillingham they suddenly came in sight of the sea, and the most amazing crowd of shipping of all sorts that it is possible to imagine.

For after the sailors could no longer come up the Thames, they came on to the Essex coast, to Harwich and Walton and Clacton, and afterwards to Foulness and Shoebury, to bring off the people. They lay in a huge sickle-shaped curve that vanished into mist at last towards the Naze. Close inshore was a multitude of fishing smacks—English, Scotch, French, Dutch, and Swedish; steam launches from the Thames, yachts, electric boats; and beyond were ships of large burden, a multitude of filthy colliers, trim merchantmen, cattle ships, passenger boats, petroleum tanks, ocean tramps, an old white transport even, neat white and grey liners from Southampton and Hamburg; and along the blue coast across the Blackwater my brother could make out dimly a dense swarm of boats chaffering with the people on the beach, a swarm which also extended up the Blackwater almost to Maldon. Most of the decks of these vessels brimmed with sailors and refugees but here and there among this motley fleet sat ships that were strangely vacant. My brother guessed the dead were aboard these ships and now claimed them as their own after making a meal of the passengers and crew. The creatures were trapped aboard these vessels with no way off except to disappear under the water's surface once more and stumble along until they chanced into a spot where they could reach and scale the hull of another ship.

About a couple of miles out lay an ironclad, very low in the water, almost, to my brother's perception, like a waterlogged ship. This was the ram *Thunder Child*. It was the only warship in sight, but far away to the right over the smooth surface of the sea—for that day there was a dead calm—lay a serpent of black smoke to mark the next ironclads of the Channel Fleet, which hovered in an extended line, steam up and ready for action, across the Thames estuary during the course of the Martian conquest, vigilant and yet powerless to prevent it.

At the sight of the sea, Mrs. Elphinstone, in spite of the assurances of her sister-in-law, gave way to panic. She had never been out of England before, she would rather die than trust herself friendless in a foreign country, and so forth. She seemed, poor woman, to imagine that the French and the Martians might prove very similar. She had been growing increasingly hysterical, fearful, and depressed during the two days' journeyings. Her great idea was to return to Stanmore. Things had been always well and safe at Stanmore. They would find George at Stanmore.

It was with the greatest difficulty they could get her down to the beach, where presently my brother succeeded in attracting the attention of some men on a paddle steamer from the Thames. They sent a boat and drove a bargain for thirty-six pounds for the three. The steamer was going, these men said, to Ostend.

It was about two o'clock when my brother, having paid their fares at the gangway, found himself safely aboard the steamboat with his charges. There was food aboard, albeit at exorbitant prices, and the three of them contrived to eat a meal on one of the seats forward.

There were already a couple of score of passengers aboard, some of whom had expended their last money in securing a passage, but the captain lay off the Blackwater until five in the afternoon, picking up passengers until the seated decks were even dangerously crowded. He would probably have remained longer had it not been for the sound of guns that began about that hour in the south. As if in answer, the ironclad seaward fired a small gun and hoisted a string of flags. A jet of smoke sprang out of her funnels.

Some of the passengers were of opinion that this firing came from Shoeburyness, until it was noticed that it was growing louder. At the same time, far away in the southeast the masts and upperworks of three ironclads rose one after the other out of the sea, beneath clouds of black smoke. But my brother's attention speedily reverted to the distant firing in the south. He fancied he saw a column of smoke rising out of the distant grey haze.

The little steamer was already flapping her way eastward of the big crescent of shipping, and the low Essex coast was growing blue and hazy, when a Martian appeared, small and faint in the remote distance, advancing along the muddy coast from the direction of Foulness. At that the captain on the bridge swore at the top of his voice with fear and anger at his own delay, and the paddles seemed infected with his terror. Every soul aboard stood at the bulwarks or on the seats of the steamer and stared at that distant shape, higher than the trees or church towers inland, and advancing with a leisurely parody of a human stride.

It was the first Martian my brother had seen, and he stood, more amazed than terrified, watching this Titan advancing deliberately towards the shipping, wading farther and farther into the water as the coast fell away. Then, far away beyond the Crouch, came another, striding over some stunted trees, and then yet another, still farther off, wading deeply through a shiny mudflat that seemed to hang halfway up between sea and sky. They were all stalking seaward, as if to intercept the escape of the multitudinous vessels that were crowded between Foulness and the Naze. In spite of the throbbing exertions of the engines of the little paddleboat, and the pouring foam that her wheels flung behind her, she receded with terrifying slowness from this ominous advance.

Glancing northwestward, my brother saw the large crescent of shipping already writhing with the approaching terror; one ship passing behind another, another coming round from broadside to end on, steamships whistling and giving off volumes of steam, sails being let out, launches rushing hither and thither. He was so fascinated by this and by the creeping danger away to the left that he had no eyes for anything seaward. And then a swift movement of the steamboat (she had suddenly come round to avoid being run down) flung him headlong from the seat upon which he was standing. There was a shouting all about him, a trampling of feet, and a cheer that seemed to be answered faintly. The steamboat lurched and rolled him over upon his hands.

He sprang to his feet and saw to starboard, and not a hundred yards from their heeling, pitching boat, a vast iron bulk like the blade of a plough tearing through the water, tossing it on either side in huge waves of foam that leaped towards the steamer, flinging her paddles helplessly in the air, and then sucking her deck down almost to the waterline.

A douche of spray blinded my brother for a moment. When his eyes were clear again he saw the monster had passed and was rushing landward. Big iron upperworks rose out of this headlong structure, and from that twin funnels projected and spat a smoking blast shot with fire. It was the torpedo ram, *Thunder Child,* steaming headlong, coming to the rescue of the threatened shipping.

Keeping his footing on the heaving deck by clutching

the bulwarks, my brother looked past this charging leviathan at the Martians again, and he saw the three of them now close together, and standing so far out to sea that their tripod supports were almost entirely submerged. Thus sunken, and seen in remote perspective, they appeared far less formidable than the huge iron bulk in whose wake the steamer was pitching so helplessly. It would seem they were regarding this new antagonist with astonishment. To their intelligence, it may be, the giant was even such another as themselves. The *Thunder Child* fired no gun, but simply drove full speed towards them. It was probably her not firing that enabled her to get so near the enemy as she did. They did not know what to make of her. One shell, and they would have sent her to the bottom forthwith with the Heat-Ray.

She was steaming at such a pace that in a minute she seemed halfway between the steamboat and the Martians— a diminishing black bulk against the receding horizontal expanse of the Essex coast.

Suddenly the foremost Martian lowered his tube and discharged a canister of the black gas at the ironclad. It hit her starboard side and glanced off in an inky jet that rolled away to seaward, an unfolding torrent of Black Smoke, from which the ironclad drove clear. To the watchers from the steamer, low in the water and with the sun in their eyes, it seemed as though she were already among the Martians.

They saw the gaunt figures separating and rising out of the water as they retreated shoreward, and one of them raised the camera-like generator of the Heat-Ray. He held it pointing obliquely downward, and a bank of steam sprang from the water at its touch. It must have driven through the iron of the ship's side like a white-hot iron rod through paper.

A flicker of flame went up through the rising steam, and then the Martian reeled and staggered. In another moment he was cut down, and a great body of water and steam shot high in the air. The guns of the *Thunder Child* sounded through the reek, going off one after the other, and one shot splashed the water high close by the steamer, ricocheted towards the other flying ships to the north, and smashed a smack to matchwood.

But no one heeded that very much. At the sight of the Martian's collapse the captain on the bridge yelled inarticulately, and all the crowding passengers on the steamer's stern shouted together. And then they yelled again. For, surging out beyond the white tumult, drove something long and black, the flames streaming from its middle parts, its ventilators and funnels spouting fire.

She was alive still; the steering gear, it seems, was intact and her engines working. She headed straight for a second Martian, and was within a hundred yards of him when the Heat-Ray came to bear. Then with a violent thud, a blinding flash, her decks, her funnels, leaped upward. The Martian staggered with the violence of her explosion, and in another moment the flaming wreckage, still driving forward with the impetus of its pace, had struck him and crumpled him up like a thing of cardboard. My brother shouted involuntarily. A boiling tumult of steam hid everything again.

"Two!" yelled the captain.

Everyone was shouting. The whole steamer from end to

end rang with frantic cheering that was taken up first by one and then by all in the crowding multitude of ships and boats that was driving out to sea.

The steam hung upon the water for many minutes, hiding the third Martian and the coast altogether. And all this time the boat was paddling steadily out to sea and away from the fight; and when at last the confusion cleared, the drifting bank of black vapour intervened, and nothing of the *Thunder Child* could be made out, nor could the third Martian be seen. But the ironclads to seaward were now quite close and standing in towards shore past the steamboat.

The little vessel continued to beat its way seaward, and the ironclads receded slowly towards the coast, which was hidden still by a marbled bank of vapour, part steam, part black gas, eddying and combining in the strangest way. The fleet of refugees was scattering to the northeast; several smacks were sailing between the ironclads and the steamboat. After a time, and before they reached the sinking cloud bank, the warships turned northward, and then abruptly went about and passed into the thickening haze of evening southward. The coast grew faint, and at last indistinguishable amid the low banks of clouds that were gathering about the sinking sun.

Then suddenly out of the golden haze of the sunset came the vibration of guns, and a form of black shadows moving. Everyone struggled to the rail of the steamer and peered into the blinding furnace of the west, but nothing was to be distinguished clearly. A mass of smoke rose slanting and barred the face of the sun. The steamboat throbbed on its way through an interminable suspense.

The sun sank into grey clouds, the sky flushed and dark-ened, the evening star trembled into sight. It was deep twi-light when the captain cried out and pointed. My brother strained his eyes. Something rushed up into the sky out of the greyness—rushed slantingly upward and very swiftly into the luminous clearness above the clouds in the western sky; something flat and broad, and very large, that swept round in a vast curve, grew smaller, sank slowly, and van-ished again into the grey mystery of the night. And as it flew it rained down darkness upon the land. Perhaps soon there would be no one living left at all and then the Earth would belong to the dead and the alien visitors. My brother hoped the dead would at least trouble the Martians in whatever their plans were for this world.

BOOK TWO

———⧫———

THE EARTH UNDER
THE MARTIANS

1

UNDER FOOT

In the first book I have wandered so much from my own adventures to tell of the experiences of my brother that all through the last two chapters I and the curate have been lurking in the empty house at Halliford whither we fled to escape the Black Smoke. Holed up in our own little fortress of relative safety behind barred doors and filled with fear as we listened to the dead roam the country outside. There I will resume. We stopped there all Sunday night and all the next day—the day of the panic—in a little island of daylight, cut off by the Black Smoke from the rest of the world. We could do nothing but wait in aching inactivity during those two weary days.

They were far from peaceful and not just from the phantoms of our fears and worries. More than once, the dead gathered on the doorstep in small packs of threes and fours to beat their decaying fists on the thick wood of the door. They would spit and snarl in fury, demanding entrance as if they somehow smelled our warm flesh inside.

The worst of it came our second night. The door finally gave way to their endless hammering and a group of three of the things broke in. The curate was on watch but had fallen asleep on the floor between the entrance and the living room. So tired was he that it took the full breaking of the door to wake him. He sat up at once as the things came at him, rolling to his feet. He slept with a kitchen knife lying beside him as there were no better weapons to be found within the confines of the house we'd made our shelter. As the fastest of the dead reached him, he slashed out at its face, cutting through its nose and scarring its eyes. The blind thing kept coming, confused by its loss of vision, but unhindered by the pain (for the dead were incapable of feeling any). The curate grabbed the thing and shoved it behind him as I, now awake myself, came lunging from the living room with a heavy piece of firewood gripped tightly in my hands like sword. I met the next of the creatures' head by swinging with all my might. The blow took it in the side of its head and it toppled to the floor with a large dent in its skull.

The curate made a move against the last of the creatures, ignoring the stumbling blind thing behind him, and rammed his knife into its eye socket, burying the blade to its hilt. He tossed the falling body from his path and slammed the door shut, pressing his back against it in a panic though no more of the creatures had showed themselves so far. I finished off the blind monster, knocking it to the floor and bashing its head until it rested in a pool of cold red and black pus. I raced to his side. Together, one of us holding the door, the other working with determined zeal, we nailed the door back to its frame and replaced the boards that had covered it, making sure it was as securely in place as we could make it. We then took the couch I had slept on and shoved it over and up against the door to give it additional support, all the while cursing ourselves for not doing it earlier.

We both were hungry and tired beyond measure. Our minds again wandered to our worries and fears for our kin. My own mind was occupied by anxiety for my wife. I figured her at Leatherhead, terrified, in danger, mourning me already as a dead man. I could see her and our friend holed up much as we were here, fending off the dead who surely by now had discovered their place of refuge. I paced the rooms and cried aloud when I thought of how I was cut off from her, of all that might happen to her in my absence. My cousin, I knew, was brave enough for any emergency, but he was not the sort of man to realise danger quickly, to rise promptly. What was needed now was not bravery, but circumspection. My only consolation was to believe that the Martians were moving Londonward and away from her. All they had to do in order to survive was hold out against the dead and the dead alone. Not an easy task by any measure but one that could be achieved as my own struggle here had proved. Such vague anxieties keep the mind sensitive and painful. I grew very weary and irritable with the curate's perpetual ejaculations; I tired of the sight of his selfish despair. I even came close to thinking of murdering myself, being trapped with this insufferable ingrate. The world had ended and law was a thing of the past yet I knew God was still present. The Father in Heaven watched over us or we would surely not have been alive now. I stilled my anger and vowed I would not surrender myself to the horror that the things around here had become. After some ineffectual remonstrance I kept away from him, staying in a room—evidently a children's schoolroom—containing globes, forms, and copybooks. When he followed me thither, I went to a box room at the top of the house and, in order to be alone with my aching miseries, locked myself in. I could only pray if the dead gained entry again that I would be able to stand against them alone.

We were hopelessly hemmed in by the Black Smoke all that day and the morning of the next. There were signs of people in the next house on Sunday evening—a face at a window and moving lights, and later the slamming of a door. But I do not know who these people were, nor what became of them. For all I knew, they could have been dead. Mindless creatures that had wandered inside a house and now bumped their way through it, unable to find their way out again. We saw nothing of them the next day. The Black Smoke drifted slowly riverward all through Monday morning, creeping nearer and nearer to us, driving at last along the roadway outside the house that hid us.

A Martian came across the fields about midday, laying the stuff with a jet of superheated steam that hissed against the walls, smashed all the windows it touched, and scalded the curate's hand as he fled out of the front room. When at last we crept across the sodden rooms and looked out again, the country northward was as though a black snowstorm had passed over it. Scores of truly dead corpses covered the ground, trampled underneath Martian feet. Looking towards the river, we were astonished to see an unaccountable redness mingling with the black of the scorched meadows.

For a time we did not see how this change affected our position, save that we were relieved of our fear of the Black Smoke. But later I perceived that we were no longer hemmed in, that now we might get away. The dead in the area had cleared with the smoke. The creatures must have grown tired in their vain search for flesh in this area and made their way to better hunting grounds. So soon as I realised that the way of escape was open, my dream of action returned. But the curate was lethargic, unreasonable.

"We are safe here," he repeated; "safe here."

I resolved to leave him—would that I had! Wiser now for the artilleryman's teaching, I sought out food and drink. I had found oil and rags for my burns, and I also took a hat and a flannel shirt that I found in one of the bedrooms. When it was clear to him that I meant to go alone—had reconciled myself to going alone—he suddenly roused himself to come. And all being quiet throughout the afternoon, we started about five o'clock, as I should judge, along the blackened road to Sunbury.

In Sunbury, and at intervals along the road, were dead bodies lying in contorted attitudes, the corpses riddled with bullet holes from the long past stand of the military, and others who looked to have been cooked after death by the Martians' heat weapons. Horses covered the ground as well as men, overturned carts and luggage, all covered thickly with black dust. That pall of cindery powder made me think of what I had read of the destruction of Pompeii. We got to Hampton Court without misadventure, our minds full of strange and unfamiliar appearances, and at Hampton Court our eyes were relieved to find a patch of green that had escaped the suffocating drift. We went through Bushey Park, with its deer going to and fro under the chestnuts, and some men and women hurrying in the distance towards Hampton, though we did not know if they were alive or dead, and so we came to Twickenham. As we drew closer we saw these folk were indeed still breathing. These were the first people we saw.

Away across the road the woods beyond Ham and Petersham were still afire. Twickenham was uninjured by either Heat-Ray or Black Smoke, and there were more people about here, though none could give us news. For the most part they were like ourselves, taking advantage of a lull to shift their quarters. I have an impression that many of the houses here were still occupied by scared inhabitants, too frightened even for flight. Here too the evidence of a hasty rout was abundant along the road. I remember most vividly three smashed bicycles in a heap, pounded into the road by the wheels of subsequent carts. We crossed Richmond Bridge about half past eight. We hurried across the exposed bridge, of course, but I noticed floating down the stream a number of red masses, some many feet across. I did not know what these were—there was no time for scrutiny—and I put a more horrible interpretation on them than they deserved. Here again on the Surrey side were black dust that had once been smoke, and dead bodies—a heap near the approach to the station—that had been burnt in the flames of a pyre of human construction. Mostly only their bones remained, but we had no glimpse of the Martians until we were some way towards Barnes.

We saw in the blackened distance a group of three people running down a side street towards the river, but otherwise it seemed deserted. These folk, however, were clearly dead and their cries of hunger rode on the wind, haunting us. We steered clear of them, taking cover until they were long out of sight and then continued on. Up the hill Richmond town was burning briskly; outside the town of Richmond there was no trace of the Black Smoke.

Then suddenly, as we approached Kew, came a number of people running, and the upperworks of a Martian fighting-machine loomed in sight over the housetops, not a hundred yards away from us. We stood aghast at our danger, and had the Martian looked down we must immediately have perished. We were so terrified that we dared not go on, but turned aside and hid in a shed in a garden. There the curate crouched, weeping silently, and refusing to stir again.

But my fixed idea of reaching Leatherhead would not let me rest, and in the twilight I ventured out again. I went through a shrubbery, and along a passage beside a big house standing in its own grounds, and so emerged upon the road towards Kew. My heart froze in my chest as I heard the cries of the dead in the distance and paused where I stood, sure that they were coming for me. I remember thanking God time and time again as the screams grew more distant and I realised that the things already had other prey. The curate I left in the shed, but he came hurrying after me as if to make sure I was okay. I think, though, more than anything, his tortured mind couldn't stand the thought of being alone.

That second start was the most foolhardy thing I ever did. For it was manifest the Martians were about us. No sooner had the curate overtaken me than we saw either the fighting-machine we had seen before or another, far away across the meadows in the direction of Kew Lodge. Four or five little black figures hurried before it across the green-grey of the field, and in a moment it was evident this Martian pursued them. In three strides he was among them, and they ran radiating from his feet in all directions. He used no Heat-Ray to destroy them, but picked them up one by one. Apparently he tossed them into the great metallic carrier which projected behind him, much as a workman's basket hangs over his shoulder.

It was the first time I realised that the Martians might have any other purpose than destruction with defeated humanity. We stood for a moment petrified, then turned and fled through a gate behind us into a walled garden, fell into, rather than found, a fortunate ditch, and lay there, scarce daring to whisper to each other until the stars were out.

I suppose it was nearly eleven o'clock before we gathered courage to start again, no longer venturing into the road, but sneaking along hedgerows and through plantations, and watching keenly through the darkness, he on the right and I on the left, for the Martians, who seemed to be all about us. In one place we blundered upon a scorched and blackened area, now cooling and ashen, and a number of scattered dead bodies of men, burned horribly about the heads and trunks but with their legs and boots mostly intact; and of dead horses, fifty feet, perhaps, behind a line of four ripped guns and smashed gun carriages.

Sheen, it seemed, had escaped destruction, but the place was silent and deserted. Here we happened on no dead, resting peacefully or otherwise, though the night was too dark for us to see into the side roads of the place. In Sheen my companion suddenly complained of faintness and thirst, and we decided to try one of the houses. At the very least it would offer us safety from the dead and keep us out of view of both the creatures and the Martian machines alike.

The first house we entered, after a little difficulty with the window, was a small semi-detached villa, and I found nothing eatable left in the place but some mouldy cheese. There was, however, water to drink; and I took a hatchet, which promised to be useful in our next housebreaking. Its blade would also come in very useful if our luck failed us and we did encounter the dead.

We then crossed to a place where the road turns towards Mortlake. Here there stood a white house within a walled garden, and in the pantry of this domicile we found a store of food—two loaves of bread in a pan, an uncooked steak, and the half of a ham. I give this catalogue so precisely because, as it happened, we were destined to subsist upon this store for the next fortnight. Bottled beer stood under a shelf, and there were two bags of haricot beans and some limp lettuces. This pantry opened into a kind of wash-up kitchen, and in this was firewood; there was also a cupboard, in which we found nearly a dozen of burgundy, tinned soups and salmon, and two tins of biscuits.

As we gathered our bounty, a noise sounded from the

house's back room. I crept quietly towards it, leaving the curate staring in terror after me. The fight had left the man and he was now utterly useless. I reached the rear room and cautiously peeked inside it. Something black leaped at me from within and I staggered backwards, swinging the hatchet's blade through the air. My back made contact with the hallway wall, bringing my retreat to a halt as I looked down to see a black cat racing away through the house. The breath flooded out of me in relief. I peered into the room again to find it empty and made my way back to the curate. Once we were a bit more settled and the rest of the house was checked, we decided food was the most urgent of our needs.

We sat in the adjacent kitchen in the dark—for we dared not strike a light for fear it would bring unwanted company—and ate bread and ham, and drank beer out of the same bottle. The curate, who was still timorous and restless, was now, oddly enough, for pushing on, and I was urging him to keep up his strength by eating when the thing happened that was to imprison us.

"It can't be midnight yet," I said, and then came a blinding glare of vivid green light. Everything in the kitchen leaped out, clearly visible in green and black, and vanished again. And then followed such a concussion as I have never heard before or since. So close on the heels of this as to seem instantaneous came a thud behind me, a clash of glass, a crash and rattle of falling masonry all about us, and the plaster of the ceiling came down upon us, smashing into a multitude of fragments upon our heads. I was knocked headlong across the floor against the oven handle and stunned. I was insensible for a long time, the curate told me, and when

I came to we were in darkness again, and he, with a face wet, as I found afterwards, with blood from a cut forehead, was dabbing water over me.

For some time I could not recollect what had happened. Then things came to me slowly. A bruise on my temple asserted itself.

"Are you better?" asked the curate in a whisper.

At last I answered him. I sat up.

"Don't move," he said. "The floor is covered with smashed crockery from the dresser. You can't possibly move without making a noise, and I fancy *they* are outside."

"The dead?" I asked, my mind instantly assuming a large pack of the things had found us, forgetting the circumstances that had brought me low.

The curate shook his head and gestured upwards as if at a giant.

We both sat quite silent, so that we could scarcely hear each other breathing. Everything seemed deadly still, but once something near us, some plaster or broken brickwork, slid down with a rumbling sound. Outside and very near was an intermittent, metallic rattle.

"That!" said the curate, when presently it happened again.

"Yes," I said. "But what is it?" I asked again.

"A Martian!" said the curate.

I listened.

"It was not like the Heat-Ray," I said, and for a time I was inclined to think one of the great fighting-machines had stumbled against the house, as I had seen one stumble against the tower of Shepperton Church.

Our situation was so strange and incomprehensible that for three or four hours, until the dawn came, we scarcely moved. I sat thinking about the events of the past days and for some reason of the dead. I wondered what had created them. Surely not the Martians. They seemed put off by the mindless things. They did not see them as a threat unless they were outside their great machines. I could scarcely believe that a race so advanced with such powerful tools at their disposal would need to turn our dead against us in order to make a bid for our world. Was this God's judgment? No. These were not the end times spoken of in the Bible.

I stared into the darkness, lost in thoughts beyond my understanding as a mortal man whose knowledge of science was, at best, limited.

And then the light filtered in, not through the window, which remained black, but through a triangular aperture between a beam and a heap of broken bricks in the wall behind us. The interior of the kitchen we now saw greyly for the first time.

The window had been burst in by a mass of garden mould, which flowed over the table upon which we had been sitting and lay about our feet. Outside, the soil was banked high against the house. At the top of the window frame we could see an uprooted drainpipe. The floor was littered with smashed hardware; the end of the kitchen towards the house was broken into, and since the daylight shone in there, it was evident the greater part of the house had collapsed. Contrasting vividly with this ruin was the neat dresser, stained in the fashion, pale green, and with a number of copper and tin vessels below it, the wallpaper imitating blue and white tiles, and a couple of coloured supplements fluttering from the walls above the kitchen range.

As the dawn grew clearer, we saw through the gap in the wall the body of a Martian, standing sentinel, I suppose, over the still glowing cylinder. At the sight of that we crawled as circumspectly as possible out of the twilight of the kitchen into the darkness of the scullery.

Abruptly the right interpretation dawned upon my mind.

"The fifth cylinder," I whispered, "the fifth shot from Mars, has struck this house and buried us under the ruins!"

For a time the curate was silent, and then he whispered:

"God have mercy upon us!"

I heard him presently whimpering to himself. This was far worse than the horde of the dead I had feared upon waking from my fall.

Save for that sound we lay quite still in the scullery; I for my part scarce dared breathe, and sat with my eyes fixed on the faint light of the kitchen door. I could just see the curate's face, a dim, oval shape, and his collar and cuffs. Outside there began a metallic hammering, then a violent hooting, and then again, after a quiet interval, a hissing like the hissing of an engine. These noises, for the most part problematical, continued intermittently, and seemed if anything to increase in number as time wore on. Presently a measured thudding and a vibration that made everything about us quiver and the vessels in the pantry ring and shift, began and continued. Once the light was eclipsed, and the ghostly kitchen doorway became absolutely dark. For many hours we must have crouched there, silent and shivering, until our tired attention failed. . . .

At last I found myself awake and very hungry. I am inclined to believe we must have spent the greater portion of a day before that awakening. My hunger was at a stride so insistent that it moved me to action. I told the curate I was going to seek food, and felt my way towards the pantry. He made me no answer, but so soon as I began eating the faint noise I made stirred him up and I heard him crawling after me.

2

WHAT WE SAW FROM THE RUINED HOUSE

After eating we crept back to the scullery, and there I must have dozed again, for when presently I looked round I was alone. The thudding vibration continued with wearisome persistence. I whispered for the curate several times, and at last felt my way to the door of the kitchen. It was still daylight, and I perceived him across the room, lying against the triangular hole that looked out upon the Martians. His shoulders were hunched, so that his head was hidden from me.

I could hear a number of noises almost like those in an engine shed; and the place rocked with that beating thud.

Through the aperture in the wall I could see the top of a tree touched with gold and the warm blue of a tranquil evening sky. For a minute or so I remained watching the curate, and then I advanced, crouching and stepping with extreme care amid the broken crockery that littered the floor.

I touched the curate's leg and he started so violently that a mass of plaster went sliding down outside and fell with a loud impact. His face told me he had taken me as one of the dead who somehow managed to get into the house unseen. I gripped his arm, fearing he might cry out, and for a long time we crouched motionless. At last, he calmed and the madness left his eyes enough for me to know that he saw me as who I was. Then I turned to see how much of our rampart remained. The detachment of the plaster had left a vertical slit open in the debris, and by raising myself cautiously across a beam I was able to see out of this gap into what had been overnight a quiet suburban roadway. Vast, indeed, was the change that we beheld.

The fifth cylinder must have fallen right into the midst of the house we had first visited. The building had vanished, completely smashed, pulverised, and dispersed by the blow. The cylinder lay now far beneath the original foundations—deep in a hole, already vastly larger than the pit I had looked into at Woking. The earth all round it had splashed under that tremendous impact—"splashed" is the only word—and lay in heaped piles that hid the masses of the adjacent houses. It had behaved exactly like mud under the violent blow of a hammer. Our house had collapsed backward; the front portion, even on the ground floor, had been destroyed completely; by a chance the kitchen and scullery had escaped, and stood buried now under soil and ruins, closed in by tons of earth on every side save towards the cylinder. Over that aspect we hung now on the very edge of the great circular pit the Martians were engaged in making. The heavy beating sound was evidently just behind us, and ever and again a bright green vapour drove up like a veil across our peephole. Around the pit, two of the Martian giants stood watch against the dead. Every so often their Heat-Rays would blaze into the night and the smell of burning human flesh would drift to us on the wind.

The cylinder was already opened in the centre of the pit, and on the farther edge of the pit, away from the machines standing guard against the dead, amid the smashed and gravel-heaped shrubbery, one of the great fighting-machines, deserted by its occupant, stood stiff and tall against the evening sky. At first I scarcely noticed the pit and the cylinder, although it has been convenient to describe them first, on account of the extraordinary glittering mechanism I saw busy in the excavation, and on account of the strange creatures that were crawling slowly and painfully across the heaped mould near it.

The mechanism it certainly was that held my attention first. It was one of those complicated fabrics that have since been called handling-machines, and the study of which has already given such an enormous impetus to terrestrial invention. As it dawned upon me first, it presented a sort of metallic spider with five jointed, agile legs, and with an extraordinary number of jointed levers, bars, and reaching and clutching tentacles about its body. Most of its arms were retracted, but with three long tentacles it was fishing out a number of rods, plates, and bars which lined the covering and apparently strengthened the walls of the cylinder. These, as it extracted them, were lifted out and deposited upon a level surface of earth behind it.

Its motion was so swift, complex, and perfect that at first I did not see it as a machine, in spite of its metallic glitter. The fighting-machines were co-ordinated and animated to an extraordinary pitch, but nothing to compare with this. People who have never seen these structures, and have only the ill-imagined efforts of artists or the imperfect descriptions of such eye-witnesses as myself to go upon, scarcely realise that living quality.

I recall particularly the illustration of one of the first pamphlets to give a consecutive account of the war. The artist had evidently made a hasty study of one of the fighting-machines, and there his knowledge ended. He presented them as tilted, stiff tripods, without either flexibility or subtlety, and with an altogether misleading monotony of effect. The pamphlet containing these renderings had a considerable vogue, and I mention them here simply to warn the reader against the impression they may have created. They were no more like the Martians I saw in action than a Dutch doll is like a human being. To my mind, the pamphlet would have been much better without them as they would've without their depictions of the dead. The artist tasked to render images of the monstrous things for the pamphlet drew the creatures in a cartoon-like manner that not only failed to capture the horror of the rotting fiends but also made them seem a joke.

At first, I say, the handling-machine did not impress me

as a machine, but as a crablike creature with a glittering integument, the controlling Martian whose delicate tentacles actuated its movements seeming to be simply the equivalent of the crab's cerebral portion. But then I perceived the resemblance of its grey-brown, shiny, leathery integument to that of the other sprawling bodies beyond, and the true nature of this dexterous workman dawned upon me. With that realisation my interest shifted to those other creatures, the real Martians. Already I had had a transient impression of these, and the first nausea no longer obscured my observation. Moreover, I was concealed and motionless, and under no urgency of action.

They were, I now saw, the most unearthly creatures it is possible to conceive. They were huge round bodies—or, rather, heads—about four feet in diameter, each body having in front of it a face. This face had no nostrils—indeed, the Martians do not seem to have had any sense of smell, but it had a pair of very large dark-coloured eyes, and just beneath this a kind of fleshy beak. In the back of this head or body—I scarcely know how to speak of it—was the single tight tympanic surface, since known to be anatomically an ear, though it must have been almost useless in our dense air. In a group round the mouth were sixteen slender, almost whiplike tentacles, arranged in two bunches of eight each. These bunches have since been named rather aptly, by that distinguished anatomist, Professor Howes, the *hands*. Even as I saw these Martians for the first time they seemed to be endeavouring to raise themselves on these hands, but of course, with the increased weight of terrestrial conditions, this was impossible. There is reason to suppose that on Mars they may have progressed upon them with some facility.

The internal anatomy, I may remark here, as dissection has since shown, was almost equally simple. The greater part of the structure was the brain, sending enormous nerves to the eyes, ear, and tactile tentacles. Besides this were the bulky lungs, into which the mouth opened, and the heart and its vessels. The pulmonary distress caused by the denser atmosphere and greater gravitational attraction was only too evident in the convulsive movements of the outer skin.

And this was the sum of the Martian organs. Strange as it may seem to a human being, all the complex apparatus of digestion, which makes up the bulk of our bodies, did not exist in the Martians. They were heads—merely heads. Entrails they had none. They did not eat, much less digest. Instead, they took the fresh, living blood of other creatures, and *injected* it into their own veins. I have myself seen this being done, as I shall mention in its place. But, squeamish as I may seem, I cannot bring myself to describe what I could not endure even to continue watching. Let it suffice to say, blood obtained from a still living animal, in most cases from a human being, was run directly by means of a little pipette into the recipient canal. . . .

The bare idea of this is no doubt horribly repulsive to us, but at the same time I think that we should remember how repulsive our carnivorous habits would seem to an intelligent rabbit.

The physiological advantages of the practice of injection are undeniable, if one thinks of the tremendous waste of human time and energy occasioned by eating and the digestive process. Our bodies are half made up of glands and tubes and organs, occupied in turning heterogeneous food into blood. The digestive processes and their reaction upon the nervous system sap our strength and colour our minds. Men go happy or miserable as they have healthy or unhealthy livers, or sound gastric glands. But the Martians were lifted above all these organic fluctuations of mood and emotion.

Their undeniable preference for men as their source of nourishment is partly explained by the nature of the remains of the victims they had brought with them as provisions from Mars. These creatures, to judge from the shrivelled remains that have fallen into human hands, were bipeds with flimsy, silicious skeletons (almost like those of the silicious sponges) and feeble musculature, standing about six feet high and having round, erect heads, and large eyes in flinty sockets. Two or three of these seem to have been brought in each cylinder, and all were killed before earth was reached. It was just as well for them, for the mere attempt to stand upright upon our planet would have broken every bone in their bodies. It made no sense to me that they would have caused the happenings with the dead as this would kill off the very food source they traveled to this world in search of. And of the dead themselves, why did they hunger for the flesh of the living? Their internal organs did not function. This would be proven time and time again by scientists in search of answers in the days after the invasion. The best explanation to be put forth as yet is that the dead ran on instinct alone. One of the greatest instincts in a living being is to seek nourishment and as thus the mindless creatures believe they need to eat and are driven by this force. Even this theory, though, falls short when one is asked why the dead prey only on humans. Never once in the days of the invasion by the Martians or in the studies ran thereafter has anyone ever seen the dead eat the meat of an animal. If the basic drive for sustenance was the sole reason for their hunger, would it not fill it in any fashion it could? Perhaps we are never to know the answer to this riddle.

Again I turned my attention to the Martian monsters outside our place of hiding and began to study them, seeking to capture in my mind every detail of them that I could.

And while I am engaged in this description, I may add in this place certain further details which, although they were not all evident to us at the time, will enable the reader who is unacquainted with them to form a clearer picture of these offensive creatures.

In three other points their physiology differed strangely from ours. Their organisms did not sleep, any more than the heart of man sleeps. Since they had no extensive muscular mechanism to recuperate, that periodical extinction was unknown to them. They had little or no sense of fatigue, it would seem. On earth they could never have moved without effort, yet even to the last they kept in action. In twenty-four hours they did twenty-four hours of work, as even on earth is perhaps the case with the ants.

In the next place, wonderful as it seems in a sexual world, the Martians were absolutely without sex, and therefore without any of the tumultuous emotions that arise from that difference among men. A young Martian, there can now be no dispute, was really born upon earth during the war, and it was found attached to its parent, partially *budded* off, just as young lilybulbs bud off, or like the young animals in the fresh-water polyp.

In man, in all the higher terrestrial animals, such a method of increase has disappeared; but even on this earth it was certainly the primitive method. Among the lower animals, up even to those first cousins of the vertebrated animals, the Tunicates, the two processes occur side by side, but finally the sexual method superseded its competitor altogether. On Mars, however, just the reverse has apparently been the case.

It is worthy of remark that a certain speculative writer of quasi-scientific repute, writing long before the Martian invasion, did forecast for man a final structure not unlike the actual Martian condition. His prophecy, I remember, appeared in November or December, 1893, in a long-defunct publication, the *Pall Mall Budget,* and I recall a caricature of it in a pre-Martian periodical called *Punch*. He pointed out—writing in a foolish, facetious tone—that the perfection of mechanical appliances must ultimately supersede limbs; the perfection of chemical devices, digestion; that such organs as hair, external nose, teeth, ears, and chin were no longer essential parts of the human being, and that the tendency of natural selection would lie in the direction of their steady diminution through the coming ages. The brain alone remained a cardinal necessity. Only one other part of the body had a strong case for survival, and that was the hand, "teacher and agent of the brain." While the rest of the body dwindled, the hands would grow larger.

There is many a true word written in jest, and here in the Martians we have beyond dispute the actual accomplishment of such a suppression of the animal side of the organism by the intelligence. To me it is quite credible that the Martians may be descended from beings not unlike ourselves, by a gradual development of brain and hands (the latter giving rise to the two bunches of delicate tentacles at last) at the expense of the rest of the body. Without the body the brain would, of course, become a mere selfish intelligence, without any of the emotional substratum of the human being.

The last salient point in which the systems of these creatures differed from ours was in what one might have thought a very trivial particular. Micro-organisms, which cause so much disease and pain on earth, have either never appeared upon Mars or Martian sanitary science eliminated them ages ago. A hundred diseases, all the fevers and contagions of human life, consumption, cancers, tumours and such morbidities, never enter the scheme of their life. And speaking of the differences between the life on Mars and terrestrial life, I may allude here to the curious suggestions of the red weed.

Apparently the vegetable kingdom in Mars, instead of having green for a dominant colour, is of a vivid blood-red tint. At any rate, the seeds which the Martians (intentionally or accidentally) brought with them gave rise in all cases to red-coloured growths. Only that known popularly as the red weed, however, gained any footing in competition with terrestrial forms. The red creeper was quite a transitory growth, and few people have seen it growing. For a time, however, the red weed grew with astonishing vigour and luxuriance. It spread up the sides of the pit by the third or fourth day of our imprisonment, and its cactus-like branches formed a carmine fringe to the edges of our triangular window. And afterwards I found it broadcast throughout the country, and especially wherever there was a stream of water.

The Martians had what appears to have been an auditory organ, a single round drum at the back of the head-body, and eyes with a visual range not very different from ours except that, according to Philips, blue and violet were as black to them. It is commonly supposed that they communicated by sounds and tentacular gesticulations; this is asserted, for instance, in the able but hastily compiled pamphlet (written evidently by someone not an eye-witness of Martian actions) to which I have already alluded, and which, so far, has been the chief source of information concerning them. Now no surviving human being saw so much of the Martians in action as I did. I take no credit to myself for an accident, but the fact is so. And I assert that I watched them closely time after time, and that I have seen four, five, and (once) six of them sluggishly performing the most elaborately complicated operations together without either sound or gesture. Their peculiar hooting invariably preceded feeding; it had no modulation, and was, I believe, in no sense a signal, but merely the expiration of air preparatory to the suctional operation. I have a certain claim to at least an elementary knowledge of psychology, and in this matter I am convinced—as firmly as I am convinced of anything—that the Martians interchanged thoughts without any physical intermediation. And I have been convinced of this in spite of strong preconceptions. Before the Martian invasion, as an occasional reader here or there may remember, I had written with some little vehemence against the telepathic theory.

The Martians wore no clothing. Their conceptions of ornament and decorum were necessarily different from ours; and not only were they evidently much less sensible of changes of temperature than we are, but changes of pressure do not seem to have affected their health at all seriously. Yet though they wore no clothing, it was in the other artificial additions to their bodily resources that their great superiority over man lay. We men, with our bicycles and road-skates, our Lilienthal soaring-machines, our guns and sticks and so forth, are just in the beginning of the evolution that the Martians have worked out. They have become practically mere brains, wearing different bodies according to their needs just as men wear suits of clothes and take a bicycle in a hurry or an umbrella in the wet. And of their appliances, perhaps nothing is more wonderful to a man than the curious fact that what is the dominant feature of almost all human devices in mechanism is absent—the *wheel* is absent; among all the things they brought to earth there is no trace or suggestion of their use of wheels. One would have at least expected it in locomotion. And in this connection it is curious to remark that even on this earth Nature has never hit upon the wheel, or has preferred other expedients to its development. And not only did the Martians either not know of (which is incredible), or abstain from, the wheel, but in their apparatus singularly little use is made of the fixed pivot or relatively fixed pivot, with circular motions thereabout confined to one plane. Almost all the joints of the machinery present a complicated system of sliding parts moving over small but beautifully curved friction bearings. And while upon this matter of detail, it is remarkable that the long leverages of their machines are in most cases actuated by a sort of sham musculature of the disks in an elastic sheath; these disks become polarised and drawn closely and powerfully together when traversed by a current of electricity. In this way the curious parallelism to animal motions, which was so striking and disturbing to the human beholder, was attained. Such quasi-muscles abounded in the crablike handling-machine which, on my first peeping out of the slit, I watched unpacking the cylinder. It seemed infinitely more alive than the actual Martians lying beyond it in the sunset light, panting, stirring ineffectual tentacles, and moving feebly after their vast journey across space.

As I studied the Martians from my place of concealment, I watched two of the things arguing inside the pit. I must assume that is what they were doing as one flopped its long tentacles in a fit of rage. The two of them removed a sort of device from the cylinder and it sprang to life. I have not the words to fully describe it. It was a small box that projected patterns of light into the air above it. I stared at this marvelous device as it formed perfect images of the Martian cylinders in flight from the red world of their birth. The cylinders sailed through the stars and the void of space before my eyes. As they reached our blue and green world, I was taken aback by how appealing our world must have looked from space. It was so beautiful, a mass of swirling colors of life. Then the cylinders hit our sky. Flames erupted over their hulls as they entered our world but something far stranger happened when the flames fell away: their gleaming hulls were surrounded by white clouds and blue skies. The Martians did something to the device and the image closed in on one of the ships. Tiny purple flakes of some unknown substance flew, flaking off the ship's hull as it screeched at unimaginable speed towards the ground below. These flakes rode the wind to Earth as well. One of the Martians kept pointing at them in an unsettling manner with the point of his tentacle and making a grunting-like noise. The other Martian waved its tentacles in the air and whistled back. I did not know it at the time but as I later thought about my viewing of this event, I believe the Martians were discussing the dead plague and the circumstances which gave it birth. Somewhere in the void among the stars something unknown to them attached itself to their ships like a kind of mold and grew there during their voyage. As they entered the Earth's atmosphere, it was loosed into our air. Whatever this strange mold or element was, it was surely the source of the dead's hungry un-life. It confirmed my own take on the matter of the dead. The Martians did not create them intentionally and they, like we, needed to dispose of the walking corpses. For us, it was a matter of survival, and to them, they were beginning to worry that their entire food supply would become tainted and useless to them from the effects of this plague.

While I was still watching their sluggish motions in the sunlight, and noting each strange detail of their form, the curate reminded me of his presence by pulling violently at my arm. I turned to a scowling face, and silent, eloquent lips. I was angered by his desire to take my place for his turn of viewing the monsters. He wanted the slit, which permitted only one of us to peep through; and so I had to forego watching them for a time while he enjoyed that privilege. As he watched, I thought about what I had seen and how it must upset the Martians' plans. Even today, no one on Earth really understands the dead plague or what caused it. Most still attribute it to a sort of radiation emanating from the cylinders themselves but this theory fails and cannot be defended as the dead plague was not confined to where the cylinders fell. It spread like a cancer across most of the world during the invasion and the days after. I have told no one of the images of light I saw that day in the house where we hid. I wonder what the world of science would make of it, if I did?

When I looked again, the busy handling-machine had already put together several of the pieces of apparatus it had taken out of the cylinder into a shape having an unmistakable likeness to its own; and down on the left a busy little digging mechanism had come into view, emitting jets of green vapour and working its way round the pit, excavating and embanking in a methodical and discriminating manner. This it was which had caused the regular beating noise, and the rhythmic shocks that had kept our ruinous refuge quivering. It piped and whistled as it worked. So far as I could see, the thing was without a directing Martian at all.

It also bore armaments against the dead. When one of the things by some chance evaded the giant machines that stood watch and approached the pit where the Martians were outside and unprotected, a small gun mechanism popped up from its top and unfolded itself it. A beam of light brighter than the hottest fire would erupt from it and cut the dead to pieces with the sharpness of a surgeon's fine blade. I was thankful this machine was for defensives purposes and was not sent out in search of survivors like myself and the curate.

3

THE DAYS
OF IMPRISONMENT

The arrival of a yet another fighting-machine drove us from our peephole into the scullery, for we feared that from his elevation the Martian might see down upon us behind our barrier. At a later date we began to feel less in danger of their eyes, for to an eye in the dazzle of the sunlight outside our refuge must have been blank blackness, but at first the slightest suggestion of approach drove us into the scullery in heart-throbbing retreat. Outside a new war raged. The three fighting machines of the Martians, the two who had stood guard over the pit we spied on, and this newcomer, at last turned their full attention to the city's dead. The sound of their Heat-Rays being fired was continuous. The dead made terrible noises as they were set upon by the Martians. Having no weapons, the dead gave them next to no resistance yet the battle was still hopeless to the invaders. The dead were so great in number and the Martians' supplies were not infinite. Finally, the giant machines gave up their rampage and returned to guard the pit. Inside it, the two creatures I had studied so closely as they argued before were at work on something new, but I could not fathom what it might be. They kept glancing at the light images which now showed things beyond my understanding as a mortal man born of Earth. I feared the time would come when the giant machines would grow tired of attacking the dead in the open streets of the city and turn upon the houses and shelters with their weapons in the hopes of destroying any of the dead that may be residing in such structures. If the mighty machines gained so much as a spark of an idea that we might be within this place, our lives would be over. Yet terrible as was the danger we incurred, the attraction of peeping was for both of us irresistible. And I recall now with a sort of wonder that, in spite of the infinite danger in which we were between starvation and a still more terrible death, we could yet struggle bitterly for that horrible privilege of sight. We would race across the kitchen in a grotesque way between eagerness and the dread of making a noise, and strike each other, and thrust a kick, within a few inches of exposure.

The fact is that we had absolutely incompatible dispositions and habits of thought and action, and our danger and isolation only accentuated the incompatibility. At Halliford I

had already come to hate the curate's trick of helpless excla-
mation, his stupid rigidity of mind. His endless muttering
monologue vitiated every effort I made to think out a line of
action, and drove me at times, thus pent up and intensified,
almost to the verge of craziness. He was as lacking in re-
straint as a silly woman. He would weep for hours together,
and I verily believe that to the very end this spoiled child
of life thought his weak tears in some way efficacious. And
I would sit in the darkness unable to keep my mind off him
by reason of his importunities. He ate more than I did, and
it was in vain I pointed out that our only chance of life was
to stop in the house until the Martians had done with their
pit, that in that long patience a time might presently come
when we should need food. He ate and drank impulsively in
heavy meals at long intervals. He slept little. Again, I considered killing him myself in order to ensure that at least
one of us would survive this ordeal and again God stayed
my hand. God was all I had left in these moments of fear,
hunger, and desperation. I prayed often and tried to keep to
myself as much as possible in the limited space we occupied
together. I could not bring myself to take a life in a world
where so many had been snuffed out already.

As the days wore on, his utter carelessness of any con-
sideration so intensified our distress and danger that I had,
much as I loathed doing it, to resort to threats, and at last to
blows. It took all my effort not to strangle him in his sleep
or plant the blade of our hatchet between his eyes. It would
end both his threat as a living idiot and as a risen monster
with but a single blow. My anger was clear and evident. Our
last fight left him with a large bruise that covered most of

the left side of his face and with several missing teeth. That brought him to reason for a time. But he was one of those weak creatures, void of pride, timorous, anaemic, hateful souls, full of shifty cunning, who face neither God nor man, who face not even themselves.

It is disagreeable for me to recall and write these things, but I set them down that my story may lack nothing. Those who have escaped the dark and terrible aspects of life will find my brutality, my flash of rage in our final tragedy, easy enough to blame; for they know what is wrong as well as any, but not what is possible to tortured men. But those who have been under the shadow, who have gone down at last to elemental things, will have a wider charity.

And while within we fought out our dark, dim contest of whispers, snatched food and drink, and gripping hands and blows, without, in the pitiless sunlight of that terrible June, was the strange wonder, the unfamiliar routine of the Martians in the pit. Let me return to those first new experiences of mine. After a long time I ventured back to the peephole, to find that the newcomers had been reinforced by the occupants of no fewer than three of the fighting-machines. These last had brought with them certain fresh appliances that stood in an orderly manner about the cylinder. The second handling-machine was now completed, and was busied in serving one of the novel contrivances the big machine had brought. This was a body resembling a milk can in its general form, above which oscillated a pear-shaped receptacle, and from which a stream of white powder flowed into a circular basin below.

The oscillatory motion was imparted to this by one tentacle of the handling-machine. With two spatulate hands the handling-machine was digging out and flinging masses of clay into the pear-shaped receptacle above, while with another arm it periodically opened a door and removed rusty and blackened clinkers from the middle part of the machine. Another steely tentacle directed the powder from the basin along a ribbed channel towards some receiver that was hidden from me by the mound of bluish dust. From this unseen receiver a little thread of green smoke rose vertically into the quiet air. As I looked, the handling-machine, with a faint and musical clinking, extended, telescopic fashion, a tentacle that had been a moment before a mere blunt projection, until its end was hidden behind the mound of clay. In another second it had lifted a bar of white aluminium into sight, untarnished as yet, and shining dazzlingly, and deposited it in a growing stack of bars that stood at the side of the pit. Between sunset and starlight this dexterous machine must have made more than a hundred such bars out of the crude clay, and the mound of bluish dust rose steadily until it topped the side of the pit.

The contrast between the swift and complex movements of these contrivances and the inert panting clumsiness of their masters was acute, and for days I had to tell myself repeatedly that these latter were indeed the living of the two things.

The curate had possession of the slit when the first men, both living and dead, were brought to the pit. I was sitting below, huddled up, listening with all my ears. He made a sudden movement backward, and I, fearful that we were observed, crouched in a spasm of terror. He came sliding down

the rubbish and crept beside me in the darkness, inarticulate, gesticulating, and for a moment I shared his panic.
His gesture suggested a resignation of the slit, and after
a little while my curiosity gave me courage, and I rose up,
stepped across him, and clambered up to it. At first I could
see no reason for his frantic behaviour. I had yet to witness
the actual feeding of the Martians on man. The twilight
had now come, the stars were little and faint, but the pit
was illuminated by the flickering green fire that came from
the aluminium-making. The whole picture was a flickering
scheme of green gleams and shifting rusty black shadows,
strangely trying to the eyes. Over and through it all went
the bats, heeding it not at all. The sprawling Martians were
no longer to be seen, the mound of blue-green powder had
risen to cover them from sight, and a fighting-machine, with
its legs contracted, crumpled, and abbreviated, stood across
the corner of the pit. And then, amid the clangour of the
machinery, came a drifting suspicion of human voices, that I
entertained at first only to dismiss.

I crouched, watching this fighting-machine closely, satis-
fying myself now for the first time that the hood did indeed
contain a Martian. As the green flames lifted I could see the
oily gleam of his integument and the brightness of his eyes.
And suddenly I heard a yell, and saw a long tentacle reaching over the shoulder of the machine to the little cage that
hunched upon its back. Then something—something struggling violently—was lifted high against the sky, a black,
vague enigma against the starlight; and as this black object
came down again, I saw by the green brightness that it was
a man. For an instant he was clearly visible. He was a stout,

ruddy, middle-aged man, well dressed; three days before, he must have been walking the world, a man of considerable consequence. I could see his staring eyes and gleams of light on his studs and watch chain. He vanished behind the mound, and for a moment there was silence. And then began a shrieking and a sustained and cheerful hooting from the Martians. It took all my resolve to endure bearing witness to this horrid display. When the screaming ended, another of the giant machines that also bore a small cage upon its back reached inside it with a tentacle and pulled forth a dead man. The corpse struggled and gnashed its teeth at the metal tentacle that held it. Another machine took a step forward, reaching out to snap the bones off the thing's arms and legs, leaving only its head mobile. The dead thing was lowered into the pit with the Martians. They did not feed on it as they had the living human. Instead, they set about examining it as a man would a diseased rat in a lab. One of them sampled its blood and spat it out with an inhuman coughing sound. There were more arguments inside the pit and more dancing images of things that looked like the very forms of cells magnified under a powerful microscope projected from their tiny handheld device. Then the Martians produced a bladed instrument not unlike a knife of terrestrial origin and went to work on the dead man, cutting him open, first at the chest, then at the stomach. They dug through his innards as I fought not to vomit from the utter sickness of their display and disregard for the sanctity of the human body. At last, I could take no more and I retreated from the slit.

I slid down the rubbish, struggled to my feet, clapped

my hands over my ears, and bolted into the scullery. The curate, who had been crouching silently with his arms over his head, looked up as I passed, cried out quite loudly at my desertion of him, and came running after me.

That night, as we lurked in the scullery, balanced between our horror and the terrible fascination this peeping had, although I felt an urgent need of action I tried in vain to conceive some plan of escape; but my thoughts kept returning to the Martians' dissection of the dead man's corpse. Clearly they were studying the dead now. I wondered if they were trying to design a way to deal with them and end the dead plague before it consumed us all and left them hungry and wanting. I tried once more to turn my thoughts back to a plan of escape but afterwards, during the second day, I was able to consider our position with great clearness. The curate, I found, was quite incapable of discussion; this new and culminating atrocity had robbed him of all vestiges of reason or forethought. Practically he had already sunk to the level of an animal. But as the saying goes, I gripped myself with both hands. It grew upon my mind, once I could face the facts, that terrible as our position was, there was as yet no justification for absolute despair. Our chief chance lay in the possibility of the Martians making the pit nothing more than a temporary encampment. Or even if they kept it permanently, they might not consider it necessary to guard it, and a chance of escape might be afforded us. The dead were no longer anywhere near as much as a problem as they had been. The Martians had cleared most of the foul creatures from the city out of their own need for safety and to be left alone. I also weighed very carefully the possibility of our digging a way out in a direction away from the pit, but the chances of our emerging within sight of some sentinel fighting-machine seemed at first too great. And I should have had to do all the digging myself. The curate would certainly have failed me.

It was on the third day, if my memory serves me right, that I saw the lad killed. It was the second occasion on which I actually saw the Martians feed. After that experience I avoided the hole in the wall for the better part of a day. I could not endure watching more die to their abominable need for living blood nor could I watch them continue to experiment upon the dead. This they continued in some fashion throughout every passing hour as they too tried to make sense of how the things were born from their arrival. I suspect they knew far more of medicine and science than we would for many years if we survived as a species. Their machines were clear evidence of this on a mechanical level. Their knowledge of medical things surely outweighed our own by an equal factor as well. I went into the scullery, removed the door, and spent some hours digging with my hatchet as silently as possible; but when I had made a hole about a couple of feet deep the loose earth collapsed noisily, and I did not dare continue. I lost heart, and lay down on the scullery floor for a long time, having no spirit even to move. And after that I abandoned altogether the idea of escaping by excavation. As I sat there, broken in spirit, I heard movement from the curate's direction. I hurried as quietly as I could back to where he lay to see him gesturing outside the house with feverish zeal. My heart sank and I knew the Martians had found us. Then I saw what upset him so. A man, long dead and stinking of decay, had found his way into our shelter. He crawled slowly and deliberately towards the curate with a determination of a dog that has treed its prey. The man was a mess and gore oozed from every inch of his flesh. His clothes were long gone and burnt off of him, except for a few charred tattered bits clung to melted flesh. Snapping his teeth, he continued his slow advance and I moved to meet him. The curate sat so struck with fear he was unable to move as I crawled by him on my hands and knees to bury the hatchet's blade into the dead man's skull. I struck the blade into the creature's head. At once, his damaged body dropped to the floor and moved no more. I sat there, breathing hard and fighting off sickness from his smell, before I yanked the blade free and cleaned it on the dirt around us. I left the curate where he sat whispering miseries to himself and returned to my own corner to lose myself in my thoughts of our situation and its direness.

It says much for the impression the Martians had made upon me that at first I entertained little or no hope of our escape being brought about by their overthrow through any human effort. But on the fourth or fifth night I heard a sound like heavy guns.

It was very late in the night, and the moon was shining brightly. The Martians had taken away the excavating-machine, and, save for a fighting-machine that stood in the remoter bank of the pit and a handling-machine that was buried out of my sight in a corner of the pit immediately beneath my peephole, the place was deserted by them. Except for the pale glow from the handling-machine and the bars and patches of white moonlight the pit was in darkness, and, except for the clinking of the handling-machine, quite still. That night was a beautiful serenity; save for one planet, the moon seemed to have the sky to herself. I heard a dog howling, and that familiar sound it was that made me listen. Then I heard quite distinctly a booming exactly like the sound of great guns. Six distinct reports I counted, and after a long interval six again. And that was all.

Whether it was humankind making an attempt to reclaim the areas taken by the Martians or the otherworldly creatures combating the dead, I did not know.

4

⫸◆⫷

THE DEATH
OF THE CURATE

It was on the sixth day of our imprisonment that I peeped for the last time, and presently found myself alone. Instead of keeping close to me and trying to oust me from the slit, the curate had gone back into the scullery. I was struck by a sudden thought. I went back quickly and quietly into the scullery. In the darkness I heard the curate drinking. I snatched in the darkness, and my fingers caught a bottle of burgundy.

For a few minutes there was a tussle. The bottle struck the floor and broke, and I desisted and rose. We stood panting and threatening each other. In the end I planted myself

between him and the food, and told him of my determination to begin a discipline. I divided the food in the pantry,
into rations to last us ten days. I would not let him eat any
more that day. In the afternoon he made a feeble effort to
get at the food. I had been dozing, but in an instant I was
awake. All day and all night we sat face to face, I weary
but resolute, and he weeping and complaining of his immediate hunger. It was, I know, a night and a day, but to me
it seemed—it seems now—an interminable length of time.
Our only company was the body of the burnt man whom we
had no true means to dispose of. We had pushed him into a
corner and covered him with the remains of a blanket, doing
our best to stay clear of him as much as possible. I feared for
our health being confined thus with the corpse. It would be
only a matter of time until it made us sick from its decay but
there was nothing to be done for it. My main focus stayed on
our continually dwindling supplies and the curate's unwise
desires in his wretched childlike manner.

And so our widened incompatibility ended at last in
open conflict. For two vast days we struggled in undertones
and wrestling contests. There were times when I beat and
kicked him madly, times when I cajoled and persuaded
him, and once I tried to bribe him with the last bottle of
burgundy, for there was a rain-water pump from which I
could get water. But neither force nor kindness availed; he
was indeed beyond reason. He would neither desist from
his attacks on the food nor from his noisy babbling to himself. My patience was pushed to its limits and drew ever
nearer a point from which there would be no return. The
rudimentary precautions to keep our imprisonment endur-

able he would not observe. Slowly I began to realise the complete overthrow of his intelligence, to perceive that my sole companion in this close and sickly darkness was a man insane.

From certain vague memories I am inclined to think my own mind wandered at times. I had strange and hideous dreams whenever I slept. The images of the dead man being cut apart like an animal by the Martians haunted me. Often too when I dozed, I saw the dead in their legions roaming the streets, glazed eyes and yellow teeth, with snarling expressions of rage. I could feel cold hands touching me in my dreams, tearing at my skin, and teeth breaking it, pulling parts of me in separate directions as the horde fought over my limbs and entrails. It sounds paradoxical, but I am inclined to think that the weakness and insanity of the curate warned me, braced me, and kept me a sane man.

On the eighth day he began to talk aloud instead of whispering, and nothing I could do would moderate his speech.

"It is just, O God!" he would say, over and over again. "It is just. On me and mine be the punishment laid. We have sinned, we have fallen short. There was poverty, sorrow; the poor were trodden in the dust, and I held my peace. I preached acceptable folly—my God, what folly!—when I should have stood up, though I died for it, and called upon them to repent—repent! . . . Oppressors of the poor and needy . . . ! The wine press of God! We sinners have overflowed the depths of Hell and have now spread to the face of the Earth in the form of demons and monsters of rot. Woe be unto us all!"

Then he would suddenly revert to the matter of the food I

withheld from him, praying, begging, weeping, at last threatening. He began to raise his voice—I prayed him not to. He perceived a hold on me—he threatened he would shout and bring the Martians upon us. For a time that scared me; but any concession would have shortened our chance of escape beyond estimating. I defied him, although I felt no assurance that he might not do this thing. His sanity and any shards of it that may have remained in the first days of imprisonment were completely gone and broken. But that day, at any rate, he did not. He talked with his voice rising slowly, through the greater part of the eighth and ninth days—threats, entreaties, mingled with a torrent of half-sane and always frothy repentance for his vacant sham of God's service, such as made me pity him. Then he slept awhile, and began again with renewed strength, so loudly that I must needs make him desist.

"Be still!" I implored.

He rose to his knees, for he had been sitting in the darkness near the copper.

"I have been still too long," he said, in a tone that must have reached the pit, "and now I must bear my witness. Woe unto this unfaithful city! Woe! Woe! Woe! Woe! Woe! To the inhabitants of the earth by reason of the other voices of the trumpet—"

"Shut up!" I said, rising to my feet, and in a terror lest the Martians should hear us.

"Nay," shouted the curate, at the top of his voice, standing likewise and extending his arms. "Speak! The word of the Lord is upon me!"

In three strides he was at the door leading into the kitchen.

"I must bear my witness! I go! It has already been too long delayed."

I put out my hand and felt the meat chopper hanging to the wall. In a flash I was after him. I was fierce with fear. Before he was halfway across the kitchen I had overtaken him. With one last touch of humanity I turned the blade back and struck him with the butt. He went headlong forward and lay stretched on the ground. For a moment, I was actually flooded with a sense of retribution for my days of suffering made worse by his company. I stumbled over him and stood panting. He lay still. My heart raced as I wondered if I struck him too hard and that he might rise up with a bestial need to feed. If that happened, I was as good as dead myself. The noise of such a battle would attract the Martians to us if they had not heard us already. Then I noticed the blood leaking from his ears and knew he would not be rising either alive or dead.

Suddenly I heard a noise without, the run and smash of slipping plaster, and the triangular aperture in the wall was darkened. I looked up and saw the lower surface of a handling-machine coming slowly across the hole. One of its gripping limbs curled amid the debris; another limb appeared, feeling its way over the fallen beams. I stood petrified, staring. Then I saw through a sort of glass plate near the edge of the body the face, as we may call it, and the large dark eyes of a Martian, peering, and then a long metallic snake of tentacle came feeling slowly through the hole.

I turned by an effort, stumbled over the curate, and stopped at the scullery door. The tentacle was now some way, two yards or more, in the room, and twisting and turning, with queer sudden movements, this way and that. For a while I stood fascinated by that slow, fitful advance. Then, with a faint, hoarse cry, I forced myself across the scullery. I trembled violently; I could scarcely stand upright. I opened the door of the coal cellar, and stood there in the darkness staring at the faintly lit doorway into the kitchen, and listening. Had the Martian seen me? What was it doing now?

Something was moving to and fro there, very quietly; every now and then it tapped against the wall, or started on its movements with a faint metallic ringing, like the movements of keys on a split-ring. Then a heavy body—I knew too well what—was dragged across the floor of the kitchen towards the opening. Irresistibly attracted, I crept to the door and peeped into the kitchen. In the triangle of bright outer sunlight I saw the Martian, in its Briareus of a handling-machine, scrutinizing the curate's head. I thought at once that it would infer my presence from the mark of the blow I had given him.

I crept back to the coal cellar, shut the door, and began to cover myself up as much as I could, and as noiselessly as possible in the darkness, among the firewood and coal therein. Every now and then I paused, rigid, to hear if the Martian had thrust its tentacles through the opening again.

Then the faint metallic jingle returned. I traced it slowly feeling over the kitchen. Presently I heard it nearer—in the scullery, as I judged. I thought that its length might be insufficient to reach me. I prayed copiously. It passed, scraping faintly across the cellar door. An age of almost intolerable suspense intervened; then I heard it fumbling at the latch! It had found the door! The Martians understood doors!

It worried at the catch for a minute, perhaps, and then the door opened.

In the darkness I could just see the thing—like an elephant's trunk more than anything else—waving towards me and touching and examining the wall, coals, wood and ceiling. It was like a black worm swaying its blind head to and fro.

Once, even, it touched the heel of my boot. I was on the verge of screaming; I bit my hand. For a time the tentacle was silent. I could have fancied it had been withdrawn. Presently, with an abrupt click, it gripped something—I thought it had me!—and seemed to go out of the cellar again.

For a minute I was not sure. Apparently it had taken a lump of coal to examine.

I seized the opportunity of slightly shifting my position, which had become cramped, and then listened. I whispered passionate prayers for safety.

Then I heard the slow, deliberate sound creeping towards me again. Slowly, slowly it drew near, scratching against the walls and tapping the furniture.

While I was still doubtful, it rapped smartly against the cellar door and closed it. I heard it go into the pantry, and the biscuit-tins rattled and a bottle smashed, and then came a heavy bump against the cellar door. Then silence that passed into an infinity of suspense.

Had it gone?

At last I decided that it had.

It came into the scullery no more; but I lay all the tenth day in the close darkness, buried among coals and firewood, not daring even to crawl out for the drink for which I craved. It was the eleventh day before I ventured so far from my security.

5

THE STILLNESS

My first act before I went into the pantry was to fasten the door between the kitchen and the scullery. But the pantry was empty; every scrap of food had gone. Apparently, the Martian had taken it all on the previous day. At that discovery I despaired for the first time. I took no food, or no drink either, on the eleventh or the twelfth day.

At first my mouth and throat were parched, and my strength ebbed sensibly. I sat about in the darkness of the scullery, in a state of despondent wretchedness. My mind ran on eating. I thought I had become deaf, for the noises of movement I had been accustomed to hear from the pit had ceased absolutely. I did not feel strong enough to crawl noiselessly to the peephole, or I would have gone there.

On the twelfth day my throat was so painful that, taking the chance of alarming the Martians, I attacked the creaking rain-water pump that stood by the sink, and got a couple of glassfuls of blackened and tainted rain water. I was greatly refreshed by this, and emboldened by the fact that no enquiring tentacle followed the noise of my pumping.

During these days, in a rambling, inconclusive way, I thought much of the curate and of the manner of his death. I also thought of my death, for if I perished, would I return as one of the dead? I knew rationally that I would. Every corpse I had thus seen rose regardless of their nature as a person, how holy or unclean they might have been in life. I did not want to become one of those . . . things. If I did, it stood to reason I would wander outside in my then mindless state and the Martians would claim me for more of their disgusting studies of the creatures. I would be sliced and diced, cut open and defiled as if reanimating were not horror enough. I wondered then what happened to the souls of those returned as the dead. Did they venture on to Heaven and Hell or were they trapped inside the rotting bodies, like cages, witnessing their actions with no control over their Earthly forms? I began to consider finding a means of taking my own life in such a manner as to ensure I would not return, but quickly cast those thoughts aside. I was not a quitter. Having endured all that I had, I would not surrender to such a coward's escape.

On the thirteenth day I drank some more water, and dozed and thought disjointedly of eating and of vague impossible plans of escape. Whenever I dozed I dreamt of horrible phantasms, of the faces of the dead, of the death of the curate, or of sumptuous dinners and the arms of my wife; but, asleep or awake, I felt a keen pain that urged me to drink again and again. The light that came into the scullery was no longer grey, but red. To my disordered imagination it seemed the colour of blood.

On the fourteenth day I went into the kitchen, and I was surprised to find that the fronds of the red weed had grown right across the hole in the wall, turning the half-light of the place into a crimson-coloured obscurity.

It was early on the fifteenth day that I heard a curious, familiar sequence of sounds in the kitchen, and, listening, identified it as the snuffing and scratching of a dog. Going into the kitchen, I saw a dog's nose peering in through a break among the ruddy fronds. This greatly surprised me. At the scent of me he barked shortly.

I thought if I could induce him to come into the place quietly I should be able, perhaps, to kill and eat him; and in any case, it would be advisable to kill him, lest his actions attracted the attention of the Martians.

I crept forward, saying "Good dog!" very softly; but he suddenly withdrew his head and disappeared.

I listened—I was not deaf—but certainly the pit was still.

I heard a sound like the flutter of a bird's wings, and a hoarse croaking, but that was all.

For a long while I lay close to the peephole, but not daring to move aside the red plants that obscured it. Once or twice I heard a faint pitter-patter like the feet of the dog going hither and thither on the sand far below me, and there were more birdlike sounds, but that was all. At length, encouraged by the silence, I looked out.

Except in the corner, where a multitude of crows hopped and fought over the skeletons of the dead the Martians had consumed, there was not a living thing in the pit.

I stared about me, scarcely believing my eyes. All the machinery had gone. Save for the big mound of greyish-blue powder in one corner, certain bars of aluminium in another, the black birds, and the skeletons of the killed, the place was merely an empty circular pit in the sand.

Slowly I thrust myself out through the red weed, and stood upon the mound of rubble. I could see in any direction save behind me, to the north, and neither Martians nor sign of Martians were to be seen. The pit dropped sheerly from my feet, but a little way along the rubbish afforded a practicable slope to the summit of the ruins. My chance of escape had come. I began to tremble.

I hesitated for some time, and then, in a gust of desperate resolution, and with a heart that throbbed violently, I scrambled to the top of the mound in which I had been buried so long.

I looked about again. To the northward, too, no Martian was visible.

When I had last seen this part of Sheen in the daylight it had been a straggling street of comfortable white and red houses, interspersed with abundant shady trees. Now I stood on a mound of smashed brickwork, clay, and gravel, over which spread a multitude of red cactus-shaped plants, knee-high, without a solitary terrestrial growth to dispute their footing. The trees near me were dead and brown, but farther a network of red thread scaled the still living stems.

The neighbouring houses had all been wrecked, but none had been burned; their walls stood, sometimes to the second story, with smashed windows and shattered doors. The red weed grew tumultuously in their roofless rooms. Below me was the great pit, with the crows struggling for its refuse. A number of other birds hopped about among the ruins. Far away I saw a gaunt cat slink crouchingly along a wall, but traces of men there were none. Even the corpses of the dead sent back to Hell by the Martian machines were gone and cleared from the streets.

The day seemed, by contrast with my recent confinement, dazzlingly bright, the sky a glowing blue. A gentle breeze kept the red weed that covered every scrap of unoccupied ground gently swaying. And oh! the sweetness of the air!

As the days of terror passed for the curate and I inside our hiding place, the war raged on in the world at large. The Martians slowly continued their advance with the calm speed of an enemy who knows that victory is already theirs and at hand. It was the war with the dead that took its toll on mankind now. Those risen from the hold of the Reaper pressed on harder and far faster than the slow and deliberate invaders from another world who brought this plague into our lives. Beyond the boundaries of the sections of our Earth under Martian foot, mankind fought on. The dead left us no choice. It was either stand against them and contain them here and now before the masses that had risen from the Black Smoke and the cities, or watch them spread their filth, continuing to grow in numbers as they went. America and other countries that had yet to feel the wrath of the Martian weapons made short work of the dead. Their military forces and organized parties of police and civilians halted the worst outbreaks of the dead with hails of bullets and cannon fire. These governments implemented hastily drafted new laws that ordered all bodies be beheaded or shot in the brain and promptly burned within minutes of a soul's passing. Whole new branches of police and armed forces were transferred or newly commissioned to this task and this task alone. The present threat of the dead was given greater importance than the stories of the invaders from another planet and rightly so. One guards against the robber lurking in the shadows outside one's house first, not the one who may come the next week.

I knew not if those countries also endeavored to strengthen themselves against the coming of the Martians or lay defenses to waylay them. Surely with so much of their military and resources and even their populaces fixated on the dead plague, I cannot see how they would have. But as to here in the country I call home, man's spirit was already broken under the Martian heel. Even the bravest of men would no longer stand against the mechanical giants and their Heat-Rays of certain death, though they might have stood a chance if they had. Never again during the invasion did the Martians use their Black Smoke of death. The poison created too many of the dead and only helped the monsters to grow in number, spreading their contagion. This went directly against the Martians' plans. They had no wish to see their food supply tainted in such a manner. The blood of the dead gave them no nourishment and was unusable to them. It is said that wherever time and resources permitted, the invaders now waged their own war with the dead as well. They must have hoped, if nothing else, to thin out the dead's numbers and curtail the growth of the foul creatures amidst their stock of food to be harvested.

Throughout my homeland, most people went into hiding. They sealed themselves away in cellars and behind barred doors, praying that help would come before the dead discovered them and clawed their way inside to devour them. In the areas which existed beyond the Martians' reach of power and their slow, deliberate advance, one woman rallied what was left of an army. Before the Martians came and the dead found new life, this woman worked as an editor on the staff of one of London's leading newspapers and taught classes on the art of language to those she could convince to attend. I never learned what her proper name was and it is now lost to the poorly recorded history of those dark times. It is said, though, that in those days she answered to "Becca." From whence this odd shortening of Rebecca came, I do not know. She watched her beloved London fall; her family was among the victims of the dead and their gnashing teeth. They say her voice could not be silenced, that her cries to those that retained power moved them to act. The remnants of the army gathered and laid fortifications ahead of the dead's advance. Here they held the hordes at the cost of untold lives in order to protect what remained of the human race in our part of the world. She too died in these battles. As it is told, she stood on the front lines, screaming for the men to hold firm as the dead came in wave after endless wave.

Whether or not the line would have held was never decided for the Martians finally found an answer to the dead and spared us all, even if it was only so they rather than the dead could feast on us. All of the Martians' experimenting with the dead finally produced the fruit of knowledge. Their awe-striking tripods marched to the places where the dead things gathered *en masse*. There they stood with their Heat-Rays silent. Each of the giants carried a canister like those which smothered the ground with the Black Smoke. They fired these into the ranks of the dead. Wherever they landed these containers sprayed a bright blue gas into the air. This gas floated through the ranks of the dead, dissolving the creatures into mounds of thick, goopy, corroded flesh that was not recognizable as anything that had lived. The gas melted everything organic in nature wherever it was released: plants, trees, animals . . . everything. The Martians destroyed the bulk of the dead in this manner, even advancing close to the human line of defense in order to employ their gas against the dead. When these canisters were launched at the great battle between the living and the dead where Becca led her troops to preserve what was left of man, the order to retreat went up. Men scurried like rats before the power of the Martians but even so hundreds met their end in those blue vapours. I cannot imagine what a horrid death it must have been to watch your flesh dripping off of you or what the pain must have been like.

Once most of the dead were gone, the Martians pulled back inside their pre-established borders to continue their preparations for the second round of the war with man and fed on those already within their grasp.

Thus it was that one of man's enemies eliminated the threat of the other. The dead were not wholly wiped out but now their numbers were so low that there was little threat of them eradicating the human race before the Martians could claim it as their own. The dead that were left scattered over the land, mostly wandering aimlessly in packs of two or three still in search of men to consume. These small groups were easily dealt with. A single prepared man or woman could survive an encounter with them as long as they stayed calm and used their head. One war was ended but one's outcome was yet to be decided, though to most it seemed the Martians had won and were merely taking their time in collecting their spoils.

After the curate's death, when I finally emerged into the world, I was shocked at how much had changed under the Martians' reign during my time of hiding.

6

⮞⬦⬸

THE WORK
OF FIFTEEN DAYS

For some time I stood tottering on the mound regardless of my safety. I stared out into a world of such change, it left me stunned. Within that noisome den from which I had emerged I had thought with a narrow intensity only of our immediate security. I had not realised what had been happening to the world, had not anticipated this startling vision of unfamiliar things. I had expected to see Sheen in ruins—I found about me the landscape, weird and lurid, of another planet. It was as if the Martians were redesigning our world to match the one they had come from.

For that moment I touched an emotion beyond the common range of men, yet one that the poor brutes we dominate know only too well. I felt as a rabbit might feel returning to his burrow and suddenly confronted by the work of a dozen busy navvies digging the foundations of a house. I felt the first inkling of a thing that presently grew quite clear in my mind, that oppressed me for many days, a sense of dethrone-ment, a persuasion that I was no longer a master, but an animal among the animals, under the Martian heel. With us it would be as with them, to lurk and watch, to run and hide; the fear and empire of man had passed away.

But so soon as this strangeness had been realised it passed, and my dominant motive became the hunger of my long and dismal fast. In the direction away from the pit I saw, beyond a red-covered wall, a patch of garden ground unbur-ied. This gave me a hint, and I went knee-deep, and some-times neck-deep, in the red weed. The density of the weed gave me a reassuring sense of hiding. The wall was some six feet high, and when I attempted to clamber it I found I could not lift my feet to the crest. So I went along by the side of it. I let out a scream as a hand clutched my ankle amid the red weeds. I could not see my assailant but I kicked hard at where I thought the attacker's head must be. My foot made contact and I heard a wet, splattering sound. The hold on my foot released. I staggered backwards, trying to regain my fac-ulties. After checking my ankle and seeing it was uninjured, I steeled my courage and cautiously moved forward to see who or what lurked under the sea of red. I parted the weeds and discovered the body of a dead man. He was grossly de-cayed to the point that when my foot struck him his head popped like an over ripe melon, covering the soil beneath the red weeds with black pus. My heart thundered in my chest. What if there were more of the things among these weeds? I wondered. I picked up my pace as much as I dared and moved forward on my path around the wall as quickly as I could and came to a corner and a rock work that enabled me to get to the top, and tumble into the garden I coveted. Here the red weeds were not as thick and tall and I was very glad for it. I found some young onions, a couple of gladiolus bulbs, and a quantity of immature carrots, all of which I secured, and, scrambling over a ruined wall, went on my way through scarlet and crimson trees towards Kew—it was like walking through an avenue of gigantic blood drops—possessed with two ideas: to get more food, and to limp, as soon and as far as my strength permitted, out of this accursed unearthly region of the pit. I managed to find a stick and used it to part the weeds before me as I went, much like a gardener in the summer time checking for snakes among the weeds of an overgrown field in need of cutting.

Some way farther, in a grassy place, was a group of mushrooms which also I devoured, and then I came upon a brown sheet of flowing shallow water, where meadows used to be. These fragments of nourishment served only to whet my hunger. At first I was surprised at this flood in a hot, dry summer, but afterwards I discovered that it was caused by the tropical exuberance of the red weed. Directly this extraordinary growth encountered water it straightway became gigantic and of unparalleled fecundity. Its seeds were simply poured down into the water of the Wey and Thames, and its swiftly growing and Titanic water fronds speedily choked both those rivers.

At Putney, as I afterwards saw, the bridge was almost lost in a tangle of this weed, and at Richmond, too, the Thames water poured in a broad and shallow stream across the meadows of Hampton and Twickenham. As the water spread the weed followed them, until the ruined villas of the Thames valley were for a time lost in this red swamp, whose margin I explored, and much of the desolation the Martians had caused was concealed.

In the end the red weed succumbed almost as quickly as it had spread. A cankering disease, due, it is believed, to the action of certain bacteria, presently seized upon it. Now by the action of natural selection, all terrestrial plants have acquired a resisting power against bacterial diseases—they never succumb without a severe struggle, but the red weed rotted like a thing already dead. The fronds became bleached, and then shrivelled and brittle. They broke off at the least touch, and the waters that had stimulated their early growth carried their last vestiges out to sea.

My first act on coming to this water was, of course, to slake my thirst. I drank a great deal of it and, moved by an impulse, gnawed some fronds of red weed; but they were watery, and had a sickly, metallic taste. I gave no thought to the toxins that they may contain, doing so without thinking. No ill effects befell me however by the grace of God. I found the water was sufficiently shallow for me to wade securely, although the red weed impeded my feet a little; but the flood evidently got deeper towards the river, and I turned back to Mortlake. I managed to make out the road by means of occasional ruins of its villas and fences and lamps, and so presently I got out of this spate and made my way to the hill going up towards Roehampton and came out on Putney Common.

Here the scenery changed from the strange and unfamiliar to the wreckage of the familiar: patches of ground exhibited the devastation of a cyclone, and in a few score yards I would come upon perfectly undisturbed spaces, houses with their blinds trimly drawn and doors closed, as if they had been left for a day by the owners, or as if their inhabitants slept within. There were, of course, other houses with doors swaying on broken hinges and with shattered windows from where the dead had forced their way inside to make a meal of the poor souls who dwelt there. The red weed was less abundant; the tall trees along the lane were free from the red creeper. I hunted for food among the trees, finding nothing, and I also raided a couple of silent houses. I did so carefully, fully believing I would encounter at least one of the dead in these abandoned places. I did not, but neither did I find the much needed supplies I sought because the houses had already been broken into and ransacked. I rested for the remainder of the daylight in a shrubbery, being, in my enfeebled condition, too fatigued to push on. At the time, I had yet to learn of the great battle with the dead that occurred far from where I sat or the Martians' new blue gas. I worried that the dead would happen upon me and I would not be able to fight, much less run, in my weakened state.

All this time I saw no human beings either, and no signs of the Martians. I encountered a couple of hungry-looking dogs, but both hurried circuitously away from the advances I made them. Near Roehampton I had seen two human skeletons—not bodies, but skeletons, picked clean—and in the wood by me I found the crushed and scattered bones of several cats and rabbits and the skull of a sheep. But though I gnawed parts of these in my mouth, there was nothing to be got from them.

After sunset I struggled on along the road towards Putney, where I think the Heat-Ray must have been used for some reason, perhaps in a battle with the dead as the Martians advanced. And in the garden beyond Roehampton I got a quantity of immature potatoes, sufficient to stay my hunger. From this garden one looked down upon Putney and the river. The aspect of the place in the dusk was singularly desolate: blackened trees, blackened, desolate ruins, and down the hill the sheets of the flooded river, red-tinged with the weed. And over all—silence. It filled me with indescribable terror to think how swiftly that desolating change had come.

For a time I believed that mankind had been swept out of existence, and that I stood there alone, the last man left alive. The thought made me sick to think all of human culture and history had been swept aside so easily and I was now the sole remaining vestige of mankind on this world. I wept for a while, thinking there would be no more plays, no more moving books of prose or poems. There would be no tomorrow when mankind could reach for the stars themselves as our conquerors had. Hard by the top of Putney Hill I came upon another skeleton, with the arms dislocated and removed several yards from the rest of the body. As I proceeded I became more and more convinced that the extermination of mankind was, save for such stragglers as myself, already accomplished in this part of the world. The

Martians, I thought, had gone on and left the country desolated, seeking food elsewhere. Perhaps even now they were destroying Berlin or Paris, or it might be they had gone northward. Of the whereabouts of the dead, at that time, I could only imagine they had followed the great machines of the invaders onward into the world.

I prayed the rest of the world, given more warning of the Martians and what they were capable of, would make a better stand against them than we had here.

7

THE MAN
ON PUTNEY HILL

I spent that night in the inn that stands at the top of Putney Hill, sleeping in a made bed for the first time since my
flight to Leatherhead. I will not tell the needless trouble I had
breaking into that house—afterwards I found the front door
was on the latch—nor how I ransacked every room for food,
until just on the verge of despair, in what seemed to me to be
a servant's bedroom, I found a rat-gnawed crust and two tins
of pineapple. The place had been already searched and emp-
tied. In the bar I afterwards found some biscuits and sand-
wiches that had been overlooked. The latter I could not eat,
they were too rotten, but the former not only stayed my hun-

ger, but filled my pockets. I lit no lamps, fearing some Martian might come beating that part of London for food in the night or that perhaps some of the dead lingered behind where most of the creatures seemed departed. Before I went to bed I had an interval of restlessness, and prowled from window to window, peering out for some sign of these monsters. I had locked the doors and barricaded them, taking great pains to make sure they would give me warning even if they failed to keep the dead out. I slept little. As I lay in bed I found myself thinking consecutively—a thing I do not remember to have done since my last argument with the curate. During all the intervening time my mental condition had been a hurrying succession of vague emotional states or a sort of stupid receptivity. But in the night my brain, reinforced, I suppose, by the food I had eaten, grew clear again, and I thought.

Three things struggled for possession of my mind: the killing of the curate, the whereabouts of the Martians and the dead, and the possible fate of my wife. The former gave me no sensation of horror or remorse to recall; I saw it simply as a thing done, a memory infinitely disagreeable but quite without the quality of remorse. I saw myself then as I see myself now, driven step by step towards that hasty blow, the creature of a sequence of accidents leading inevitably to that. I felt no condemnation; yet the memory, static, unprogressive, haunted me. In the silence of the night, with that sense of the nearness of God that sometimes comes into the stillness and the darkness, I stood my trial, my only trial, for that moment of wrath and fear. I retraced every step of our conversation from the moment when I had found him crouching beside me, heedless of my thirst, and pointing to

the fire and smoke that streamed up from the ruins of Weybridge. We had been incapable of co-operation—grim chance
had taken no heed of that. Had I foreseen, I should have left
him at Halliford. But I did not foresee; and crime is to foresee and do. And I set this down as I have set all this story
down, as it was. There were no witnesses—all these things
I might have concealed. But I set it down, and the reader
must form his judgment as he will.

And when, by an effort, I had set aside that picture of
a prostrate body, I faced the problem of the Martians and
the fate of my wife. For the former I had no data; I could
imagine a hundred things, and so, unhappily, I could for the
latter. And suddenly that night became terrible. I found myself sitting up in bed, staring at the dark. I found myself
praying that the Heat-Ray might have suddenly and pain-
lessly struck her out of being for this was a fate far more
favorable than others. It was more likely that the dead
had found her at Leatherhead than the invaders. I could
see her screaming behind barred doors as the dead broke
through the wood with their massive numbers. I could hear
the gunshots of those trying to defend her, her footsteps as
she ran upstairs after those same men fell to dead claws. I
imagined her tucking away in a bedroom or closet and holding her breath, asking God to let the things pass her by. I
could see the terror in her eyes when she was discovered
and feel every bite the yellow teeth took of her, tearing her
flesh, as she struggled vainly against rotting hands. Since
the night of my return from Leatherhead I had not prayed. I
had uttered prayers, fetish prayers, had prayed as heathens
mutter charms when I was in extremity; but now I prayed

indeed, pleading steadfastly and sanely, face to face with the darkness of God. Strange night! Strangest in this, that so soon as dawn had come, I, who had talked with God, crept out of the house like a rat leaving its hiding place—a creature scarcely larger, an inferior animal, a thing that for any passing whim of our masters might be hunted and killed. Perhaps they also prayed confidently to God. Surely, if we have learned nothing else, this war has taught us pity—pity for those witless souls that suffer our dominion.

The morning was bright and fine. I made a quick search of the establishment for a weapon as I did not want to travel unarmed. I had no luck with regards to firearms or anything proper with which to defend myself. In the end, I settled by taking a fire poker, figuring I could use it both as a club of sorts and a small impaling instrument if the situation demanded such. Finally, I set forth, looking up at the sky above me.

The eastern sky glowed pink, and was fretted with little golden clouds. In the road that runs from the top of Putney Hill to Wimbledon was a number of poor vestiges of the panic torrent that must have poured Londonward on the Sunday night after the fighting began. There was a little two-wheeled cart inscribed with the name of Thomas Lobb, Greengrocer, New Malden, with a smashed wheel and an abandoned tin trunk; there was a straw hat trampled into the now hardened mud, and at the top of West Hill a lot of blood-stained glass about the overturned water trough. My movements were languid, my plans of the vaguest. I had an idea of going to Leatherhead, though I knew that there I had the poorest chance of finding my wife. Certainly, unless death had overtaken them suddenly or the dead had trapped them and eventually broken their way inside, my cousins and she would have fled thence; but it seemed to me I might find or learn there whither the Surrey people had fled. I knew I wanted to find my wife, that my heart ached for her and the world of men, but I had no clear idea how the finding might be done. I was also sharply aware now of my intense loneliness. From the corner I went, under cover of a thicket of trees and bushes, to the edge of Wimbledon Common, stretching wide and far.

That dark expanse was lit in patches by yellow gorse and broom; there was no red weed to be seen, and as I prowled, hesitating, on the verge of the open, the sun rose, flooding it all with light and vitality. I came upon a busy swarm of little frogs in a swampy place among the trees. I stopped to look at them, drawing a lesson from their stout resolve to live. And presently, turning suddenly, with an odd feeling of being watched, I beheld something crouching amid a clump of bushes. I stood regarding this. I made a step towards it, and it rose up and became a man armed with a cutlass. I approached him slowly. He stood silent and motionless, regarding me.

As I drew nearer I perceived he was dressed in clothes as dusty and filthy as my own; he looked, indeed, as though he had been dragged through a culvert. Nearer, I distinguished the green slime of ditches mixing with the pale drab of dried clay and shiny, coaly patches. His black hair fell over his eyes, and his face was dark and dirty and sunken, so that at first I did not recognise him. There was a red cut across the lower part of his face.

"Stop!" he cried, when I was within ten yards of him, and I stopped. His voice was hoarse. "Where do you come from?" he said.

I noticed the dried blood covering his weapon's edge and hoped it belong to dead monsters that he slew and not passersby such as myself.

I thought, surveying him.

"I come from Mortlake," I said. "I was buried near the pit the Martians made about their cylinder. I have worked my way out and escaped. What has transpired? Where are the dead?"

"There is no food about here," he said, ignoring my questions. "This is my country. All this hill down to the river, and back to Clapham, and up to the edge of the common. There is only food for one. Which way are you going?"

I answered slowly.

"I don't know," I said. "I have been buried in the ruins of a house thirteen or fourteen days. I don't know what has happened."

He looked at me doubtfully, then started, and looked with a changed expression.

"I've no wish to stop about here. You have no need to fear my intentions," said I. "I think I shall go to Leatherhead, for my wife was there."

He shot out a pointing finger.

"It is you," said he; "the man from Woking. And you weren't killed at Weybridge?"

I recognised him at the same moment.

"You are the artilleryman who came into my garden."

"Good luck!" he said. "We are lucky ones! Fancy *you*!" He

put out a hand, and I took it. "I crawled up a drain," he said. "But they didn't kill everyone. And after they went away I got off towards Walton across the fields. I rejoined some troops there and we fought the dead in the streets. There was no choice but to retreat and hide. This we did but the dead followed us. Soon our ammunition was exhausted and our numbers dwindled. As the dead made their final great push to get inside, I leaped from a window at the rear of the house and made my way here. I have lived here alone except for the occasional intrusion of the dead since then. But— It's not sixteen days altogether—and your hair is grey." He looked over his shoulder suddenly. "Only a rook," he said. "One gets to know that birds have shadows these days. This is a bit open. Let us crawl under those bushes and talk."

"Have you seen any Martians?" I said. "Since I crawled out—"

"They've gone away across London," he said. "I guess they've got a bigger camp there. Of a night, all over there, Hampstead way, the sky is alive with their lights. It's like a great city, and in the glare you can just see them moving. By daylight you can't. But nearer—I haven't seen them—" (he counted on his fingers) "five days. Then I saw a couple across Hammersmith way carrying something big. And the night before last"—he stopped and spoke impressively—"it was just a matter of lights, but it was something up in the air. I believe they've built a flying-machine, and are learning to fly."

I stopped, on hands and knees, for we had come to the bushes.

"Fly!"

"Yes," he said, "fly."

I went on into a little bower, and sat down.

"It is all over with humanity," I said. "If they can do that they will simply go round the world."

He nodded. "Assuming the dead haven't wiped us all out first. And, yes, they will fly to the rest of the world in their machines," he continued, referring to the Martians. "But—It will relieve things over here a bit. And besides—" He looked at me. "Aren't you satisfied it *is* up with humanity? I am. We're down; we're beat."

I stared. Strange as it may seem, I had not arrived at this fact—a fact perfectly obvious so soon as he spoke. I had still held a vague hope; rather, I had kept a lifelong habit of mind. He repeated his words, "We're beat." They carried absolute conviction.

"It's all over," he said. "They've lost *one*—just *one*. And they've made their footing good and crippled the greatest power in the world. They've walked over us. The death of that one at Weybridge was an accident. And these are only pioneers. They kept on coming. These green stars—I've seen none these five or six days, but I've no doubt they're falling somewhere every night. Nothing's to be done. We're under! We're beat! And least you not forgot the dead. Their numbers are daunting and growing each day. I dare say even if we were to drive back the Martians, the dead would, given time, make equally short work of us."

I made him no answer. I sat staring before me, trying in vain to devise some countervailing thought.

"This isn't a war," said the artilleryman. "It never was a war, any more than there's war between man and ants."

Suddenly I recalled the night in the observatory.

"After the tenth shot they fired no more—at least, until the first cylinder came."

"How do you know?" said the artilleryman. I explained. He thought. "Something wrong with the gun," he said. "But what if there is? They'll get it right again. And even if there's a delay, how can it alter the end? It's just men and ants. There's the ants builds their cities, live their lives, have wars, revolutions, until the men want them out of the way, and then they go out of the way. That's what we are now—just ants. Only—"

"Yes," I said.

"We're eatable ants regardless of who gets us."

We sat looking at each other.

"And what will the Martians do with us?" I said.

"That's what I've been thinking," he said; "that's what I've been thinking. After Weybridge and my escape from death alongside the other soldiers, I went south—thinking. I saw what was up. Most of the people were hard at it squealing and exciting themselves. But I'm not so fond of squealing. I've been in sight of death once or twice; I'm not an ornamental soldier, and at the best and worst, death—it's just death. And it's the man that keeps on thinking comes through. I saw everyone tracking away south. Says I, 'Food won't last this way,' and I turned right back. I went for the Martians like a sparrow goes for man. All round"—he waved a hand to the horizon—"they're starving in heaps, bolting, treading on each other, the dead among them, spreading their disease . . ."

He saw my face, and halted awkwardly.

"No doubt lots who had money and got the chance have gone away to France," he said. He seemed to hesitate whether to apologise, met my eyes, and went on: "There's food all about here. Canned things in shops; wines, spirits, mineral waters; and the water mains and drains are empty. The dead are mostly gone from these parts. Any that are left . . ." He swished his cutlass through the air before me with a grin tracing the outline of his lips. "Well, I was telling you what I was thinking about the Martians. 'Here's intelligent things,' I said, 'and it seems they want us for food. First, they'll smash us up—ships, machines, guns, cities, all the order and organisation. All that will go. If we were the size of ants we might pull through. But we're not. It's all too bulky to stop. That's the first certainty.' Eh?"

I assented.

"It is; I've thought it out. Very well, then—next; at present we're caught as we're wanted. A Martian has only to go a few miles to get a crowd on the run. And I saw one, one day, out by Wandsworth, picking houses to pieces and routing among the wreckage. But they won't keep on doing that. So soon as they've settled all our guns and ships, and smashed our railways, and done all the things they are doing over there, they will begin catching us systematic, picking the best and storing us in cages and things. That's what they will start doing in a bit. They haven't begun on us yet. Don't you see that? I do not know what they will do about the dead. Surely they can not take nourishment from stale putrid blood. I believe they too will have to settle up things with the dead as fast as they can."

"Not begun!" I exclaimed.

"Not begun. All that's happened so far is through our not having the sense to keep quiet—worrying them with guns and such foolery. And losing our heads, and rushing off in crowds to where there wasn't any more safety than where we were. They don't want to bother us yet. They're making their things—making all the things they couldn't bring with them, getting things ready for the rest of their people. Very likely that's why the cylinders have stopped for a bit, for fear of hitting those who are here. And instead of our rushing about blind, on the howl, or getting dynamite on the chance of busting them up, we've got to fix ourselves up according to the new state of affairs. That's how I figure it out. It isn't quite according to what a man wants for his species, but it's about what the facts point to. And that's the principle I acted upon. Cities, nations, civilisation, progress—it's all over. That game's up. We're beat."

"But if that is so, what is there to live for?"

The artilleryman looked at me for a moment.

"There won't be any more blessed concerts for a million years or so; there won't be any Royal Academy of Arts, and no nice little feeds at restaurants. If it's amusement you're after, I reckon the game is up. If you've got any drawing-room manners or a dislike to eating peas with a knife or dropping aitches, you'd better chuck 'em away. They ain't no further use."

"You mean—"

"I mean that men like me are going on living—for the sake of the breed. I tell you, I'm grim set on living. And if I'm not mistaken, you'll show what insides *you've* got, too, before long. We aren't going to be exterminated. The Martians won't let that happen. As I said, they will find a way to deal with the dead. And I don't mean to be caught either, and tamed and fattened and bred like a thundering ox. Ugh! Fancy those brown creepers!"

"You don't mean to say—"

"I do. I'm going on, under their feet. I've got it planned; I've thought it out. We men are beat. We don't know enough. We've got to learn before we've got a chance. And we've got to live and keep independent while we learn. See! That's what has to be done."

I stared, astonished, and stirred profoundly by the man's resolution.

"Great goodness!" cried I. "But you are a man indeed!" And suddenly I gripped his hand.

"Eh!" he said, with his eyes shining. "I've thought it out, eh?"

"Go on," I said.

"Well, those who mean to escape their catching must get ready. I'm getting ready. Mind you, it isn't all of us that are made for wild beasts; and that's what it's got to be. That's why I watched you. I had my doubts. You're slender. I didn't know that it was you, you see, or just how you'd been buried. All these—the sort of people that lived in these houses, and all those little clerks that used to live down that way—they'd be no good. They haven't any spirit in them—no proud dreams and no proud lusts; and a man who hasn't one or the other! What is he but funk and precautions? They just used to skedaddle off to work—I've seen hundreds of 'em, bit of breakfast in hand, running wild and shining to catch their little season-ticket train,

for fear they'd get dismissed if they didn't; working at busi-
nesses they were afraid to take the trouble to understand;
skedaddling back for fear they wouldn't be in time for
dinner; keeping indoors after dinner for fear of the back
streets, and sleeping with the wives they married, not
because they wanted them, but because they had a bit of
money that would make for safety in their one little miserable skedaddle through the world. Lives insured and a bit
invested for fear of accidents. And on Sundays—fear of the
hereafter. As if Hell was built for rabbits! Well, the Martians
will just be a godsend to these. Nice roomy cages, fattening
food, careful breeding, no worry. After a week or so chasing
about the fields and lands on empty stomachs, they'll come
and be caught cheerful. They'll be quite glad after a bit.
They'll wonder what people did before there were Martians
to take care of them. And the bar loafers, and mashers, and
singers—I can imagine them. I can imagine them," he said,
with a sort of sombre gratification. "There'll be any amount
of sentiment and religion loose among them. There's hundreds of things I saw with my eyes that I've only begun to
see clearly these last few days. There's lots will take things
as they are—fat and stupid; and lots will be worried by a
sort of feeling that it's all wrong, and that they ought to be
doing something. Now whenever things are so that a lot
of people feel they ought to be doing something, the weak,
and those who go weak with a lot of complicated thinking,
always make for a sort of do-nothing religion, very pious
and superior, and submit to persecution and the will of the
Lord. Very likely you've seen the same thing. It's energy
in a gale of funk, and turned clean inside out. These cages

will be full of psalms and hymns and piety. And those of a less simple sort will work in a bit of—what is it?—eroticism."

He paused.

"Very likely these Martians will make pets of some of them; train them to do tricks—who knows?—get sentimental over the pet boy who grew up and had to be killed. And some, maybe, they will train to hunt us."

"No," I cried, "that's impossible! No human being—"

"What's the good of going on with such lies?" said the artilleryman. "There's men who'd do it cheerful. What nonsense to pretend there isn't!"

And I succumbed to his conviction.

"If they come after me," he said; "My, if they come after me!" and subsided into a grim meditation.

I sat contemplating these things. I could find nothing to bring against this man's reasoning. In the days before the invasion no one would have questioned my intellectual superiority to his—I, a professed and recognised writer on philosophical themes, and he, a common soldier; and yet he had already formulated a situation that I had scarcely realised.

"What are you doing?" I said presently. "What plans have you made?"

He hesitated.

"Well, it's like this," he said. "What have we to do? We have to invent a sort of life where men can live and breed, safe from the dead if the invaders don't deal with them, and be sufficiently secure to bring the children up. Yes—wait a bit, and I'll make it clearer what I think ought to be done.

The tame ones will go like all tame beasts; in a few generations they'll be big, beautiful, rich-blooded, stupid—rubbish! The risk is that we who keep wild will go savage—degenerate into a sort of big, savage rat. . . . You see, how I mean to live is underground. I've been thinking about the drains. Of course those who don't know drains think horrible things; but under this London are miles and miles—hundreds of miles—and a few days' rain and London empty will leave them sweet and clean. The main drains are big enough and airy enough for anyone. Then there's cellars, vaults, stores, from which bolting passages may be made to the drains. And the railway tunnels and subways. Eh? You begin to see? And we form a band—able-bodied, clean-minded men. We're not going to pick up any rubbish that drifts in. Weaklings go out again."

"As you meant me to go?"

"Well—I parleyed, didn't I?"

"We won't quarrel about that. Go on."

"Those who stop obey orders. Able-bodied, clean-minded women we want also—mothers and teachers. No lackadaisical ladies—no blasted rolling eyes. We can't have any weak or silly. Life is real again, and the useless and cumbersome and mischievous have to die. They ought to die. They ought to be willing to die. It's a sort of disloyalty, after all, to live and taint the race. And they can't be happy. Moreover, dying's none so dreadful; it's the funking makes it bad. And in all those places we shall gather. Our district will be London. And we may even be able to keep a watch, and run about in the open when the Martians keep away. Play cricket, perhaps. That's how we shall save the race. Eh? It's a possible thing? But saving the race is nothing in itself. As I say, that's only being rats. It's saving our knowledge and adding to it is the thing. There men like you come in. There's books, there's models. We must make great safe places down deep, and get all the books we can; not novels and poetry swipes, but ideas, science books. That's where men like you come in. We must go to the British Museum and pick all those books through. Especially we must keep up our science—learn more. We must watch these Martians. Some of us must go as spies. When it's all working, perhaps I will. Get caught, I mean. And the great thing is, we must leave the Martians alone. We mustn't even steal. If we get in their way, we clear out. We must show them we mean no harm. Yes, I know. But they're intelligent things, and they won't hunt us down if they have all they want, and think we're just harmless vermin."

The artilleryman paused and laid a brown hand upon my arm.

"After all, it may not be so much we may have to learn before—Just imagine this: four or five of their fighting machines suddenly starting off—Heat-Rays right and left, and not a Martian in 'em. Not a Martian in 'em, but men—men who have learned the way how. It may be in my time, even—those men. Fancy having one of them lovely things, with its Heat-Ray wide and free! Fancy having it in control! What would it matter if you smashed to smithereens at the end of the run, after a bust like that? I reckon the Martians'll open their beautiful eyes! Can't you see them, man? Can't you see them hurrying, hurrying—puffing and blowing and hooting to their other mechanical affairs? Something out of gear in every case. And swish, bang, rattle, swish! Just as they are fumbling over it, *swish* comes the Heat-Ray, and, behold! Man has come back to his own."

For a while the imaginative daring of the artilleryman, and the tone of assurance and courage he assumed, completely dominated my mind. I believed unhesitatingly both in his forecast of human destiny and in the practicability of his astonishing scheme, and the reader who thinks me susceptible and foolish must contrast his position, reading steadily with all his thoughts about his subject, and mine, crouching fearfully in the bushes and listening, distracted by apprehension. We talked in this manner through the early morning time, and later crept out of the bushes, and, after scanning the sky for Martians and the surroundings for the lingering dead, hurried precipitately to the house on Putney Hill where he had made his lair. It was the coal cellar of the place, and when I saw the work he had spent a week upon—it was a burrow scarcely ten yards long, which he designed to reach to the main drain on Putney Hill—I had my first inkling of the gulf between his dreams and his powers. Such a hole I could have dug in a day. But I believed in him sufficiently to work with him all that morning until past midday at his digging. We had a garden barrow and shot the earth we removed against the kitchen range. We refreshed ourselves with a tin of mock turtle soup and wine from the neighbouring pantry. I found a curious relief from the aching strangeness of the world in this steady labour. As we worked, I turned his project over in my mind, and presently objections and doubts began to arise; but I worked there all the morning, so glad was I to find myself with a purpose again. After working an hour I began to speculate on the distance one had to go before the cloaca was reached, the chances we had of missing it altogether. My immediate trouble was why we should dig this long tunnel, when it was possible to get into the drain at once down one of the manholes, and work back to the house. It seemed to me, too, that the house was inconveniently chosen, and required a needless length of tunnel. I also began to think of the dead. If they came into this dark underground, we would be trapped, having no choice but to fight through their ranks in order to escape to the world above. And just as I was beginning to face these things, the artilleryman stopped digging, and looked at me.

"We're working well," he said. He put down his spade. "Let us knock off a bit" he said. "I think it's time we reconnoitred from the roof of the house."

I was for going on, and after a little hesitation he resumed his spade; and then suddenly I was struck by a thought. I stopped, and so did he at once.

"Why were you walking about the common," I said, "instead of being here?"

"Taking the air," he said. "I was coming back. It's safer by night."

"But the work?"

"Oh, one can't always work," he said, and in a flash I saw the man plain. He hesitated, holding his spade. "We ought to reconnoitre now," he said, "because if any of the dead or the blasted Martians come near they may hear the spades and drop upon us unawares."

I was no longer disposed to object. We went together to

the roof and stood on a ladder peeping out of the roof door. No Martians were to be seen, and we ventured out on the tiles, and slipped down under shelter of the parapet. The dead were not to be seen either. The whole of the area was vacant but for us.

From this position a shrubbery hid the greater portion of Putney, but we could see the river below, a bubbly mass of red weed, and the low parts of Lambeth flooded and red. The red creeper swarmed up the trees about the old palace, and their branches stretched gaunt and dead, and set with shrivelled leaves, from amid its clusters. It was strange how entirely dependent both these things were upon flowing water for their propagation. About us neither had gained a footing; laburnums, pink mays, snowballs, and trees of arborvitae, rose out of laurels and hydrangeas, green and brilliant into the sunlight. Beyond Kensington dense smoke was rising, and that and a blue haze hid the northward hills.

The artilleryman began to tell me of the sort of people who still remained in London.

"One night last week," he said, "some fools got the electric light in order, and there was all Regent Street and the Circus ablaze, crowded with painted and ragged drunkards, men and women, dancing and shouting till dawn. They took turns fighting off the dead so they could indulge in this lunacy. How they were not overrun I do not know. A man who was there told me. And as the day came they became aware of a fighting-machine standing near by the Langham and looking down at them. Heaven knows how long he had been there. It must have given some of them a nasty turn. He came down the road towards them, and picked up nearly a hundred too drunk or frightened to run away."

Grotesque gleam of a time no history will ever fully describe!

From that, in answer to my questions, he came round to his grandiose plans again. He grew enthusiastic. He talked so eloquently of the possibility of capturing a fighting-machine that I more than half believed in him again. But now that I was beginning to understand something of his quality, I could divine the stress he laid on doing nothing precipitately. And I noted that now there was no question that he personally was to capture and fight the great machine.

After a time we went down to the cellar. Neither of us seemed disposed to resume digging, and when he suggested a meal, I was nothing loath. He became suddenly very generous, and when we had eaten he went away and returned with some excellent cigars. We lit these, and his optimism glowed. He was inclined to regard my coming as a great occasion.

"There's some champagne in the cellar," he said.

"We can dig better on this Thames-side burgundy," said I.

"No," said he; "I am host today. Champagne! Besides, we've a heavy enough task before us! Let us take a rest and gather strength while we may. Look at these blistered hands!"

And pursuant to this idea of a holiday, he insisted upon playing cards after we had eaten. He taught me euchre, and after dividing London between us, I taking the northern side and he the southern, we played for parish points. Grotesque and foolish as this will seem to the sober reader, it is absolutely true, and what is more remarkable, I found the card game and several others we played extremely interesting.

Strange mind of man! that, with our species upon the edge of extermination or appalling degradation, with no clear prospect before us but the chance of a horrible death, we could sit following the chance of this painted pasteboard, and playing the "joker" with vivid delight. Afterwards he taught me poker, and I beat him at three tough chess games. When dark came we decided to take the risk, and lit a lamp.

After an interminable string of games, we supped, and the artilleryman finished the champagne. We went on smoking the cigars. He was no longer the energetic regenerator of his species I had encountered in the morning. He was still optimistic, but it was a less kinetic, a more thoughtful optimism. I remember he wound up with my health, proposed in a speech of small variety and considerable intermittence. I took a cigar, and went upstairs to look at the lights of which he had spoken that blazed so greenly along the Highgate hills.

At first I stared unintelligently across the London valley. The northern hills were shrouded in darkness; the fires near Kensington glowed redly, and now and then an orange-red tongue of flame flashed up and vanished in the deep blue night. All the rest of London was black. Then, nearer, I perceived a strange light, a pale, violet-purple fluorescent glow, quivering under the night breeze. For a space I could not understand it, and then I knew that it must be the red weed from which this faint irradiation proceeded. With that realisation my dormant sense of wonder, my sense of the proportion of things, awoke again. I glanced from that to Mars, red and clear, glowing high in the west, and then gazed long and earnestly at the darkness of Hampstead and Highgate.

I remained a very long time upon the roof, wondering at the grotesque changes of the day. I recalled my mental states from the midnight prayer to the foolish card-playing. I had a violent revulsion of feeling. I remember I flung away the cigar with a certain wasteful symbolism. My folly came to me with glaring exaggeration. I seemed a traitor to my wife and to my kind; I was filled with remorse. I resolved to leave this strange, undisciplined dreamer of great things to his drink and gluttony, and to go on into London. There, it seemed to me, I had the best chance of learning what the Martians and my fellow men were doing. I was still upon the roof when the late moon rose.

8

DEAD LONDON

After I had parted from the artilleryman, I went down the hill, and by the High Street across the bridge to Fulham. The red weed was tumultuous at that time, and nearly choked the bridge roadway; but its fronds were already whitened in patches by the spreading disease that presently removed it so swiftly.

At the corner of the lane that runs to Putney Bridge station I found a man lying. He was as black as a sweep with the black dust, alive, but helplessly and speechlessly drunk. I could get nothing from him but curses and furious lunges at my head. I think I should have stayed by him but for the brutal expression of his face.

There was black dust along the roadway from the bridge

onwards, and it grew thicker in Fulham. The streets were horribly quiet. I got food—sour, hard, and mouldy, but quite eatable—in a baker's shop here. Some way towards Walham Green the streets became clear of powder, and I passed a white terrace of houses on fire; the noise of the burning was an absolute relief. Going on towards Brompton, the streets were quiet again.

Where there was no black powder, it was curiously like a Sunday in the City, with the closed shops, the houses locked up and the blinds drawn, the desertion, and the stillness. In some places plunderers had been at work, but rarely at other than the provision and wine shops. A jeweller's window had been broken open in one place, but apparently the thief had been disturbed, and a number of gold chains and a watch lay scattered on the pavement. I did not trouble to touch them. Farther on was a tattered woman in a heap on a doorstep; the hand that hung over her knee was gashed and bled down her rusty brown dress, and a smashed magnum of champagne formed a pool across the pavement. She seemed asleep, but she was dead. As I drew nearer to her I saw the hole in her forehead where a bullet entered and blood long dried had seeped forth.

The farther I penetrated into London, the profounder grew the stillness. But it was not so much the stillness of death—it was the stillness of suspense, of expectation. At any time the destruction that had already singed the north-western borders of the metropolis, and had annihilated Ealing and Kilburn, might strike among these houses and leave them smoking ruins. It was a city condemned and derelict. . . .

In South Kensington the streets were clear of the dead and of black powder. It was near South Kensington that I first heard the howling. It crept almost imperceptibly upon my senses. It was a sobbing alternation of two notes, "Ulla, ulla, ulla, ulla," keeping on perpetually. When I passed streets that ran northward it grew in volume, and houses and buildings seemed to deaden and cut it off again. It came in a full tide down Exhibition Road. I stopped, staring towards Kensington Gardens, wondering at this strange, remote wailing. It was as if that mighty desert of houses had found a voice for its fear and solitude.

"Ulla, ulla, ulla, ulla," wailed that superhuman note—great waves of sound sweeping down the broad, sunlit roadway, between the tall buildings on each side. I turned northwards, marvelling, towards the iron gates of Hyde Park. I had half a mind to break into the Natural History Museum and find my way up to the summits of the towers, in order to see across the park. But I decided to keep to the ground, where quick hiding was possible, and so went on up the Exhibition Road. All the large mansions on each side of the road were empty and still, and my footsteps echoed against the sides of the houses. At the top, near the park gate, I came upon a strange sight—a bus overturned, and the skeleton of a horse picked clean. I knew at once this was the work of the Martians or other men because the dead would not partake of the flesh of animals. I puzzled over this for a time, and then went on to the bridge over the Serpentine. The voice grew stronger and stronger, though I could see nothing above the housetops on the north side of the park, save a haze of smoke to the northwest.

"Ulla, ulla, ulla, ulla," cried the voice, coming, as it seemed to me, from the district about Regent's Park. The desolating cry worked upon my mind. The mood that had sustained me passed. The wailing took possession of me. I found I was intensely weary, footsore, and now again hungry and thirsty.

It was already past noon. Why was I wandering alone in this city of the dead? Why was I alone when all London was lying in state, and in its black shroud? I felt intolerably lonely. My mind ran on old friends that I had forgotten for years. I thought of the poisons in the chemists' shops, of the liquors the wine merchants stored; I recalled the two sodden creatures of despair, who so far as I knew, shared the city with myself. . . .

I came into Oxford Street by the Marble Arch, and here again were black powder and several bodies, and an evil, ominous smell from the gratings of the cellars of some of the houses. I grew very thirsty after the heat of my long walk. With infinite trouble I managed to break into a public-house and get food and drink. I was weary after eating, and went into the parlour behind the bar, and slept on a black horse-hair sofa I found there.

I awoke to find that dismal howling still in my ears, "Ulla, ulla, ulla, ulla." It was now dusk, and after I had routed out some biscuits and a cheese in the bar—there was a meat safe, but it contained nothing but maggots—I wandered on through the silent residential squares to Baker Street—Portman Square is the only one I can name—and so came out at last upon Regent's Park. And as I emerged from the top of Baker Street, I saw far away over the trees in the clearness of the sunset the hood of the Martian giant from which this howling proceeded. I was not terrified. I came upon him as if it were a matter of course. I watched him for some time, but he did not move. He appeared to be standing and yelling, for no reason that I could discover.

I tried to formulate a plan of action. That perpetual sound of "Ulla, ulla, ulla, ulla," confused my mind. Perhaps I was too tired to be very fearful. Certainly I was more curious to know the reason of this monotonous crying than afraid. I turned back away from the park and struck into Park Road, intending to skirt the park, went along under the shelter of the terraces, and got a view of this stationary, howling Martian from the direction of St. John's Wood. A couple of hundred yards out of Baker Street I heard a yelping chorus, and saw first a dog with a piece of putrescent red meat in his jaws coming headlong towards me, and then a pack of starving mongrels in pursuit of him. He made a wide curve to avoid me, as though he feared I might prove a fresh competitor. As the yelping died away down the silent road, the wailing sound of "Ulla, ulla, ulla, ulla," reasserted itself.

I came upon the wrecked handling-machine halfway to St. John's Wood station. At first I thought a house had fallen across the road. It was only as I clambered among the ruins that I saw, with a start, this mechanical Samson lying, with its tentacles bent and smashed and twisted, among the ruins it had made. The forepart was shattered. It seemed as if it had driven blindly straight at the house, and had been overwhelmed in its overthrow. It seemed to me then that this might have happened by a handling-machine escaping from the guidance of its Martian. I could not clamber among the ruins to see it, and the twilight was now so far advanced that the blood with which its seat was smeared, and the gnawed gristle of the Martian that the dogs had left, were invisible to me.

Wondering still more at all that I had seen, I pushed on towards Primrose Hill. Far away, through a gap in the trees, I saw a second Martian, as motionless as the first, standing in the park towards the Zoological Gardens, and silent. A little beyond the ruins about the smashed handling-machine I came upon the red weed again, and found the Regent's Canal, a spongy mass of dark-red vegetation.

As I crossed the bridge, the sound of "Ulla, ulla, ulla, ulla," ceased. It was, as it were, cut off. The silence came like a thunderclap.

The dusky houses about me stood faint and tall and dim; the trees towards the park were growing black. All about me the red weed clambered among the ruins, writhing to get above me in the dimness. Night, the mother of fear and mystery, was coming upon me. But while that voice sounded the solitude, the desolation, had been endurable; by virtue of it London had still seemed alive, and the sense of life about me had upheld me. Then suddenly a change, the passing of something—I knew not what—and then a stillness that could be felt. Nothing but this gaunt quiet.

London about me gazed at me spectrally. The windows in the white houses were like the eye sockets of skulls. About me my imagination found a thousand noiseless enemies moving. Terror seized me, a horror of my temerity. In front of me the road became pitchy black as though it was tarred, and I saw a contorted shape lying across the pathway. I could not bring myself to go on. I turned down St. John's Wood Road, and ran headlong from this unendurable stillness towards Kilburn. I hid from the night and the silence, until long after midnight, in a cabmen's shelter in Harrow Road. But before the dawn my courage returned, and while the stars were still in the sky I turned once more towards Regent's Park. I missed my way among the streets, and presently saw down a long avenue, in the half-light of the early dawn, the curve of Primrose Hill. On the summit, towering up to the fading stars, was a third Martian, erect and motionless like the others.

An insane resolve possessed me. I would die and end it. And I would save myself even the trouble of killing myself. I marched on recklessly towards this Titan, and then, as I drew nearer and the light grew, I saw that a multitude of black birds was circling and clustering about the hood. At that my heart gave a bound, and I began running along the road.

I hurried through the red weed that choked St. Edmund's Terrace (I waded breast-high across a torrent of water that was rushing down from the waterworks towards the Albert Road), and emerged upon the grass before the rising of the sun. Great mounds had been heaped about the crest of the hill, making a huge redoubt of it—it was the final and largest place the Martians had made—and from behind these heaps there rose a thin smoke against the sky. Against the sky line an eager dog ran and disappeared. The thought that had flashed into my mind grew real, grew credible. I felt no fear, only a wild, trembling exultation, as I ran up the hill towards the motionless monster. Out of the hood hung lank shreds of brown, at which the hungry birds pecked and tore.

In another moment I had scrambled up the earthen rampart and stood upon its crest, and the interior of the redoubt was below me. A mighty space it was, with gigantic machines here and there within it, huge mounds of material and strange shelter places. And scattered about it, some in their overturned war-machines, some in the now rigid handling-machines, and a dozen of them stark and silent and laid in a row, were the Martians—*dead!*—slain by the putrefactive and disease bacteria against which their systems were unprepared; slain as the red weed was being slain; slain, after all man's devices had failed, by the humblest things that God, in His wisdom, has put upon this earth.

For so it had come about, as indeed I and many men might have foreseen had not terror and disaster blinded our minds. These germs of disease have taken toll of humanity since the beginning of things—taken toll of our prehuman ancestors since life began here. But by virtue of this natural selection of our kind we have developed resisting power; to no germs do we succumb without a struggle, and to many—those that cause putrefaction in dead matter, for instance—our living frames are altogether immune. But there are no bacteria in Mars, and directly these invaders arrived, directly they drank and fed, our microscopic allies began to work their overthrow. Already when I watched them they were irrevocably doomed, dying and rotting even as they went to and fro. It was inevitable. By the toll of a billion deaths man has bought his birthright of the earth, and it is his against all comers; it would still be his were the

Martians ten times as mighty as they are. For neither do men live nor die in vain.

Here and there they were scattered, nearly fifty altogether, in that great gulf they had made, overtaken by a death that must have seemed to them as incomprehensible as any death could be. To me also at that time this death was incomprehensible. All I knew was that these things that had been alive and so terrible to men were dead. For a moment I believed that the destruction of Sennacherib had been repeated, that God had relented, that the Angel of Death had slain them in the night.

I stood staring into the pit, and my heart lightened gloriously, even as the rising sun struck the world to fire about me with his rays. The pit was still in darkness; the mighty engines, so great and wonderful in their power and complexity, so unearthly in their tortuous forms, rose weird and vague and strange out of the shadows towards the light. A multitude of dogs, I could hear, fought over the bodies that lay darkly in the depth of the pit, far below me. Across the pit on its farther lip, flat and vast and strange, lay the great flying-machine with which they had been experimenting upon our denser atmosphere when decay and death arrested them. Death had come not a day too soon. At the sound of a cawing overhead I looked up at the huge fighting-machine that would fight no more for ever, at the tattered red shreds of flesh that dripped down upon the overturned seats on the summit of Primrose Hill.

I turned and looked down the slope of the hill to where, enhaloed now in birds, stood those other two Martians that I had seen overnight, just as death had overtaken them. The one had died, even as it had been crying to its companions; perhaps it was the last to die, and its voice had gone on perpetually until the force of its machinery was exhausted. They glittered now, harmless tripod towers of shining metal, in the brightness of the rising sun.

All about the pit, and saved as by a miracle from everlasting destruction, stretched the great Mother of Cities. Those who have only seen London veiled in her sombre robes of smoke can scarcely imagine the naked clearness and beauty of the silent wilderness of houses.

Eastward, over the blackened ruins of the Albert Terrace and the splintered spire of the church, the sun blazed dazzling in a clear sky, and here and there some facet in the great wilderness of roofs caught the light and glared with a white intensity.

Northward were Kilburn and Hampsted, blue and crowded with houses; westward the great city was dimmed; and southward, beyond the Martians, the green waves of Regent's Park, the Langham Hotel, the dome of the Albert Hall, the Imperial Institute, and the giant mansions of the Brompton Road came out clear and little in the sunrise, the jagged ruins of Westminster rising hazily beyond. Far away and blue were the Surrey hills, and the towers of the Crystal Palace glittered like two silver rods. The dome of St. Paul's was dark against the sunrise, and injured, I saw for the first time, by a huge gaping cavity on its western side.

And as I looked at this wide expanse of houses and factories and churches, silent and abandoned; as I thought of the multitudinous hopes and efforts, the innumerable hosts of lives that had gone to build this human reef, and of the swift and ruthless destruction that had hung over it all; when I realised that the shadow had been rolled back, and that men might still live in the streets, and this dear vast dead city of mine be once more alive and powerful, I felt a wave of emotion that was near akin to tears.

The torment was over. Even that day the healing would begin. The survivors of the people scattered over the country—leaderless, lawless, foodless, like sheep without a shepherd—the thousands who had fled by sea, would begin to return; the pulse of life, growing stronger and stronger, would beat again in the empty streets and pour across the vacant squares. Whatever destruction was done, the hand of the destroyer was stayed. All the gaunt wrecks, the blackened skeletons of houses that stared so dismally at the sunlit grass of the hill, would presently be echoing with the hammers of the restorers and ringing with the tapping of their trowels. At the thought I extended my hands towards the sky and began thanking God. In a year, thought I—in a year . . .

With overwhelming force came the thought of myself, of my wife, and the old life of hope and tender helpfulness that had ceased forever.

9

———⬥———

WRECKAGE

And now comes the strangest thing in my story. Yet, perhaps, it is not altogether strange. I remember, clearly and coldly and vividly, all that I did that day until the time that I stood weeping and praising God upon the summit of Primrose Hill. And then I forget.

Of the next three days I know nothing. The dead were gone, vanished as quickly as they rose. The Martians had discovered a way to kill them off in droves. The remaining ones were so scattered and few, that I made my journey in relative peace and without much fear. I have learned since that, so far from my being the first discoverer of the Martian overthrow, several such wanderers as myself had already discovered this on the previous night though I was one of the last to hear of the dead's destruction by the invaders. One man—the first—had gone to St. Martin's-le-Grand, and, while I sheltered in the cabmen's hut, had contrived to telegraph to Paris. Thence the joyful news had flashed all over the world; a thousand cities, chilled by ghastly apprehensions, suddenly flashed into frantic illuminations; they knew of it in Dublin, Edinburgh, Manchester, Birmingham, at the time when I stood upon the verge of the pit. Already men, weeping with joy, as I have heard, shouting and staying their work to shake hands and shout, were making up trains, even as near as Crewe, to descend upon London. The church bells that had ceased a fortnight since suddenly caught the news, until all England was bell-ringing. Men on cycles, lean-faced, unkempt, scorched along every country lane shouting of unhoped deliverance, shouting to gaunt, staring figures of despair. And for the food! Across the Channel, across the Irish Sea, across the Atlantic, corn, bread, and meat were tearing to our relief. All the shipping in the world seemed going Londonward in those days. But of all this I have no memory. I drifted—a demented man. I found myself in a house of kindly people, who had found me on the third day wandering, weeping, and raving through the streets of St. John's Wood. They have told me since that I was singing some insane doggerel about "The Last Man Left Alive! Hurrah! The Last Man Left Alive!" Troubled as they were with their own affairs, these people, whose name, much as I would like to express my gratitude to them, I may not even give here, nevertheless cumbered themselves with me, sheltered me, and protected me from myself. Apparently they had learned something of my story from me during the days of my lapse.

Very gently, when my mind was assured again, did they break to me what they had learned of the fate of Leatherhead. Two days after I was imprisoned it had been destroyed, with every soul in it, by a Martian. He had swept it out of existence, as it seemed, without any provocation, as a boy might crush an ant hill, in the mere wantonness of power.

I was a lonely man, and they were very kind to me. I was a lonely man and a sad one, and they bore with me. I remained with them four days after my recovery. All that time I felt a vague, a growing craving to look once more on whatever remained of the little life that seemed so happy and bright in my past. It was a mere hopeless desire to feast upon my misery. They dissuaded me. They did all they could to divert me from this morbidity. But at last I could resist the impulse no longer, and, promising faithfully to return to them, and parting, as I will confess, from these four-day friends with tears, I went out again into the streets that had lately been so dark and strange and empty.

Already they were busy with returning people; in places even there were shops open, and I saw a drinking fountain running water. Armed soldiers still walked the streets but in small numbers, each man on watch for any of the lingering dead until a proper police force could be reestablished.

I remember how mockingly bright the day seemed as I went back on my melancholy pilgrimage to the little house at Woking, how busy the streets and vivid the moving life about me. So many people were abroad everywhere, busied in a thousand activities, that it seemed incredible that any great proportion of the population could have been slain. But then I noticed how yellow were the skins of the people I met, how shaggy the hair of the men, how large and bright their eyes, and that every other man still wore his dirty rags. Their faces seemed all with one of two expressions—a leaping exultation and energy or a grim resolution. Save for the expression of the faces, London seemed a city of tramps. The vestries were indiscriminately distributing bread sent us by the French government. The ribs of the few horses showed dismally. Haggard special constables with white badges stood at the corners of every street. I saw little of the mischief wrought by the Martians until I reached Wellington Street, and there I saw the red weed clambering over the buttresses of Waterloo Bridge.

At the corner of the bridge, too, I saw one of the common contrasts of that grotesque time—a sheet of paper flaunting against a thicket of the red weed, transfixed by a stick that kept it in place. It was the placard of the first newspaper to resume publication—the *Daily Mail*. I bought a copy for a blackened shilling I found in my pocket. Most of it was in blank, but the solitary compositor who did the thing had amused himself by making a grotesque scheme of advertisement stereo on the back page. The matter he printed was emotional; the news organisation had not as yet found its way back. I learned nothing fresh except that already in one week the examination of the Martian mechanisms had yielded astonishing results. Among other things, the article assured me what I did not believe at the time, that the "Secret of Flying," was discovered. At Waterloo I found the free trains that were taking people to their homes. The first rush was already over. There were few people in the train, and I was in no mood for casual conversation. I got a compartment to myself, and sat with folded arms, looking greyly at the sunlit devastation that flowed past the windows. And just outside the terminus the train jolted over temporary rails, and on either side of the railway the houses were blackened ruins. To Clapham Junction the face of London was grimy with powder of the Black Smoke, in spite of two days of thunderstorms and rain, and at Clapham Junction the line had been wrecked again; there were hundreds of out-of-work clerks and shop-men working side by side with the customary navvies, and we were jolted over a hasty relaying.

All down the line from there the aspect of the country was gaunt and unfamiliar; Wimbledon particularly had suffered. Walton, by virtue of its unburned pine woods, seemed the least hurt of any place along the line. The Wandle, the Mole, every little stream, was a heaped mass of red weed, in appearance between butcher's meat and pickled cabbage. The Surrey pine woods were too dry, however, for the festoons of the red climber. Beyond Wimbledon, within sight of the line, in certain nursery grounds, were the heaped masses of earth about the sixth cylinder. A number of people were standing about it, and some sappers were busy in the midst of it. Over it flaunted a Union Jack, flapping cheerfully in the morning breeze. The nursery grounds were everywhere crimson with the weed, a wide expanse of livid colour cut with purple shadows, and very painful to the eye. One's gaze went with infinite relief from the scorched greys and sullen reds of the foreground to the blue-green softness of the eastward hills.

The line on the London side of Woking station was still undergoing repair, so I descended at Byfleet station and took the road to Maybury, past the place where I and the artilleryman had talked to the hussars, and on by the spot where the Martian had appeared to me in the thunderstorm. Here, moved by curiosity, I turned aside to find, among a tangle of red fronds, the warped and broken dog cart with the whitened bones of the horse scattered and gnawed. For a time I stood regarding these vestiges. . . .

Then I returned through the pine wood, neck-high with red weed here and there, and so came home past the College Arms. A man standing at an open cottage door greeted me by name as I passed.

I looked at my house with a quick flash of hope that faded immediately. The door had been forced; it was unfast and was opening slowly as I approached.

It slammed again. The curtains of my study fluttered out of the open window from which I and the artilleryman had watched the dawn. No one had closed it since. The smashed bushes were just as I had left them nearly four weeks ago. I stumbled into the hall, and the house felt empty. The stair carpet was ruffled and discoloured where I had crouched, soaked to the skin from the thunderstorm the night of the catastrophe. Our muddy footsteps I saw still went up the stairs.

I followed them to my study, and found lying on my

writing-table still, with the selenite paper weight upon it, the sheet of work I had left on the afternoon of the opening of the cylinder. For a space I stood reading over my abandoned arguments. It was a paper on the probable development of Moral Ideas with the development of the civilising process; and the last sentence was the opening of a prophecy: *"In about two hundred years,"* I had written, *"we may expect—"* The sentence ended abruptly. I remembered my inability to fix my mind that morning, scarcely a month gone by, and how I had broken off to get my *Daily Chronicle* from the newsboy. I remembered how I went down to the garden gate as he came along, and how I had listened to his odd story of "Men from Mars."

I came down and went into the dining room. There were the mutton and the bread, both far gone now in decay, and a beer bottle overturned, just as I and the artilleryman had left them. My home was desolate. I perceived the folly of the faint hope I had cherished so long. And then a strange thing occurred. "It is no use," said a voice. "The house is deserted. No one has been here these ten days. Do not stay here to torment yourself. No one escaped but you."

I was startled. Had I spoken my thought aloud? I turned, and the French window was open behind me. I made a step to it, and stood looking out.

And there, amazed and afraid, even as I stood amazed and afraid, were my cousin and my wife—

They charged at me with snarling, contorted faces of rage. I backpedaled, narrowly avoiding their cold, reaching hands. I spun and raced for the kitchen with the pair on my heels. I imagined they must have died at Leatherwood and some lingering aspect of their lives before death had drawn them here to wait for me. As I entered the kitchen, I turned and hurled a chair at them, hoping to slow them down. It took my cousin dead on and dropped him. He tumbled to the floor. Hot tears burnt their paths down my cheeks as I wailed to God that this could not be. I begged for this not to be happening. But it was. I knew they must die if I was to live but didn't know if I retained the strength to commit such horror. My wife, with a bloodcurdling howl, launched herself at me. I caught her in my arms and looked into her hollow eyes. I saw the soulless void behind them and snatched up a knife from the countertop behind me with one hand while I held her head back, her teeth from my throat with the other. I shoved her off of me and slashed outward, knowing such a move was useless. The blade slit her throat but no blood spurted from the wound. She had been dead a long while and her veins were dry and barren. Yet instinct, not pain, caused her to flinch, and I kicked her in the chest, driving her back. I knocked her to the floor and pressed the knife into her right eye as she struggled underneath me. I turned the blade back and forth, grinding it into her brain until she lay still.

Cold hands grabbed my shoulders from behind and yanked me to my feet. I stood face to face with my cousin. He leaned in, his teeth snapping at my shoulder. I rammed my knee up and into him, taking away his balance with the blow's impact, and ran. I ran from the house without looking back, though I heard his snarls as he burst from the door after me. God was with me that day because a pair of soldiers were passing by on their patrol. Their rifles cracked and my cousin found peace. Peace I knew I would never find again in this life. The days of the dead and the Martians would live on in infamy as surely as my wife's hollow eyes and rotted features shall haunt my dreams.

10

THE EPILOGUE

I cannot but regret, now that I am concluding my story, how little I am able to contribute to the discussion of the many debatable questions which are still unsettled. In one respect I shall certainly provoke criticism. My particular province is speculative philosophy. My knowledge of comparative physiology is confined to a book or two, but it seems to me that Carver's suggestions as to the reason of the rapid death of the Martians is so probable as to be regarded almost as a proven conclusion. I have assumed that in the body of my narrative.

At any rate, in all the bodies of the Martians that were examined after the war, no bacteria except those already known as terrestrial species were found. That they did not bury any of their dead, and the reckless slaughter they per-petrated, point also to an entire ignorance of the putrefac-tive process. But probable as this seems, it is by no means a proven conclusion.

Neither is the composition of the Black Smoke known nor the blue smoke the beings used on the dead, which the Martians used with such deadly effect, and the generator of the Heat-Rays remains a puzzle. The terrible disasters at the Ealing and South Kensington laboratories have dis-inclined analysts for further investigations upon the latter. Spectrum analysis of the black powder points unmistak-ably to the presence of an unknown element with a brilliant group of three lines in the green, and it is possible that it combines with argon to form a compound which acts at once with deadly effect upon some constituent in the blood. But such unproven speculations will scarcely be of interest to the general reader, to whom this story is addressed. None of the brown scum that drifted down the Thames after the destruction of Shepperton was examined at the time, and now none is forthcoming.

The results of an anatomical examination of the Mar-tians, so far as the prowling dogs had left such an examina-tion possible, I have already given. But everyone is familiar with the magnificent and almost complete specimen in spirits at the Natural History Museum, and the countless drawings that have been made from it; and beyond that the interest of their physiology and structure is purely scientific.

A question of graver and universal interest is the pos-sibility of another attack from the Martians. I do not think that nearly enough attention is being given to this aspect of the matter. At present the planet Mars is in conjunction, but with every return to opposition I, for one, anticipate a renewal of their adventure. In any case, we should be prepared. It seems to me that it should be possible to define the position of the gun from which the shots are discharged, to keep a sustained watch upon this part of the planet, and to anticipate the arrival of the next attack.

In that case the cylinder might be destroyed with dynamite or artillery before it was sufficiently cool for the Martians to emerge, or they might be butchered by means of guns so soon as the screw opened. It seems to me that they have lost a vast advantage in the failure of their first surprise. Possibly they see it in the same light.

Lessing has advanced excellent reasons for supposing that the Martians have actually succeeded in effecting a landing on the planet Venus. Seven months ago now, Venus and Mars were in alignment with the sun; that is to say, Mars was in opposition from the point of view of an observer on Venus. Subsequently a peculiar luminous and sinuous marking appeared on the unillumined half of the inner planet, and almost simultaneously a faint dark mark of a similar sinuous character was detected upon a photograph of the Martian disk. One needs to see the drawings of these appearances in order to appreciate fully their remarkable resemblance in character.

At any rate, whether we expect another invasion or not, our views of the human future must be greatly modified by these events. We have learned now that we cannot regard this planet as being fenced in and a secure abiding place for Man; we can never anticipate the unseen good or evil that may come upon us suddenly out of space. It may be that in the larger design of the universe this invasion from Mars is not without its ultimate benefit for men; it has robbed us of that serene confidence in the future which is the most fruitful source of decadence, the gifts to human science it has brought are enormous, and it has done much to promote the conception of the commonweal of mankind. It may be that across the immensity of space the Martians have watched the fate of these pioneers of theirs and learned their lesson, and that on the planet Venus they have found a securer settlement. Be that as it may, for many years yet there will certainly be no relaxation of the eager scrutiny of the Martian disk, and those fiery darts of the sky, the shooting stars, will bring with them as they fall an unavoidable apprehension to all the sons of men.

The broadening of men's views that has resulted can scarcely be exaggerated. Before the cylinder fell there was a general persuasion that through all the deep of space no life existed beyond the petty surface of our minute sphere. Now we see further. If the Martians can reach Venus, there is no reason to suppose that the thing is impossible for men, and when the slow cooling of the sun makes this earth uninhabitable, as at last it must do, it may be that the thread of life that has begun here will have streamed out and caught our sister planet within its toils.

Dim and wonderful is the vision I have conjured up in my mind of life spreading slowly from this little seed bed of the solar system throughout the inanimate vastness of sidereal space. But that is a remote dream. It may be, on the other hand, that the destruction of the Martians is only a reprieve. To them, and not to us, perhaps, is the future ordained.

I must confess the stress and danger of the time have left an abiding sense of doubt and insecurity in my mind. I sit in my study writing by lamplight, and suddenly I see again the healing valley below set with writhing flames, and feel the house behind and about me empty and desolate. I go out into the Byfleet Road, and vehicles pass me, a butcher boy in a cart, a cabful of visitors, a workman on a bicycle, children going to school, and suddenly they become vague and unreal, and I hurry again with the artilleryman through the hot, brooding silence. Of a night I see the black powder darkening the silent streets, and the contorted bodies shrouded in that layer; they rise upon me tattered and dog-bitten. They gibber and grow fiercer, paler, uglier, mad distortions of humanity at last, and I wake, cold and wretched, in the darkness of the night.

I go to London and see the busy multitudes in Fleet Street and the Strand, and it comes across my mind that they are but the ghosts of the past, haunting the streets that I have seen silent and wretched, going to and fro, phantasms in a dead city, the mockery of life in a galvanised body. And strange, too, it is to stand on Primrose Hill, as I did but a day before writing this last chapter, to see the great province of houses, dim and blue through the haze of the smoke and mist, vanishing at last into the vague lower sky, to see the people walking to and fro among the flower beds on the hill, to see the sight-seers about the Martian machine that stands there still, to hear the tumult of playing children, and to recall the time when I saw it all bright and clear-cut, hard and silent, under the dawn of that last great day. . . .

And as to the dead, they still exist. Though every effort is being made to eliminate them entirely, it is an impossible thing. We are safe from them so long as we follow the new laws set forth by all the governments of the world on how to deal with the departed. There have been no large outbreaks since the days of the invasions and we have grown used to living with the threat of the things. Only in the most rural areas do they exist in any kind of real numbers.

As long as we stay vigilant, we shall not see such horrors as those of the days gone by again.

About the Authors

H. G. Wells is considered by many to be the father of science fiction. He was the author of numerous classics such as *The Invisible Man, The Time Machine, The Island of Dr. Moreau, The War of the Worlds,* and many more.

Eric S. Brown is the author of numerous zombie and horror novels such as *Bigfoot War, The Weaponer, Season of Rot, World War of the Dead,* and *How the West Went to Hell.* His short fiction has been published hundreds of times in anthologies and magazines. He was featured as an expert on the zombie genre in Jonathan Maberry's *Zombie CSU: The Forensics of the Living Dead.* He also won best nonfiction 2009 in the Preditor and Editor Awards for his ongoing column about the comic industry in *Abandoned Towers Magazine*. Eric lives in North Carolina with his wife, Shanna, his son, Merrick, and his cat, "Zoom" (named for the DC Comics Flash villain). Eric is a lifelong comic book and genre fan.

An excerpt from

ADVENTURES OF HUCKLEBERRY FINN AND ZOMBIE JIM

Mark Twain
with W. Bill Czolgosz

Coming soon from Gallery Books!

Turn the page for an
exciting preview. . . .

Free at last! Free at last!

This ain't your grandfather's *Huckleberry Finn*.

It's nineteenth-century America and a mutant strain of tuberculosis is bringing its victims back from the dead.

Sometimes they come back docile, and other times vicious. The vicious ones are sent back to Hell, but the docile ones are put to work as servants and laborers.

With so many zombies on the market, the slave trade is non-existant. The black man is at liberty, and human bondage is no more. Young Huckleberry Finn has grown up in a world that shuns the N-word, with its scornful eye set on a new class of shambling, putrid sub-humans: The Baggers.

When his abusive father comes back into his life, Huck flees down the river with Bagger Jim, seeking a life of perfect freedom.

When the pox mutates once again, causing even the tamest of baggers to become bloodthirsty monsters, the boy Finn is forced to question his relationship with his dearest, deadest friend.

In this revised take on history and classic literature, the modern age is ending before it ever begins. Huckleberry Finn will inherit a world of horror and death, and he knows the mighty Mississippi might be the only way out.

W. Bill Czolgosz alters, edits, expurgates, massacres and abridges the original Twain narrative with gusto; and delivers up a whimsy-laden trek through the rotting heart of the Zombie Apocalypse.

The people used to own other people, an' they had a word for those people. Really mean. I think the only thing I was ever taught that managed to stick with me was that the widow better never hear that word come out of my mouth. Eventually, I learned that lesson good cause o' the whuppins I got when I tried it. Can't say I ever uttered it again. I believe not. All my days. Like I say, it was the widow's whuppin' what did it.

Other than that, she was always very kind. Strict, but kind.

I remember the widow now, sure I do. An' Miss Watson, too. An' pretty much everyone else. And that's sayin' a big deal 'cause the world was full-up of people in those times.

You don't know about me without you have read a book by the name of *The Undead Adventures of Tom Sawyer*; but that ain't no matter. That book was made by Mr. Mark Twain, and he told the truth, mainly. There was things which he stretched, but mainly he told the truth. That is nothing. I never seen anybody but lied one time or another, without it was Aunt Polly, or the widow, or maybe Mary. Aunt Polly—Tom's Aunt Polly, she is—and Mary, and the Widow Douglas is all told about in that book, which is mostly a true book, with some stretchers, as I said before.

Now the way that the book winds up is this: Tom and me found the bunderlugs that the robbers had put in the cave, and when we returned 'em to the traders it made us rich. There was almost a hundred of 'em, and th' reward money was plenty big. We got six thousand dollars apiece—all gold. It was an awful sight of money when it was piled up. Well, Judge Thatcher he took it and put it out at interest, and it fetched us a dollar a day apiece all the year round—more than a body could tell what to do with. The Widow Douglas she took me for her son, and allowed she would sivilize me; but it was rough living in the house all the time, considering how dismal regular and decent the widow was in all her ways; and so when I couldn't stand it no longer I lit out. I got into my old rags and my sugar-hogshead again, and was free and satisfied. But Tom Sawyer he hunted me up and said he was going to start his own band of robbers, and I might join if I would go back to the widow and be respectable. So I went back.

The widow she cried over me, and called me a poor lost lamb, and she called me a lot of other names, too, but she never meant no harm by it. She put me in them new clothes again, and I couldn't do nothing but sweat and sweat, and feel all cramped up. Well, then, the old thing commenced again. The widow rung a bell for supper, and you had to come to time. When you got to the table you couldn't go right to eating, but you had to wait for the widow to tuck down her head and grumble a little over the victuals, though there warn't really anything the matter with them—that is, nothing only everything was cooked by itself. In a barrel of odds and ends it is different; things get mixed up, and the juice kind of swaps around, and the things go better.

After supper she got out her book and learned me about Moses and the Bulrushers, and I was in a sweat to find out all about him; but by and by she let it out that Moses had been dead a considerable long time; so then I didn't care no more about him, because I don't take *much* stock in dead people.

I do mean that when I say it, about taking stock in dead people, *most* dead people, especially these days. Folks say the world is turned on its ear. I don't know about that. Sure thing it's at a considerable wobble, though.

Pretty soon afterward I wanted to smoke, and asked the widow to let me. But she wouldn't. She said it was a mean practice and wasn't clean, and I must try to not do it any more. That is just the way with some people. They get down on a thing when they don't know nothing about it. Here she was a-bothering about Moses, which was no kin to her, and no use to anybody, being gone, you see, yet finding a power of fault with me for doing a thing that had some good in it. And she took snuff, too; of course that was all right, because she done it herself.

Her sister, Miss Watson, a tolerable slim old maid, with goggles on, had just come to live with her, and took a set at me now with a spelling-book. She worked me middling hard for about an hour, and then the widow made her ease up. I couldn't stood it much longer. Then for an hour it was deadly dull, and I was fidgety. Miss Watson would say, "Don't put your feet up there, Huckleberry;" and "Don't scrunch up like that, Huckleberry—set up straight;" and pretty soon she would say, "Don't gap and stretch like that, Huckleberry—why don't you try to behave?" Then she told me all about the bad place, and I said I wished I was there. And then she told me how boys like me was more than likely than not to catch the fissythis, and I said fissythis weren't such a bad thing, 'cause at least I'd be having adventures. She got mad then, but I didn't mean no harm. All I wanted was to go somewheres; all I wanted was a change, I warn't particular. She said it was wicked to say what I said; said she wouldn't say it for the whole world; she was going to live so as to go to the good place. Well, I couldn't see no advantage in going where she was going, so I made up my mind I wouldn't try for it. But I never said so, because it would only make trouble, and wouldn't do no good.

Now she had got a start, and she went on and told me all about the good place. She said all a body would have to do there was to go around all day long with a harp and sing, forever and ever. I asked about if the folks with fissythis got to go there, too, and she said they surely did get to go, eventually, when their material selves were all over and done with. And I asked if that included the ones who had bit people and wreaked havoc and such, and she said it probably did, as long as their hearts was right before the pox took 'em. So I didn't think much of it. But I never said so. I asked her if she reckoned Tom Sawyer would go there, and she said not by a considerable sight. I was glad about that, because I wanted him and me to be together.

Miss Watson spelled fissythis like so: PHTHISIS. That never made a lick of sense to me. She said it could get into you just for breathing air blown in from the east, and that made even less sense. She said fissythis come from London or France, but those places might's well have been China. Tom told me Napoleon defeated all the pox over there and people was living healthier than ever. But I didn't know nothing about that for myself, nor how he pulled it off. I figured that Napoleon musta been a mighty big fella.

Miss Watson she kept pecking at me, and it got tiresome and lonesome. By and by they fetched the baggers in and had prayers, and then everybody was off to bed. I went up to my room with a piece of candle, and put it on the table. Then I set down in a chair by the window and tried to think of something cheerful, but it warn't no use. I felt so lonesome I most wished I was dead. The stars were shining, and the leaves rustled in the woods ever so mournful; and I heard an owl, away off, who-whooing about somebody that was maybe finally dead, and a whippowill and a dog crying about somebody that was going to catch the pox; and the wind was trying to whisper something to me, and I couldn't make out what it was, and so it made the cold shivers run over me. Then away out in the woods I heard that kind of a sound that a ghost makes when it wants to tell about something that's on its mind and can't make itself understood, and so can't rest easy in its grave, and has to go about that way every night grieving. I got so down-hearted and scared I did wish I had some company. Pretty soon a spider went crawling up my shoulder, and I flipped it off and it lit in the candle; and before I could budge it was all shriveled up. I didn't need anybody to tell me that that was an awful bad sign and would fetch me some bad luck, so I was scared and most shook the clothes off of me. I got up and turned around in my tracks three times and crossed my breast every time; and then I tied up a little lock of my hair with a thread to keep witches away. But I hadn't no confidence. You do that when you've lost a horseshoe that you've found, instead of nailing it up over the door, but I hadn't ever heard anybody say it was any way to keep off bad luck when you'd killed a spider.

I set down again, a-shaking all over, and got out my pipe for a smoke; for the house was all as still as death now, and so the widow wouldn't know. Well, after a long time I heard the clock away off in the town go boom—boom—boom—twelve licks; and all still again—stiller than ever. Pretty soon I heard a twig snap down in the dark amongst the trees—something was a stirring. I set still and listened. Directly I could just barely hear a "me-yow! me-yow!" down there. That was good! Says I, "me-yow! me-yow!" as soft as I could, and then I put out the light and scrambled out of the window on to the shed. Then I slipped down to the ground and crawled in among the trees, and, sure enough, there was Tom Sawyer waiting for me.

We went tiptoeing along a path amongst the trees back towards the end of the widow's garden, stooping down so as the branches wouldn't scrape our heads. When we was passing by the kitchen I fell over a root and made a noise. We scrouched down and laid still. Miss Watson's big bagger, named Jim, was setting in the kitchen door; we could see him pretty clear, because there was a light behind him. He got up and stretched his neck out about a minute, listening. Then he says, gurgling:

"Who dah?"

He listened some more; then he come tiptoeing down and stood right between us; we could a touched him, nearly. Well, likely it was minutes and minutes that there warn't a sound, and we all there so close together. There was a place on my ankle that got to itching, but I dasn't scratch it; and then my ear begun to itch; and next my back, right between my shoulders. Seemed like I'd die if I couldn't scratch. Well, I've noticed that thing plenty times since. If you are with the quality, or at a funeral, or trying to go to sleep when you ain't sleepy—if you are anywheres where it won't do for you to scratch, why you will itch all over in upwards of a thousand places. Pretty soon Jim says:

"Say, who is you? Whar is you? Dog my cats if I didn' hear

sumf'n. Well, I know what I's goan to do: I's goan to set down here and listen tell I hears it agin."

So he set down on the ground betwixt me and Tom. He leaned his back up against a tree, and stretched his legs out till one of them most touched one of mine. My nose begun to itch. It itched till the tears come into my eyes. But I dasn't scratch. Then it begun to itch on the inside. Next I got to itching underneath. I didn't know how I was going to set still. This miserableness went on as much as six or seven minutes; but it seemed a sight longer than that. I was itching in eleven different places now. I reckoned I couldn't stand it more'n a minute longer, but I set my teeth hard and got ready to try. Just then Jim begun to breathe heavy; next he begun to snore and slobber—and then I was pretty soon comfortable again.

After the fissythis took him, Jim managed to keep parts of himself. He was called a half-bag or a some-bag, on account o' he could be made to understand things. That was his value. You couldn't trade or train a full bagger to do the things the black folks used to have to do. A full bagger is a damn problem. You got to go after the marbles in his head and knock'em all out 'fore you can put him down.

New York City had itself a real crisis, more times than a once.

But a half-bagger, as the widow told me, still had the potential to be of some use to folks. He could listen and, even if he couldn't learn, he could still be put to the tasks he might have known in earlier times.

Tom he made a sign to me—kind of a little noise with his mouth—and we went creeping away on our hands and knees. When we was ten foot off Tom whispered to me, and wanted to tie Jim to the tree for fun. But I said no; he might wake and make a disturbance, and then they'd find out I warn't in. Then Tom said he hadn't got candles enough, and he would slip in the kitchen and get some more. I didn't want him to try. I said Jim might wake up and come. But Tom wanted to resk it; so we slid in there and got three candles, and Tom laid five cents on the table for pay. Then we got out, and I was in a sweat to get away; but nothing would do Tom but he must crawl to where Jim was, on his hands and knees, and play something on him. I waited, and it seemed a good while, everything was so still and lonesome.

As soon as Tom was back we cut along the path, around the garden fence, and by and by fetched up on the steep top of the hill the other side of the house. Tom said he slipped Jim's hat off of his head and hung it on a limb right over him, and Jim stirred a little, but he didn't wake. Afterwards Jim said the witches be witched him and put him in a trance, and rode him all over the State, and then set him under the trees again, and hung his hat on a limb to show who done it. And next time Jim told it he said they rode him down to New Orleans; and, after that, every time he told it he spread it more and more, till by and by he said they rode him all over the world, and tired him most to death, and his back was all over saddle-boils. Jim was monstrous proud about it, and he got so he wouldn't hardly notice the other baggers. Baggers would come miles to hear Jim tell about it, and he was more looked up to than any bagger in that country. Strange baggers would stand with their rotten mouths open and look him all over, same as if he was a wonder. Jim always kept that five-center piece round his neck with a string, and said it was a charm the devil give to him with his own hands, and told him he could cure anybody with it and fetch witches whenever he wanted to just by saying something to it; but he never told what it was he said to it. Baggers would come from all around there and give Jim anything they had, just for a sight of that five-center piece; but they wouldn't touch it, because the devil had had his hands on it, just like the devil had got his hands on them, once upon a time.

That's how Tom described it to me. It was the devil what made the fissythis pox. Them baggers what caught it made a special trip all the way to Hell 'fore they got to come back changed the way they was. He said they was charmed by the boyo, though I didn't figure charm had much to do with it.

Well, when Tom and me got to the edge of the hilltop we looked away down into the village and could see three or four lights twinkling, where there was sick folks, maybe; and the stars over us was sparkling ever so fine; and down by the village was the river, a whole mile broad, and awful still and grand. We went down the hill and found Jo Harper and Ben Rogers, and two or three more of the boys, hid in the old tanyard. So we unhitched a skiff and pulled down the river two mile and a half, to the big scar on the hillside, and went ashore.

We went to a clump of bushes, and Tom made everybody swear to keep the secret, and then showed them a hole in the hill, right in the thickest part of the bushes. Then we lit the candles, and crawled in on our hands and knees. We went about two hundred yards, and then the cave opened up. Tom poked about amongst the passages, and pretty soon ducked under a wall where you wouldn't a noticed that there was a hole. We went along a narrow place and got into a kind of room, all damp and sweaty and cold, and there we stopped. Tom says:

"Now, we'll start this band of robbers and call it Tom Sawyer's Gang. Everybody that wants to join has got to take an oath, and write his name in blood."

Everybody was willing. So Tom got out a sheet of paper that he had wrote the oath on, and read it. It swore every boy to stick to the band, and never tell any of the secrets; and if anybody done anything to any boy in the band, whichever boy was ordered to kill that person and his family must do it, and he mustn't eat and he mustn't sleep till he had killed them and hacked a cross in their breasts, which was the sign of the band. And nobody that didn't belong to the band could use that mark, and if he did he must be sued; and if he done it again he must be killed. And if anybody that belonged to the band told the secrets, he must have his throat cut, and then have his carcass burnt up and the ashes scattered all around, so that not even the devil could send him back as a bagger, and his name blotted off of the list with blood and never mentioned again by the gang, but have a curse put on it and be forgot forever.

Everybody said it was a real beautiful oath, and asked Tom if he got it out of his own head. He said, some of it, but the rest was out of pirate-books and robber-books, and every gang that was high-toned had it. And there was even a couple of bag groups, smarter ones, the ones who worked in the tannery, who took a simplified form. Much less words, and easier to grunt.

Some thought it would be good to kill the *families* of boys that told the secrets. Tom said it was a good idea, so he took a pencil and wrote it in. Then Ben Rogers says:

"Here's Huck Finn, he hain't got no family; what you going to do 'bout him?"

"Well, hain't he got a father?" says Tom Sawyer.

"Yes, he's got a father, but you can't never find him these days. He used to lay drunk with the hogs in the tanyard, but he hain't been seen in these parts for a year or more."

They talked it over, and they was going to rule me out, because they said every boy must have a family or somebody to kill, or else it wouldn't be fair and square for the others. Well, nobody could think of anything to do—everybody was stumped, and set still. I was most ready to cry; but all at once I thought of a way, and so I offered them Miss Watson—they could kill her. Everybody said:

"Oh, she'll do. That's all right. Huck can come in."

Then they all stuck a pin in their fingers to get blood to sign with, and I made my mark on the paper.

"Now," says Ben Rogers, "what's the line of business of this Gang?"

"Nothing only robbery and murder," Tom said.

"But who are we going to rob?—houses, or cattle, or—"

"Stuff! Stealing cattle and such things ain't robbery; it's burglary," says Tom Sawyer. "We ain't burglars. That ain't no sort of style. We are highwaymen. We stop stages and carriages on the road, with masks on, and kill the people and take their watches and money."

"Must we always kill the people?"

"Oh, certainly. It's best. Some authorities think different, but mostly it's considered best to kill them—except some that you bring to the cave here, and keep them till they're ransomed."

"Ransomed? What's that?"

"I don't know. But that's what they do. I've seen it in books; and so of course that's what we've got to do."

"But how can we do it if we don't know what it is?"

"Why, blame it all, we've *got* to do it. Don't I tell you it's in the books? Do you want to go to doing different from what's in the books, and get things all muddled up?"

"Oh, that's all very fine to *say*, Tom Sawyer, but how in the nation are these fellows going to be ransomed if we don't know how to do it to them?—that's the thing I want to get at. Now, what do you reckon it is?"

"Well, I don't know. But per'aps if we keep them till they're ransomed, it means that we keep them till they're dead."

"Now, that's something *like*. That'll answer. Why couldn't you said that before? We'll keep them till they're ransomed to death; and a bothersome lot they'll be, too—eating up everything, and always trying to get loose."

"How you talk, Ben Rogers. How can they get loose when there's a guard over them, ready to shoot them down if they move a peg?"

"A guard! Well, that *is* good. So somebody's got to set up all night and never get any sleep, just so as to watch them. I think that's foolishness. Why can't a body take a club and ransom them as soon as they get here?"

"Because it ain't in the books so—that's why. Now, Ben Rogers, do you want to do things regular, or don't you?—that's the idea. Don't you reckon that the people that made the books knows what's the correct thing to do? Do you reckon *you* can learn 'em anything? Not by a good deal. No, sir, we'll just go on and ransom them in the regular way."

"All right. I don't mind; but I say it's a fool way, anyhow. Say, do we kill the women, too?"

"Well, Ben Rogers, if I was as ignorant as you I wouldn't let on. Kill the women? No; nobody ever saw anything in the books like that. You fetch them to the cave, and you're always as polite as pie to them; and by and by they fall in love with you, and never want to go home any more."

"Well, if that's the way I'm agreed, but I don't take no stock in it. Mighty soon we'll have the cave so cluttered up with women, and fellows waiting to be ransomed, that there won't be no place for the robbers. But go ahead, I ain't got nothing to say."

"An' what about baggers an' such?"

"They's already worth a penny or two, and we can sell 'em up-river to the other pirates and bag traders."

"But they branded already."

"It don't matter with a bagger. You just get a foot on him and slice it away as soon as it was an oiled patch of garment. Ain't nothing to it. Cut his brand off and sell the bagger up-river, fresh as a daisy. Ain't nothin' simpler."

Little Tommy Barnes was asleep now, and when they waked him up he was scared, and cried, and said he wanted to go home to his ma, and didn't want to be a robber any more. Baggers always made him scared, anyway. He couldn't look at a fella with a bone hanging out without he'd take to wailing.

So they all made fun of him, and called him cry-baby, and that made him mad, and he said he would go straight and tell all the secrets. But Tom give him five cents to keep quiet, and said we would all go home and meet next week, and rob somebody and kill some people and get rich.

Ben Rogers said he couldn't get out much, only Sundays, and so he wanted to begin next Sunday; but all the boys said it would be wicked to do it on Sunday, and that settled the thing. They agreed to get together and fix a day as soon as they could, and then we elected Tom Sawyer first captain and Jo Harper second captain of the Gang, and so started home.

I clumb up the shed and crept into my window just before day was breaking. My new clothes was all greased up and clayey, and I was dog-tired.

Well, I got a good going-over in the morning from old Miss Watson on account of my clothes; but the widow she didn't scold, but only cleaned off the grease and clay, and looked so sorry that I thought I would behave awhile if I could. Then Miss Watson she took me in the closet and prayed, but nothing come of it. She told me to pray every day, and whatever I asked for I would get it. But it warn't so. I tried it. Once I got a fish-line, but no hooks. It warn't any good to me without hooks. I tried for the hooks three or four times, but somehow I couldn't make it work. By and by, one day, I asked Miss Watson to try for me, but she said I was a fool. She never told me why, and I couldn't make it out no way.

I set down one time back in the woods, and had a long think about it. I says to myself, if a body can get anything they pray for, why don't Deacon Winn get back the money he lost on pork? Why can't the widow get back her silver snuffbox that was stole? Why can't Miss Watson fat up? Why can't a folk cure themself of the fissythis? That must be the most spoken prayer in the whole world, except for Europe. And yet folks still getting it all the time. No, says I to my self, there ain't nothing in it. I went and told the widow about it, and she said the thing a body could get by praying for it was "spiritual gifts." This was too many for me, but she told me what she meant—I must help other people, and do everything I could for other people, and look out for them all the time, and never think about myself. This was including Miss Watson, as I took it. I went out in the woods and turned it over in my mind a long time, but I couldn't see no advantage about it—except for the other people; so at last I reckoned I wouldn't worry about it any more, but just let it go. Sometimes the widow would take me one side and talk about Providence in a way to make a body's mouth water; but maybe next day Miss Watson would take hold and knock it all down again. I judged I could see that there was two Providences, and a poor chap would stand considerable show with the widow's Providence, but if Miss Watson's got him there warn't no help for him any more. I thought it all out, and reckoned I would belong to the widow's if he wanted me, though I couldn't make out how he was a-going to be any better off then than what he was before, seeing I was so ignorant, and so kind of low-down and ornery.

Pap he hadn't been seen for more than a year, and that was comfortable for me; I didn't want to see him no more. He used to always whale me when he was sober and could get his hands on me; though I used to take to the woods most of the time when he was around. Well, about this time he was found in the river drownded, about twelve mile above town, so people said. They judged it was him, anyway; said this drownded man was just his size, and was ragged, and had uncommon long hair, which was all like pap; but they couldn't make nothing out of the face, because it had been in the water so long it warn't much like a face at all. They said he was floating on his back in the water. They took him and buried him on the bank. But I warn't comfortable long, because I happened to

think of something. I knowed mighty well that a drownded man
don't float on his back, but on his face. So I knowed, then, that this
warn't pap, but a woman dressed up in a man's clothes. So I was
uncomfortable again. I judged the old man would turn up again by
and by, though I wished he wouldn't.

We played robber now and then about a month, and then I
resigned. All the boys did. We hadn't robbed nobody, hadn't killed
any people, hadn't stole any baggers and sold 'em up-river, but
only just pretended to do those things. We used to hop out of the
woods and go charging down on hog-drivers and women in carts
taking garden stuff to market, but we never hived any of them.
Tom Sawyer called the hogs "ingots," and he called the turnips and
stuff "julery," and we would go to the cave and powwow over what
we had done, and how many people we had killed and marked.
But I couldn't see no profit in it. One time Tom sent a boy to run
about town with a blazing stick, which he called a slogan (which
was the sign for the Gang to get together), and then he said he
had got secret news by his spies that next day a whole parcel of
Spanish merchants and rich A-rabs was going to camp in Cave
Hollow with two hundred elephants, and four hundred baggers in
fancy suits, and six hundred camels, and over a thousand "sumter"
mules, all loaded down with di'monds, and they didn't have only a
guard of four hundred soldiers, and so we would lay in ambuscade,
as he called it, and kill the lot and scoop the things. He said we
must slick up our swords and guns, and get ready. He never could
go after even a turnip-cart but he must have the swords and guns
all scoured up for it, though they was only lath and broomsticks,
and you might scour at them till you rotted, and then they warn't
worth a mouthful of ashes more than what they was before. I didn't
believe we could lick such a crowd of Spaniards and A-rabs, but I
wanted to see the camels and elephants, so I was on hand next day,
Saturday, in the ambuscade; and when we got the word we rushed
out of the woods and down the hill. But there warn't no Spaniards
and A-rabs, and there warn't no camels nor no elephants, nor baggers in fancy suits. It warn't anything but a Sunday-school picnic,
and only a primer-class at that. We busted it up, and chased the
children up the hollow; but we never got anything but some dough-
nuts and jam, though Ben Rogers got a rag doll, and Jo Harper got
a hymn-book and a tract; and then the teacher charged in, and
made us drop everything and cut. I didn't see no di'monds, and I
told Tom Sawyer so. He said there was loads of them there, anyway; and he said there was A-rabs there, too, and elephants and
things. I said, why couldn't we see them, then? He said if I warn't

so ignorant, but had read a book called Don Quixote, I would know without asking. He said it was all done by enchantment. He said there was hundreds of soldiers there, and elephants and treasure, and so on, but we had enemies which he called magicians; and they had turned the whole thing into an infant Sunday-school, just out of spite. I said, all right; then the thing for us to do was to go for the magicians. Tom Sawyer said I was a numskull.

"Why," said he, "a magician could call up a lot of genies, and they would hash you up like nothing before you could say Jack Robinson. They are as tall as a tree and as big around as a church."

"Well," I says, "s'pose we got some genies to help *us*—can't we lick the other crowd then?"

"How you going to get them?"

"I don't know. How do *they* get them?"

"Why, they rub an old tin lamp or an iron ring, and then the genies come tearing in, with the thunder and lightning a-ripping around and the smoke a-rolling, and everything they're told to do they up and do it. They don't think nothing of pulling a shot-tower up by the roots, and belting a Sunday-school superintendent over the head with it—or any other man."

"Who makes them tear around so?"

"Why, whoever rubs the lamp or the ring. They belong to whoever rubs the lamp or the ring, and they've got to do whatever he says. If he tells them to build a palace forty miles long out of di'monds, and fill it full of chewing-gum, or whatever you want, and fetch an emperor's daughter from China for you to marry, they've got to do it—and they've got to do it before sun-up next morning, too. And more: they've got to waltz that palace around over the country wherever you want it, you understand."

"Well," says I, "I think they are a pack of flat-heads for not keeping the palace themselves 'stead of fooling them away like that. And what's more—if I was one of them I would see a man in Jericho before I would drop my business and come to him for the rubbing of an old tin lamp."

"How you talk, Huck Finn. Why, you'd *have* to come when he rubbed it, whether you wanted to or not."

"What! and I as high as a tree and as big as a church? All right, then; I *would* come; but I lay I'd make that man climb the highest tree there was in the country."

"Shucks, it ain't no use to talk to you, Huck Finn. You don't seem to know anything, somehow—perfect saphead."

I thought all this over for two or three days, and then I reckoned I would see if there was anything in it. I got an old tin lamp and an iron ring, and went out in the woods and rubbed and rubbed till I sweat like an Injun, calculating to build a palace and sell it; but it warn't no use, none of the genies come. So then I judged that all that stuff was only just one of Tom Sawyer's lies. I reckoned he believed in the A-rabs and the elephants, but as for me I think different. It had all the marks of a Sunday-school.

The time I asked Tom why baggers was called baggers, he said it was 'cause their lungs was tore out by the devil and been replaced with burlap satchels. But that was only after he had a minute or two to ponder it over.

"The dead still gotta breathe," he said.

Well, that didn't make a lick of sense to me. So I asked Miss Watson the same question, why baggers was called baggers, and she said it was 'cause you had to tie 'em up in a sack when they expired from the fissythis. That's how you would know if they come back dull, or keeping parts of themselves, or just plain ornery. If they was shriekin' and howlin' and rippin' like wolves to get out of the bag, you had to put 'em down quick, otherwise they'd jump around and start biting everyone. Gotta cut their heads off, or smash up their brains.

That's how it was done.

Most baggers, the ones folks bought and sold and traded, they was tame an' pleasant enough; not much fer wanting anything in the world. But you couldn't know which way they'd be until after they come back. Which is why the bag—so you didn't get hurt in findin' out.

When Sy Booth got the fissythis and was on his last breath, his brothers come and tied him up good and secure and left him that way for the night. In the morning they come back and he was almost like his old self. Quiet and friendly and the like, and not one to say much. So they let him come out of the bag, hobbled his left foot, and gave him as a gift to the Church, which he loved so much in life.

I still saw him from time to time, whacking at the weeds and not doing a very good job of it.

But when Sy Booth's widow succumbed to the pox, just a few weeks after Sy, it was a whole other different story. She come back raging like the devil himself, and if she hadn't been bagged and tied, a few fellas might've lost their eyes.

That's how it goes.

When I went back to Tom Sawyer with this new information, why baggers was called baggers, and how it was they got bagged-up just to see how gentle or not-gentle they come back, he told me he knowed it all along. I told him he was just whistling out of his ear, that he'd said the story about missing lungs and potato sacks, but he denied that on the souls of his ancestors and called me a rock-head.

"Never said no such thing," he said.

Oh, he was always a big fish.

Don't miss

*ADVENTURES OF HUCKLEBERRY FINN
AND ZOMBIE JIM*

coming soon from Gallery Books!